GORE VIDAL wrote his first novel, *Williwaw* (1946), at the age of nineteen while overseas in World War II. During four decades as a writer, Vidal has written novels, plays, short stories, and essays. He has also been a political activist. As a Democratic candidate for Congress from upstate New York, he received the most votes of any Democrat in a half-century. From 1970 to 1972 he was co-chairman of the People's Party. In California's 1982 Democratic primary for U.S. Senate, he polled a half-million votes, and came in second in a field of nine.

In 1948 Vidal wrote the highly praised international best-seller *The City and the Pillar*. This was followed by *The Judgment of Paris* and the prophetic *Messiah*. In the fifties Vidal wrote plays for live television and films for Metro-Goldwyn-Mayer. One of the television plays became the successful Broadway play *Visit to a Small Planet* (1957). Directly for the theater he wrote the prize-winning hit *The Best Man* (1960). In 1964 Vidal returned to the novel with *Julian*, the story of the apostate Roman emperor. This novel has been published in many languages and editions. As Henry de Montherlant wrote: "*Julian* is the only book about a Roman emperor that I like to re-read. Vidal loves his protagonist; he knows the period thoroughly; and the book is a beautiful hymn to the twilight of paganism." During the last quarter-century Vidal has been telling the history of the United States as experienced by one family and its connections in what Gabriel Garcia Marquez has called "Gore Vidal's magnificent series of historical novels or novelized histories." They are, in chronological order, *Burr, Lincoln, 1876, Empire, Hollywood,* and *Washington, D.C.*

ted a series of satiric comedies – "Vidal's development . . . along *h* is crowned with success," wrote "I consider Vidal to be a master n world literature and which we levated to the square or to the cube. To this list Vidal added the highly praised – and controversial – *Live from Golgotha* in 1992.

Vidal has also published several volumes of essays. When the National Book Critics Circle presented him with an award (1982), the citation read: "The American tradition of independent and curious learning is kept alive in the wit and great expressiveness of Gore Vidal's criticism." In 1993, he won the National Book Award for *United States: Essays 1952–1992* and in 1995 he published his critically acclaimed and best-selling memoir, *Palimpsest*.

Vidal co-starred with Tim Robbins in the movie *Bob Roberts*.

Novels

Narratives of a Golden Age
BURR
LINCOLN
1876
EMPIRE
HOLLYWOOD
WASHINGTON, D.C.

WILLIWAW
IN A YELLOW WOOD
THE CITY AND THE PILLAR
THE SEASON OF COMFORT
A SEARCH FOR THE KING
DARK GREEN, BRIGHT RED
THE JUDGMENT OF PARIS
MESSIAH
JULIAN
MYRA BRECKINRIDGE
TWO SISTERS
MYRON
KALKI
CREATION
DULUTH
LIVE FROM GOLGOTHA

Short Stories

A THIRSTY EVIL

Plays

AN EVENING WITH
RICHARD NIXON
WEEKEND
ROMULUS
THE BEST MAN
VISIT TO A SMALL PLANET

Non-Fiction

ROCKING THE BOAT
REFLECTIONS UPON A SINKING SHIP
HOMAGE TO DANIEL SHAYS
MATTERS OF FACT AND OF FICTION
PINK TRIANGLE AND YELLOW STAR
ARMAGEDDON?
AT HOME
SCREENING HISTORY
A VIEW FROM THE DINERS CLUB
UNITED STATES: ESSAYS 1952–1992
PALIMPSEST: A MEMOIR

THE

Season of Comfort

BY

Gore Vidal

An *Abacus* Book

First published in the United States of America 1949
Copyright © Gore Vidal 1949
First published in Great Britain by
André Deutsch Limited 1996
Copyright © Gore Vidal 1996
Published by Abacus 1997

A CIP catalogue record for this book is
available from the British Library.

ISBN 0 349 11024 7

Printed and bound in Great Britain by
Clays Ltd, St Ives plc

Abacus
A Division of
Little, Brown and Company (UK)
Brettenham House
Lancaster Place
London WC2E 7EN

For Gene Vidal

Contents

Et je redoute l'hiver parce que c'est la saison du confort!

. . . J'ai vu l'enfer des femmes là-bas; . . . et il me sera loisible de posséder la vérité dans une âme et un corps.

A SEASON IN HELL by Arthur Rimbaud.

The Season of Comfort

‮≈≈≈≈≈≈≈≈≈≈≈≈≈‬

the beginning

‮≈≈≈≈≈≈≈≈≈≈≈≈≈‬

THE SUMMER was green and damp and the grass was moist all day long and there was a green-gold haze between the dark trees. The house stood on a hill and looked very white and new in the sun though only the paint was new for the house had been built before the Civil War and the family that had owned it then owned it now. And this family, the Hawkins, were even wealthier now than they had been before the Civil War, a fact that was vastly irritating to the other old families. The house was as well-cared-for as the houses the rich Northerners had bought. The Northerners had been coming South ever since the World War.

But now even the Hawkins family suffered from the heat. The house was cooler than most houses but not cool enough. The ceilings were high and the heat rose to the ceilings but there was so much heat that it remained on the floor, too: hot billowing heat; the slightest movement made one sweat. The Vice-President swore at the heat but wisely stayed in his chair on the shady terrace. His wife was a lady from an old Southern family and she did not sweat: she barely even perspired but their daughter Charlotte Giraud cursed the heat and wondered for the hundredth time if a sunstroke could cause a miscarriage.

After breakfast a hot breeze from the river came up over

the fields of the estate, through the woods of the estate, and climbed the hill to burn the Hawkins.

The Vice-President sat in his chair on the shaded terrace and fanned himself with the newspaper he was trying to read. He swore gently and wondered if he should go inside where it might be cooler but immediately it occurred to him that he'd probably stick to the seat of the chair and this thought so depressed him that he sat back in his chair, a rocking chair, and wished plaintively that he had gone to Maine for the summer as the family had originally planned. Of course, Charlotte was going to have a baby and her mother, his wife, refused to leave her daughter and, further, insisted that the child be born in the house. It made no difference to her that most of the Hawkins, including the Vice-President, had been born in hospitals. In *her* family they were born at home until that home had been sold to a New York broker in 1912, just before the War. The Vice-President was out of office then and no one in the family had been quite wealthy enough to save her family's Carolina estate. He thought of this as he sat in the rocking chair rocking quietly, careful not to strain himself, careful not to sweat. The June sun reflected brilliantly on the green grass, and green-tinted sunlight struck him in the face. He stopped fanning with the newspaper but he didn't want to read. He disliked Coolidge and the paper was full of Coolidge today. And, further, he was not really interested in politics today; he was only interested in the heat which was pressing all about him, which refused to be warded off by his white suit. He thought of his first grandchild who would be born soon and he thought of death for one was closer to death when one had grandchildren. It was something primitive and mysterious; he felt it in his stomach but he would never admit it to anyone. He wondered when he would die. Would it come suddenly, a stroke? His President had died that way. Or would it come slowly and gradually, after a long illness? He shuddered in the heat. If his grandchild was born dead he would live longer. He knew this but there was nothing he could do.

The servants, five cheerful Negroes, were very happy. They watched Miss Charlotte's stomach become a graceful curve, expanding with the future of the Hawkins family; and in the servants' dining room there was betting as to when the child would be born. The cook favored the 7th of June but that date was several days past now and still the child had not torn its way out of the darkness into the sunlight, the hot summer sun.

Mrs Hawkins, born Clara Spotsleigh, daughter of a Governor impeached, as the family said, by enemies who had themselves misappropriated funds from the State treasury, and a granddaughter of a Confederate General who had been taken captive during the first few months of the Civil War and had been imprisoned in Washington where he grew a magnificent beard and posed several times for photographs by Brady, Mrs Hawkins who, as it turned out, had married *the* Hawkins of that family, looked forward to the birth of her grandchild. She loved babies, although her interest in them diminished as they got older. But she still loved them. No one could say she didn't love Charlotte, her difficult daughter, or William, her son William, who had been killed ten years before in France. In a way her life had stopped the day she heard the news of his death but life continues even when it should, dramatically speaking, end; she put all her energies into Charlotte, her other child; but it was different with Charlotte. There was not the same relationship between daughter and mother as there'd been between mother and son. Charlotte loved only her father and Charlotte regarded all women, except herself, as foolish poorer versions of men. All men were important and her father was the most important of all the men; he had a page and a half devoted to him in the school history books. And she resents *me*, said Clara Hawkins to herself as she walked into the drawing room, lightly touching with her fingertips the heavy mahogany furniture; yes, the servants had dusted. But Charlotte was her daughter, but, oh, if she were not so close to her father. They never include me, but she *is* my daughter and I am his wife, I shall always be

13

with them, near by. She felt the familiar bitterness and lone-
liness as she walked in the drawing room, noticing that the
chandelier was dusty; she would tell George that the chandelier was dusty. Oh, it must be a boy; it must be another son,
like William.

"President and Mrs Coolidge left Washington today for a
short vacation. . . ." Maine would be cool now. There would
be fishing which, though he rather disliked it, he'd be glad
to do now. He sat up suddenly and got unstuck from the
chair; this heat was disgusting. I shall be a grandfather. "President and Mrs Coolidge. . . ."

Charlotte Giraud, born Hawkins twenty-four years ago
when the Twentieth Century was new and undeclared and her
father was a powerful man, lay on her back and wanted to
vomit; only it would be so tiring and so much trouble and it
was hot, hot.

To be cool again, to be cool, to be shivering the way Stephen
and I did in New York last winter; before this happened, before all this was inside of me.

She touched her large smooth stomach and she could feel
the beating of another heart in her stomach, in her womb;
this always frightened her; it was like being possessed by an
evil spirit but, of course, this was not an evil spirit: this was
her child or *was* it a child before it was born? It was only a
thing now, a growth with a heart of its own inside her. She
was afraid. She had had pains in the night but it hadn't
come and the doctor had said, soothingly, that it would come
any hour now, any day, and he complimented her on her
broad pelvis and told her that birth would be easy. Would
be easy!

She had refused to eat the breakfast they brought her. She
lay now on the bed with only a dressing gown on, an open
dressing gown and she could see the pink curve of her stomach
stretched taut . . . she looked away, anywhere to escape from
what was inside her. Soon her mother would come into the

14

room and ask her why she hadn't had breakfast: did she feel sick? It will soon be over.

"Charlotte, you didn't eat any breakfast. Here, I've brought you some orange juice. Do you feel better? It won't be long now." Her mother stood beside her, gray and tall; her mouth like a scar, thin and tight. Thank God this won't be a Caesarean; they leave scars. Will I die?

"I don't want it, Mother," and then she said thanks for her mother would be hurt if she were rude.

"Will you feel like getting up for lunch today?"

"I really don't know, Mother. I feel so terrible. Where's Stephen?"

"He's in Washington but he'll be back for lunch."

"I'll come down if I don't feel worse."

"I wish," said Clara Hawkins, "that you'd cover yourself. Suppose one of the servants came in now; besides you might get a chill."

"On a day like this? Really, Mother!"

The scar suffered patiently. "Suit yourself, Charlotte." She is always like this except with her father and he used to be this way when he was younger. He's more controlled now, of course. One has to be controlled when one is a Vice-President of the United States. What awful years those were! It was so much nicer when we were in the Senate. But it's better to be out of politics. There's much more money now. She's just like him only he can't do without me and she *can* do without me. Perhaps she'll be happier when Stephen has enough money to buy a house in Washington. But he won't go far in the State Department as long as those Republicans are in office. They can't be in forever, of course. Politics again. Charlotte is so beautiful; her hair is darker than mine used to be. My hair was what they called mouse-brown. Yes, I was rather like a mouse in those days but I was the one who married Bill Hawkins. What does he see in her they all said. Now they all know he relies on me and *I* couldn't live without him and the house, Charlotte and William, my son, William. It must be a boy.

The orange juice was sour and she grimaced as she drank it. She could hear her mother's regular step on the stairs. The orange juice made her sweat again and for a moment she felt like vomiting but that feeling passed. She got up unsteadily and sat for a moment on the edge of the bed; then she stood up, her back carefully arched to counteract the weight in her womb.

She went to the tall window, drew back the curtains and looked out at the trees in the sun and she could see, glittering silver between the leaves, the river, the roaring river whose sound was the first of her memories; the river which only muttered now for it had shrunk in the heat. The glare of the sun on the still green lawn hurt her eyes and she turned from the window and let the curtains drop back.

The room was airless but less hot than the direct sun. She walked uncomfortably over to her dressing table and here, before the mirror, she arranged and rearranged her hair and she tried not to think of the pain she would soon undergo; pain and release.

She looked for gray hairs but at twenty-four she had no gray hairs in spite of the pain. Her face looked tired, drawn and frightened. Will it ever be born? shall I look back on this at another time and wonder why I was afraid? Of course, I have a broad pelvis. Then as she sat before the mirror a wave of dark green came behind her eyes and she allowed herself to be carried down into a whirling pool where lights flashed. Then the nausea passed and she was aware of time again. Will it ever be born?

What difference does it make, having a grandson? What difference does it make to have one's line continued when one is dead and forgotten or, worse, the subject of dull biographies. And the future appeared to the Vice-President as a grave at Arlington and water trickling into his coffin, while a marble monument established his greatness and a grandson lived while he decomposed in a metal box. Oh, he was afraid of death. But I'm not so old. "President Coolidge . . ." Yes,

Coolidge would be dead one of these days. They would be forgotten together.

Stephen Giraud, heir to an old New Orleans name and no money, climbed the stairs quickly to see his wife who would, soon, provide him an heir, an heir for the Hawkins family, too.

She was dressing and he tried not to look at her stomach, pendulous and swollen with a life for which he was partly responsible though it was rather difficult to feel responsible, to feel anything more than a mild thankfulness that one was potent. They embraced.

"How was Washington?" Her eyes were red and he supposed that she'd been crying. It must be a strain, he thought; and he himself tried to feel the strain, to share it, but he could not.

"Hot as hell; there isn't much happening: there never is in the summer, anyway. The White House crowd's all on vacation and almost everyone else is, too."

"I don't see why they don't give you your vacation in the summer," said Charlotte, irritably pulling a specially made dress over her head and then, wearily, arranging it about her body so that as little showed as possible but what was possible was, unfortunately, more than little.

"Did you see the doctor today?" Women dramatize everything connected with sex and their natural function; was it Russia where women had children while working in the fields and, after a few minutes, went back to work? Or maybe it was Poland; it was probably Communist propaganda if it was Russia and, very likely, untrue. But American women did dramatize such things. Menstruation was a martyrdom and having a child was a descent into the abyss, a foretaste of hell, an atonement for all happiness. Really, it could not be that unpleasant. And Stephen Giraud, who had a logical mind, concluded that since it was part of a woman's function to bear children then nature had probably not made it too difficult; after all, procreation itself was a pleasure. Certain scientists did say, however, that modern women had narrower hips and pelvises but the doctor had complimented Charlotte on her broad pelvis. Damn the heat! Sweat rolled down his back and under his shirt as he walked slowly, carefully down the broad stairway into the high-ceilinged entrance hall, into the high-ceilinged and almost cool dining room where the family was gathered for dinner.

George, the Negro butler, served lamb chops.

"Thank you, George." Charlotte doesn't look at all well, thought the Vice-President who preferred lamb chops to almost any other meat; he always took two of them and now he was quite happy as he cut them neatly, noticing Charlotte and his wife and Stephen and the young man who was writing his autobiography for him: "It will be, Mr Hawkins, the picture of an age; from your Populist beginnings to your, uh, Vice-Presidency." He chuckled to himself as he thought of the days in the last century when he had been a Populist, when all the poor but ambitious young men were Populists. The Hawkins family had been well-off then but he'd had five brothers and so he had been a poor young man and Clarence, poor Clarence who died of a cancer of the throat, had been the brilliant one of the family; yet he died. It didn't do to be too brilliant. He ate the lamb chops greedily. Then the dull young man asked him a question; the young man was afraid of him. He swallowed, cleared his throat loudly; the family, long acquainted with this signal, were silent and the Vice-President said, "No, I don't expect the Democrats to win in '28. In a nation where there are two parties such as the Democratic and the Republican . . ."

"Thank you, George." Mrs Hawkins disliked lamb chops; once when she was a child her nurse had told her that lamb, all mutton, had a rank taste and this so upset her that all her life she ate lamb thinking of its rank taste and trying to tell whether it really tasted that way to her or not. The Vice-President liked it, though, and she would never have told him

that she thought lamb had a peculiarly rank taste. He looked
pale she thought, looking at her husband as he talked about
the two-party system. The weather is really much too hot and
poor Charlotte . . . she pitied Charlotte, deliberately. It must
be awful to be pregnant in June in the South. Her own preg-
nancies had all been in the fall. William; she thought of him.
What had he looked like? She was frightened, afraid that she'd
forgotten the way her son looked but, with an effort, she remembered. She always saw him walking into the library in
uniform, sitting down in a chair and putting his feet on the
couch. His hair was blond; not like mine which used to be a
mouse-brown. That poor young man she thought, glancing
at the autobiographer. She couldn't understand why they
didn't let her husband write his own memoirs; after all he had
a distinguished prose style. The speech he'd made at Denver
in 1908 was very good and he'd written it himself. Mr Bryan
had wept when he heard the speech. Dear Mr Bryan, such a
charming man he would have made a handsome President,
much handsomer than Wilson. But now she noticed that Charlotte had refused her lamb chops. She would have to say something to Charlotte; it would be painful: her daughter would
snap at her and it would interrupt Mr Hawkins but she must
say something. She must do her duty. "Charlotte, my dear, you
must eat *something*."

"No thank you, George. No, Mother. I'll be ill if I eat anything right now." She spoke until the scar became a thin slit.
Her father had paused just long enough to make sure that
nothing important had been said; then he went on talking,
his deep voice with its slight drawl, not really a Southern
voice, more a national one. He had gone to Harvard and he
had been in national politics almost as long as state politics.
He looks so distinguished, thought Charlotte and she admired his long white hair which fell untidily over his high
forehead; his nose was large and Roman, his mouth thin and,
humorously crooked, his eyes were gray and cold and his
chin receded slightly, spoiling what might have been the face

of God. The only physical difference was the chin; the chin of God did not recede and, also, God had steel-rimmed spectacles like Dr Madison the family doctor who had died several years before; next to her father he had been the most important man in the world to Charlotte as a child. But he's still magnificent, she thought squinting at her father, she was rather nearsighted; when she squinted she could not see the rather large stomach which had begun to spoil his slim figure. He gestured with his long hands as he talked.

Was her mother speaking to her? No, thank the Lord, she had stopped. Really, thought Charlotte irritably, she's impossible.

Charlotte's one wish as a child had been to grow up and escape from her mother but, though she was grown now, she still had not escaped. If only Stephen could find us a house in Washington. We have almost enough money now and Father is paying for the baby. Will it *ever* be born? If she says another word to me I'll leave the table.

Stephen, who had missed breakfast, took three lamb chops which pleased Mrs Hawkins who liked to see people eat well at her table. He looked at Charlotte and hoped she felt better than she looked. Her large hazel eyes under their thick curved brows (much her most striking feature, everyone agreed) were bloodshot. Her breasts which were normally rather small and tight were swollen now; her mouth, which was rather thin though she painted it larger, was tightly compressed and she looked a little like her mother, he thought with amusement. But Charlotte was really her father's child for she had the large Hawkins nose (modified) and the Hawkins chin; she was as beautiful as her father was handsome. Stephen always regarded the Hawkins family with a certain amount of awe. They had an energy which was unusual in their class. His own impoverished family was typical. It was good to know that an old family could produce a William Hawkins and his daughter was like him. She assumed his greatness for herself the way children of great men often do. The children of great men usually demand that the highest respect be paid their fathers but they themselves are the first to realize that great men are often as not no different from other men except in some superficial degree of fortune. But Charlotte had never, to his knowledge, questioned her father's eminence or suspected that he was really like other men. It will be nice to be famous, thought Stephen who knew someday he himself would be. He imagined himself as a Secretary of State, sitting in at Cabinet meetings and, grim-faced, threatening war to the envoy of some foreign power. He was quite hungry and the lamb chops tasted very good. If they were lucky Charlotte and he might have their own house by fall.

The Vice-President was unpleasant about money, however. Even his daughter reproached him for this. "Children should make their own way, independent of their parents. Besides you'll be rich enough when I'm dead." But he was healthy even though he looked pale today, almost as pale as Charlotte. Perhaps there was some strange bond between parent and child; when one was ill the other reacted, too. He had been close to his own mother, now dead, and he'd respected his father, also dead.

The Vice-President was still talking about the two-party system. He had the politician's habit of making even a table conversation sound like an interview with the press. Stephen fixed his face so that it appeared interested while he ate his dinner. His father-in-law liked him even though he often remarked that he, Stephen, was, unhappily, more French than American.

Stephen began to think about that wonderful day when the Democrats would be in office again. It would be easy for the son-in-law of William Hawkins to get an embassy.

"What's the matter, Charlotte? Are you sick?" Stephen stood up as Charlotte left the dining room, walking as quickly as she could.

"There's no reason to get upset," said Mrs Hawkins to her daughter who was already halfway up the stairs.

"What's wrong with Charlotte?" asked Mr Hawkins, irri-

tated that his speech had been, this time, seriously interrupted, for even the autobiographer was interested in Charlotte's withdrawal.

"All I did was ask her if she'd . . ."

They'll never get along, thought the Vice-President sadly.
They had always competed with one another for his favor and
this had always secretly pleased him. He looked disapprovingly
at Stephen: Stephen should really have gone upstairs with her.
It was a man's place to be with his wife at such a time. The
Vice-President thought in platitudes quite often. When he was
younger he had said amiable platitudes so that people would
think he was good-natured, no more intelligent than themselves; it had become a habit, however, and he thought and
said platitudes now unconsciously. Wilson spoke in platitudes
less than any President he'd known but Wilson was an intelligent fool. I'd have made a better President. If I'd agreed
with Clark at the convention I'd have . . . and he indulged
in his favorite daydream, his most bitter one: the time he'd
missed the Presidency. There had been a story at the time
that he'd stood in front of a mirror on the day of the convention and addressed himself solemnly as "Mr President
Hawkins." The story was an old one and had been told about
many other men, too. The daydream of the lost Presidency
and certain sexual memories were almost the only things he
could recall. These important things, however, he would never
tell anyone. He would die with many secrets. He would die.

That afternoon the sun and the moon shone together and
the air was strangely light; a breeze cooled, somewhat, the violent morning heat. Fireflies rose out of the lawn and their pale
lights shone green-gold and the labor began.

Now it starts, thought Clara Hawkins, and she knew exactly what it was like, knew better than the doctor who, calmly,
was arranging for the birth of a Hawkins to be called Giraud.
She helped the doctor. She brought him the things he would

22

need and she helped unpack his bag on the table beside the bed where Charlotte lay twisting.

She was pleased that her daughter should know this traditional pain; it was humbling to be reminded that one was, after all, only an animal. Her daughter knew that now. But she pitied her, too, because Charlotte was her daughter and the fear the first time was great. It will be born soon. My son . . . But now it will be *her* son. Charlotte will have a living son and I have only a dead one. William.

The Vice-President shuddered when he heard the first scream. He was in the library talking, rather absently, to the autobiographer. They both pretended not to hear the scream.

"In 1912 there was some question of my being nominated for the Presidency. After considerable discussion with other Democratic leaders it was decided that either Clark or Wilson should get the nomination. Bryan and I were ruled out. I was offered the second place on the ticket but, having suffered that peculiar oblivion once before, I refused. I withdrew and later gave Wilson the South without which he would never have been nominated. My quarrel with him, which has been somewhat overdramatized, began two years later. I was in the Senate at the time. . . ."

Why do they have to scream so? It sounds like an animal. Any minute now it'll be born and I can remember the night Charlotte was born. It's an idiot's idea having children born in the house. Clara is such an idiot about tradition. It's enough of a tradition having children in the first place. I can remember when Charlotte was born and now that child is having a child and I must sit here, detached, and watch and wait, like a ghost.

Stephen was in his room trying to read but the screams made him nervous. He was growing concerned. He understood that healthy women almost never died but now he was afraid for Charlotte. He did not love her. He disliked her temper, her egotism, but he admired her, he was fond of her and sexually he found her exciting. But this screaming was upsetting him. He tried to read a book by Michael Arlen but not even this could distract him. Soon it must be over. It could not go on forever.

It could go on forever and would.

The pain was intense but the fear was greater.

She felt as if the entire race was, for an instant, rushing through her. The future was splitting her womb open. It was terrifying, massive; she was no longer a person but part of a chain. She twisted on the bed. She was afraid.

The child struggled to be born.

Lights exploded in her head; she could no longer see the room, the doctor or her mother; she was alone with her pain.

The child was being forced out of her.

She struggled. If only she could see. If the pain would only stop for an instant and she could see, could rest for the final pushing but she could not stop now; it would continue until the child was born.

The child was partly born; it seemed reluctant to leave the darkness of the womb.

But she would scream now. She would scream until she had thrown this thing out of her, until she had dragged her child into the light the living saw.

The doctor gave her chloroform.

the christening

1

SHE PUT on her white dress. It was her handsomest dress although it was several years old and not the current fashion; but this was 1929 and, though the Hawkins had not lost as much money as their neighbors, they were not as rich as they had been a few years before. Besides now that her father was going back into politics it wouldn't do to look too prosperous when everyone else was poor. Also it was expensive for her father to have herself, Stephen and the child in the house.

"You're certainly welcome to live here as long as you like; this is your home. But I've always felt that young married people should have a home of their own. It's the basis of every successful marriage." Her mother had said this to her several times in the last two years, the years since William Hawkins Giraud had, with much pain, been born on the hottest June day in the history of the world.

But there was nothing Charlotte could do. Stephen was making very little money and their party had been beaten again. They would have to live with her father for a while longer. She had not yet escaped and Stephen didn't seem to mind. There were times when Stephen's easy acceptance of things made her furious. There were times when, if she'd had the money, she would have divorced him but she didn't have the money. Then, of course, all quarrels seemed foolish at night, in bed. They slept in the same bed. That had been his idea and it was the only good thing about their marriage. If they had had more money the marriage would have been completely serene; she was confident of that. Stephen paid her parents a certain amount every month; quite an adequate amount thought Charlotte, adjusting the white dress before the tall mirror. She admired her figure. The exercises the doctor had had her do after Bill was born had reduced her hips. She was as slim as she'd ever been; perhaps even a little slimmer.

Now the guests for the christening were coming. She could hear the sound of tires rolling over the gravel driveway in front of the house. She went to the window and looked out. A man, a politician of no great importance, and his wife were walking up to the door. She looked at the lovely day. She looked beyond the automobiles and the people; she looked out across the fields to the woods that edged the river. The leaves were brown and yellow, the red leaves were mostly gone now. The air was clear and all objects were sharply defined. A pile of leaves was burning in a meadow near the woods; the smoke rose whitely into the sky and she could smell the burning leaves as well as the damp and moldering smell of dying gardens.

She would have to go down soon. She knew she looked uncommonly well in her white dress even if it wasn't the fashion. But everyone was poor now, anyway; or, if not poor, one pretended to be. Her mother pretended to be. She spoke continually of the ruin of the family. The Vice-President would have to get a job in a University and she would do all the housework. As for Stephen and Charlotte . . . she'd sigh gloomily, enraging her daughter. The Vice-President only smiled when he listened to his wife. Actually he paid little attention to his family these days. He was preparing to run for the Senate; he was, also, occupied with maintaining the family's fortune. He was tolerant of his wife and said nothing when she prophesied disaster. He realized that she, like all

26

Southern women of her age and class, awaited daily the symbolic second coming of Sherman's army; it had destroyed their parents and it would destroy them. She could already hear the sounds of distant marching, the noise of guns.

But Charlotte couldn't understand this. She understood only that her mother thought Stephen incapable of making a living, a home for her, and this was, naturally, a reflection on herself for it is well known in the South that men are nothing more nor less than what their wives make of them. Men must be guided and driven to success. And Charlotte wondered what was the best way to guide or drive Stephen. He had made up his mind to stay in the State Department and it would be several years before he'd be making an adequate living. Of course he'd never make really enough working for the government but then, one day, they'd have the Hawkins money. But she would not think of that; she always decided not to think of that but she did just the same. She couldn't imagine a world without her family; on the other hand she couldn't imagine a livable world without money. She considered this momentarily insoluble problem as she painted her face. Nice women in the North painted their faces and quite a number did in the South although her mother by no means approved.

"Hello there, Monroe." Her father's voice came to her faintly from the drawing room. It was always strange to hear a voice through walls. She enjoyed listening to conversations through walls; partly out of curiosity and partly to remind herself that life continued outside of herself, a philosophic problem which sometimes disturbed her. She had never finished her finishing school but it was generally agreed that she had an excellent mind and she was, certainly, very good-looking. She admired her face as one admires a familiar view, a garden, a landscape during summer: with no premonition of a seasonal change.

She finished her face. She must go downstairs now. Her husband entered the room while she was putting perfume on her dress. He'd been making champagne punch in the dining room, a considerable extravagance. The Vice-President's boot-legger, though excellent, was expensive. Everyone had agreed, however, that the only Hawkins heir would have to be christened with all usual pomp. Even Clara Hawkins had agreed to this. It was natural for her to want to "keep up appearances" and if, as in this case, the appearances were also reality it made the pastime of her class and age all the more piquant.

"Ready, Charlotte?"

He stood behind her, looking over her shoulder and, as usual, without words or physical contact, there was a sexual tension between them.

She moved more slowly, aware of this. "In a minute, Stephen. Who's here?"

"All the usual people, the neighbors from the county, some politicians from the State Capitol and a few of Washington's statesmen."

"Is Bill Talbott here?" Charlotte was malicious. Talbott had been engaged to marry her once: he was very wealthy and it was often said that she'd made a mistake when she married Stephen instead. Naturally she never mentioned this to Stephen but it amused her to be nice to Talbott, to make Stephen jealous; perhaps it would even spur him to work hard, to make a name for himself. Certain things had been said to Charlotte for such a long time that she accepted them as axioms: "The hand that rocks the cradle is . . ."

"By the way," she asked, "is the baby down yet?"

"No, he's in the nursery. The nurse's bringing him down in half an hour. That's when the preacher wants to start the ceremony." Stephen sat down on the bed and crossed his legs. He watched her and it pleased her to have him watch. She readjusted her dress, her hair.

"Yes, Talbott's here," said Stephen. She was startled. She'd been thinking about the baby, about Stephen; she'd forgotten that she had asked a question.

"That's nice; he's really rather sweet. I wish you'd make some effort to like him. He might be useful, you know . . . what with all that money."

28

"You think we could get him to bribe Hoover to get me at St James?" Stephen was ironic and smiling and, worst of all, undisturbed.

"Don't be silly," said Charlotte. "You know what I mean." She had always been taught that contacts were extremely important. Some, of course, were more important than others.

"He's here with the Wilson girl."

That explained it and Charlotte frowned in the mirror. She didn't give a damn, not a damn for Talbott but this was a blow, a small but stinging blow to her pride. She disliked the Wilson girl who, though not as pretty as she, was always called "that pretty Wilson girl": since she had no personality that was the only way she could be described and now she'd caught Talbott and his money. Money was so important.

"She's so dull," said Charlotte, ready now to go downstairs.

The white dress was cool and she felt free and graceful in it, quite capable of dealing with the Wilson girl.

Stephen left the bedroom first. "I'd better get back to the punch bowl," he said. "Your mother doesn't want the politicos drinking too much."

She went out on the landing; her mother was there, breathing heavily; her normally pale face pink and the rigid line of her mouth relaxed and slightly ajar. The line became rigid the instant she was aware of Charlotte.

"I'm all out of breath," she said reproachfully in her monotonous rather querulous drawl (Charlotte had gone to a finishing school in New England and, though she was not, actually, finished, she did manage to lose her accent; an affectation which enraged her mother since it was, obviously, lost out of spite).

"You shouldn't come upstairs so fast," said Charlotte.

"I had to get you, Charlotte. Almost all the guests are here and naturally they've been asking for you. I think it's rather inconsiderate of you not to have received them. After all it's really *your* party."

"It's the baby's. Is he all ready to go down?"

"In a few minutes, I think. The nurse says he's been a perfect angel today." The baby belonged to her mother; her mother spent more time with it than she did. But Charlotte loved her child, passionately, and because she loved it so much she was often impatient with its slowness to learn. Her mother merely adored the child. Her mother was angry with her when, occasionally, she'd spanked the baby. Her mother had forgotten how often she'd spanked *her* as a child. Her mother, of course, had never spanked her brother William: stupid handsome William. Now there was another William, about to be christened and, in spite of her mother, he was hers, and the William who had been killed had also, though no one ever knew it, belonged to her, to his sister, the year that he died and she smiled when she thought of this; she had destroyed her mother by taking William from her, she had achieved, in reality, the dream of all daughters. It gave her a sense of power to allow her mother to believe that William had always been hers. Poor William who had wanted to die. She was frightened sometimes when she thought that she had been, in a way, responsible for his death; because of her he had decided to be killed in France. She had been shattered when she heard he'd been killed. She never believed in God after this.

She had really believed in God only once and that was when he became the presiding officer of the Senate, the Vice-President. Now as she walked down the stairs she recalled the mood of that time when she saw God enthroned and, for a moment, she felt like a child again as she smiled at the guests and waved to God, dethroned, sitting in a rocker by the French window.

2

Her first impression was of white skylights and green carpets. There was a great deal of noise in the room and her mother held her up on her knees. This was the first time she had ever been in this place before. She sat on her mother's knees in a balcony which overlooked an arena-like room. There were rows of desks on the floor and grown men sat at them or else wandered about the room talking to one another. It seemed natural to her that they should have desks, like the large children in the first grade of the school she'd go to next year. She had seen very little of her father lately; he had been campaigning but now he would be home much more often and this was an important day. Her mother was very gay; Charlotte had never seen her so happy. Of course, we had won the election, whatever that meant. It had had something to do with making speeches and she knew all about *them*. Charlotte had been taken to one in the town near home and her father had lifted her up when he'd finished his speech and the people had roared and shouted; she had been frightened because her father was different in front of these people; he was like another person, quick and smiling, loud, not quiet and comfortable the way he was at home. The noisy people had frightened her but later her father said she'd acted very well and that he was always frightened, too; she had not believed him. But now he was home for a while and he would go to Washington every day the way he used to, a long time ago, before the campaign.

She looked about her. The galleries were full of people. They were making a great deal of noise. Many were standing up at the back trying to watch the men at their desks. And people came over to her mother and said, "Congratulations, Mrs Hawkins. Is this your daughter? She looks just like her father."

People in the seats near them would turn and stare and say, "That's Bill Hawkins' wife." They stared curiously the way people almost always stared at her father.

"Where's Father?" she asked.

"He's in the cloakroom, dear." Her mother was more excited than she'd ever seen her before.

"Oh." Charlotte wondered whether she should ask what the cloakroom was. It sounded rather mysterious. She wondered if her father would appear wearing a cloak like the Prince in "Sleeping Beauty."

"Is the President here?" she asked finally. She had met the

President last summer and he had been very nice to her and asked her to come see him at the White House . . . if he was still there. He was the most important man in the world and Father was the second most important man; in fact, Father might even be more important for he was a great deal taller than the President and his voice was deeper. Besides Vice-President sounded more important.

"No, he's tired out after the inauguration. He's home in the White House."

"He said I could come and see him. Why don't we go see him?"

Her mother smiled patiently; she was much nicer when she was excited, excitement soothed her.

"When you're older we'll all go see him together."

Charlotte sighed. It was always the same: when she was older, and how slowly time passed. The days lasted forever. If the days lasted forever how could the years ever pass? Her last birthday was only a vague memory of cake and ice cream spilled on a pink party dress. Her next birthday might never come, might be strangled by the endless days.

Several people near by had heard her remarks about the President and they smiled at her tolerantly though interestedly and she was, unfortunately, old enough to recognize such smiles and resent them; she was too excited, though, to stay resentful.

She noticed for the first time a throne on one side of the chamber; it had many steps going up to it and men with papers walked around it but no one sat there. Charlotte was about to ask her mother whose throne this was but some intuition kept her from asking just yet. Her attention was diverted then by a fat man who stood in the arena below and waved to her mother. Her mother waved back and told her to wave, too. It was a Senator; all these men were Senators and, once, long ago, before her last birthday her father had been a Senator, too. That was before he had won the race. Somehow she could never imagine her father running in a race the way the first-grade children did. He was considered young, of course, although he seemed quite old to her but since everyone called him a young man then he must be young.

"Look, Charlotte, there's Senator Carter and that's Mr La Follette over there. And that's Senator Gore, the blind man; see him, Charlotte?"

She looked dutifully at the gray-haired, the white-haired, the no-haired men.

"Where's Father?"

"He's still in the cloakroom."

"Why doesn't he come out?"

"Because it isn't time."

"But we've been here awfully long."

Her mother's mouth was a straight line now, the way it was at home. "You're very inconsiderate, Charlotte. I brought you here especially to see this and then you whine and carry on. This is the last time I take you out with me."

Charlotte wondered whether she should cry or not; she decided not to since everyone was watching them.

"Now try and be a good girl; this is a sight you'll remember all your life." Her mother had decided she'd been too harsh. Charlotte obeyed her. Charlotte remembered this scene all her life.

Suddenly the chamber was quiet. The loud voices became a low murmur, a background. A clergyman came into the chamber with several other men. The Senators were on their feet and then Father entered, all alone.

There was a roar from the galleries and Charlotte pressed against her mother's breast could feel her mother's heart racing. Charlotte watched her father; he was a stranger now.

He was tall and pale; his face was rigid; he looked serious and his graying hair was carefully parted. "Keep the curve in the back." She had heard him say that to barbers many times. He wore a long black coat and gray striped trousers; he wore the black bow tie that he always wore.

He stood a moment by the glass door, looking at the galleries, waiting for the cheering to stop. Silence. A man came forward and escorted him to the dais where the clergyman stood, the dais in front of the throne. Words were spoken then but Charlotte did not listen, did not hear, so impressed was she by all the solemnity, by her father: she barely heard the sound of his deep voice saying something to the clergyman.

And then it happened; what she had known instinctively would happen happened. Her father climbed the steps to the throne. Her throat contracted and her heart seemed to stop; she ceased to live inside herself. He stood for a moment looking around the quiet chamber and then, slowly, he sat down on the throne. There was a loud sigh from the gallery. They relaxed but Charlotte could not relax for there on a throne, surrounded by men at desks, was God, her father.

There was more ceremony; in twos the Senators approached the dais, like animals entering Noah's ark. But she paid no attention to them; instead she stared at her father, her eyes fixed on his pale face. This was something very simple, very clear but it had never occurred to her before. The God her mother had taught her to pray to and sing about in the unpleasant dark church at home was, in reality, her own father who sat on a throne. She wondered why no one had explained this to her before. She would ask William when she got home. He was in bed, recovering from measles. William, who knew a great deal, would, doubtless, know all about this, too. She wouldn't ask her mother. It was something her mother wouldn't understand.

She watched her father and she wondered if she would be afraid of him; God was a rather dreadful person if what they said about him in Church was true.

Then they left the gallery.

The cloakroom was not at all mysterious. It was lined with big couches and the chandeliers, hanging from the gold-decorated ceiling, made it look like a palace.

Her father was surrounded by men. Some people were trying to take his picture. He was smiling and looked different, not at all like the man enthroned. He posed for one picture with a large black hammer in his hand. Then, the picture taken, he broke through the crowd and came over to where

Charlotte and her mother stood. He kissed them both. He was very gay.

"How was I, Clara?"

"Marvelous, Bill. Are you free now?"

"For a little while. Let's go to the Senate dining room. I've never been so hungry. Well, what'd you think of it, little girl?"

"I liked it."

"Is that so?" He picked her up and put her on his shoulder. She felt odd and sick for a moment, afraid. A man took their picture and the people watching them laughed. He carried her like this down the cold gray corridors of the Capitol and she thought she would die but she didn't. She even managed to eat a large dinner but she watched him all the time and gradually her fear went away. She never thought of God again, though, except as her father on a throne. Later when she grew up, she never thought of God at all.

Her father brushed his white hair out of his eyes and changed position in the chair by the drawing-room window. "Where the hell's the punch?" he asked and the men around him, politicians, looked anxious and obedient, frightened of him. Finally one man left the room to get him some. Charlotte watched from the doorway.

She was not quite ready to make her entrance. She had a slight, barely perceptible case of stage fright. As a child she had hated going into a room full of people who would stare at her but she had loved parties; she still did. She had wished then, she wished now, that all life was a party: polite, gracious, quick-moving, stylized, set to music preferably and, of course, with dancing.

Some people saw her in the hall, recognized her and spoke to her. She was charming but she was a little irritated that she had had to say her lines before she'd actually decided to step out on the stage. The people left her.

It had been such a long time since her first party, the one she'd never gone to. She was fourteen then and already she could imagine a man beside her and children within her.

3

Father was in the study: a brown wood room, dark, with many books in it, mostly law books. He was sitting at his desk, his chin on his chest. She could see the lines about his mouth; they had grown deeper in the last few years. A slight double chin overflowed on his stiff collar. His eyes were closed and the perpetual frown, the famous frown (not severe but, rather, earnest) was only a thin shallow line between his thick graying eyebrows. His hair was unbrushed and, unbrushed, it curled beautifully. She envied him his curling hair, envied him being a man and Godlike.

He breathed deeply, he was not asleep, only dozing, dreaming. He was no longer Vice-President. The campaign (and she knew now what a campaign was) had been violent. Terrible things had been said about him and, though the election was several years past, he still seemed stunned by it; the loud cigar-smoking, hard-drinking men who used to come regularly to the house no longer came. Sometimes the papers said he was running for the House, the Senate, the Governorship and even the Presidency but these statements were as untrue as everything else one read in the newspapers. "Never believe what you see in the papers." She had heard that all her life.

Now he sat in his chair with unopened mail on the desk before him and he tried to sleep. Recently he had made a few speeches in the State but he almost never went over to Washington. He wrote articles, answered mail and rode horseback. Her mother was worried about him and, at times, she'd ask him why he hadn't accepted someone's invitation to go to Maine, Nevada, Oregon. But he would merely look at her as if he hadn't heard and she would say nothing more.

Charlotte sat down in a chair beside him. One of his hands, the one with the heavy gold encrested ring ("it belonged to old Sir John or at least that's what the antiquarian said") hung limply over the edge of the desk. She looked at his hand: long with large white nails; the veins stood out on the back, blue and knotted.

Suddenly the dark eyes looked at her. The regular breathing stopped, the double chin was pulled back into place, the hand moved, became a fist, straightened out, touched a letter and then, oriented, rested upon the desk.

"Been dozing. What time is it?"

"About six, Father."

"Ring the bell, will you? I want my drink now." He had scotch and water every evening before dinner. She rang the bell; George brought the scotch.

"Here you are, Mr Hawkins."

"Thanks. Late today."

"Yes, sir." George left.

"Where's your mother?" He drank slowly.

"She's upstairs; I think she has a headache or something. William's coming home. He got a week's leave and he'll be home Tuesday."

"That's good news." The Vice-President had been opposed to the war; he disliked Wilson personally and he regarded the entire business as Mr Wilson's doing. There were many advantages in being a war-time President. When war was declared, however, he called on the White House to give the President his support. The President had been cordial and the interview was a success, appealing to the histrionic sense of both men. The Vice-President then released a statement supporting Mr Wilson and shortly afterwards his son William was commissioned a Second Lieutenant.

It was 1917 now and the war in France seemed quite exciting and romantic to Charlotte. It was just like the Crusades. The Kaiser and his ridiculous son were the Saracens; the identity of the sepulcher in this instance was somewhat vague but obviously it existed. Soon William would go to France: handsome and now glamorous William who had only recently, with much effort, graduated from college.

"William must be awfully handsome in his uniform. Was he when you saw him, Father?"

"All young men are handsome," said her father sourly; he

37

had wanted always to be young but now he was old and his hair had turned white.

"I can't wait to see him." She couldn't understand her father's attitude. The thought of young men made her think of the most important thing in the world: the party she was going to tonight; she would wear her first evening dress. Her mother had realized at last that she was no longer a child, a fact which Charlotte had known for almost two years and had tried, until now unsuccessfully, to impress upon her mother. At last her mother had agreed that during the Christmas holidays, when there were many sub-debutante parties in the county, Charlotte could go to these parties, wearing an evening dress. They selected a white one. The color of virginity, her father had said.

"Tonight I wear the dress."

"The dress? Oh . . ." He smiled. "I want to see you in it. Whose party are you going to?"

"Cynthia Warren's."

"They're a Northern family, aren't they?"

"Yes and Cynthia says her father is a great admirer of yours."

"That makes them all right then?"

"Well, yes." Charlotte didn't always understand her father but she liked to humor him; he was so childish sometimes; she felt quite grown up when she was with him. But he could frighten her when he was angry and resembled a man she had seen once long ago when she was a child, a man on a throne.

"Charlotte, your dinner's ready. You're eating early tonight." Her mother stood in the doorway, her eyes bloodshot. Charlotte knew her mother had been drinking. Only Charlotte knew her mother drank to cure her headaches, for once, two years ago, she had gone into her mother's room and found her hiding a bottle in a drawer; there was a half empty glass on the night table. Her mother didn't see her and Charlotte, pleased to have discovered something that might eventually be used against her mother, never mentioned it. She always watched her mother carefully afterwards and soon she could tell whether she'd been drinking or not. She found that her mother drank a great deal but never in public. She was known as a teetotaler. If her father knew about all this he never showed it and his wife's reputation was quite pure: she never smoked, drank, painted her face or used bad language. If she had not had two children there might have been talk that she was innocent of that pedestrian act.

"Yes, Mother," said Charlotte, dutifully getting up.

"Let me see you before you go," said her father, opening his mail.

Charlotte was jubilant and important as she went upstairs; her mother followed her, unsteadily and not at all jubilantly.

Dinner was on a tray in her room. She ate quickly while her mother took the white dress from the closet.

"I *do* think it's a little old for you, Charlotte," she said, smoothing the dress on the bed.

"Now *really*, Mother," said Charlotte, her mouth full.

"Don't speak with your mouth full. I *do* think it's a little old, though. Young girls never wore evening dresses when I was your age."

"Everyone does now," Charlotte drank her milk so fast that she belched.

"Charlotte! Your manners've been terrible lately."

Clara Hawkins was not at all well and her daughter understood, vaguely, what the trouble was: menopause which is, very likely, the origin of all the evil in the world, a painful change, dramatic as all change is.

Mrs Hawkins suffered from it bravely. She drank occasionally, only occasionally. Then the Vice-President was home all the time which was a strain; he made her nervous. And there was William. He would go overseas soon and he would be killed; she knew this and her prescience made her wonder sometimes whether she would go mad or not.

Some of these things Charlotte knew about her mother; others she was merely aware of without actually knowing. But tonight the most important thing was her evening dress and the party at Cynthia Warren's.

"At least you might say that you were sorry."

"Sorry? for what?"

"For . . . that noise you made."

"Oh, Mother!"

"Now don't you use that tone with me. I'll not have it."

Charlotte, angry, said nothing. She went into the bathroom and started to undress.

"Answer me, Charlotte. When I say something to you, answer." Her mother's voice was maddening.

"What do you want me to answer?" she asked, coolly.

"How can you be so rude to your own mother? I'm glad your father can't hear the way you speak to me."

"I'm glad he can't hear the way *you* speak to me," snapped Charlotte.

"What do you mean?" Her mother appeared in the doorway of the bathroom, her face red, angry.

"Because then he'd know how you acted when you were drunk." She had said it; she was appalled at what she had said. In a second she had destroyed her own carefully constructed sense of power; she had released her most powerful weapon, her best defense, too soon. Her mother's face had gone pale, yellowish; her mouth was open as though all the strength had gone out of her face, her mind. Then slowly she recovered and Charlotte, horrified at what she had said, stood beside the washbasin.

"How dare you," said her mother slowly. "How *dare* you say this to me?" And she slapped Charlotte as hard as she could in the face.

Charlotte collapsed then; she was hysterical, furious at herself for having destroyed her own power. Her mother left her in the bathroom. She kept on crying.

"What's the matter here?" Her father was in the bedroom. He had climbed the stairs quickly.

"Charlotte's been rude to me," said her mother and her mother's voice trembled.

He came into the bathroom. She was bent over the washbasin, crying into it as though she wanted to collect her tears.

40

"Don't cry," he said, patting her shoulder. "You'd better get dressed for your party."

"She's not going to the party."

"Now, Clara, I think you should let her go."

"She's not going," said Clara Hawkins and her voice was uneven, almost hysterical. "She must be taught. She can't say such things to me," and she picked up the white dress and put it in the closet.

4

Charlotte, wearing a white dress, entered the drawing room and joined the party for her son's christening.

"Here's Charlotte at last!"

"What a lovely day for a christening!"

"How old is the child? two or three?"

"You look very handsome, dear," said the Vice-President, putting his glass of punch down on the floor beside his chair. She smiled and walked over to him. He remembered, too. "Thank you, Father," she said.

There were almost fifty people in the room and yet, though they all smoked and the women wore perfume, the room smelled of the roses she had arranged herself and of autumn smoke from the dry leaves which were burned every day in the meadows around the house.

On a large table was a punch bowl, brought in from the dining room. Stephen stood behind it, slim and dark and, probably, amused.

Her mother moved grayly about the other end of the room, mechanically being a hostess as she'd mechanically been a hostess for over thirty years. She amused Charlotte now; there was a time when her mother's coldness had disturbed her but now she only pitied her and was amused. Her mother had been drinking, she noticed. She could tell by the red-rimmed eyes and the slight trembling of the hands. Clara Hawkins, seeing that her daughter was looking at her hands, folded them, one in the other, and moved on to another part of the room.

"Hello, Talbott."

"Hello, Charlotte; you're looking beautiful. You know Miss Wilson, don't you?"

"Why certainly, for years. What've you been up to?"

"Polo mostly. I've been in Santa Barbara."

"How's California?"

"Pretty nice; the polo's wonderful."

"But the people . . . I hear they're. . . ."

"Well yes. . . ."

"Unbearable," said Miss Wilson who once, at seven, had spent a month in Santa Monica. "Utterly impossible."

"So I understand," said Charlotte smiling to show that she was friendly.

"I guess some of them are," said Talbott.

"When do we see your child?" Miss Wilson was also friendly.

"Soon. He'll be down soon."

"Can he talk?"

"Not very well."

"I love children," said Miss Wilson looking at Talbott. Her family had lost their money, in the Pierce administration; his family had made theirs in the Grant administration and still had it.

"Make a lot of noise," said Talbott and, seeing a young man he liked, he separated himself from the two women who, in turn, with the inevitability of amoebas, also separated.

Her mother's voice came to her through the noise of voices. "This is a picture of my son William; he was killed in 1918, in the war."

William.

The word made her uneasy, made her remember things she'd tried to forget.

"William was only twenty-one; he had a mind just like his father's." No, that wasn't true; he didn't have a mind like his father's. He wasn't even very intelligent but everyone had loved him then almost as much as they loved the ghost now.

"William's going overseas." Her mother read this at the breakfast table.

"How do you know?" asked the Vice-President. "He can't say, can he?" Clara Hawkins put the letter down. She hadn't read that he was going overseas.

"I can tell, though," she said. "He's got a week's leave. He said last time he was here that his next leave would be the last one. He's coming tomorrow."

"Will he really be sent to France?" Charlotte was fifteen and completely grown though her mother still would not admit it. She was home from school because of the influenza epidemic.

"Yes, he'll go to France," said her father. "I wish sometimes I could go, too."

"Don't be silly, Bill; you're much too old."

"Of course, but there's something moving about the thought of men dying in a war; something youthful and sad."

"What on earth are you talking about?" asked Clara Hawkins who could already see the blood on her son's body.

"Nothing at all. I was daydreaming. I think I'll go over to Washington today."

"It'll do you good to visit around the Hill." Her husband had grown more and more strange to her; she would have been happy if he'd even run for Governor of the state (an office neither of them liked because of the provincialism of the state capital; no one suspected, of course, that they felt this way).

"Charlotte, go and tell George to fix William's room for him."

The next morning William, blond and clean, slim and muscular, his hair cut so close that it was like a gold light on his skull, stood in the hall and kissed his mother, Charlotte, and shook his father's hand.

He looked well in his olive-drab tunic with the high collar and, fortunately, his calves were sufficiently developed to make the puttees look a little less absurd on him than they did on some men.

"You look thin, William."

"I've never weighed more." He put his arm around her.

43

"Let's go in the study and have a drink," said his father, resenting youth, adoring his son.

They went into the study and George appeared with liquor and William shook hands with him, to George's delight.

William and his mother sat on the couch near the desk, the window behind them: they were both silhouettes though the light came golden through William's hair. Charlotte sat on the hearth rug, striking a rather theatrical pose. Her father sat at his desk, the light in his face.

Her mother, of course, drank nothing; she never drank. The episode of a year ago had never been referred to again. Her mother had treated her coldly ever since. She still corrected her but her corrections were automatic. Charlotte much preferred this new relationship. Her mother, a bleak figure against white light, sat beside her son.

"Well, how's it been?" asked the Vice-President. He was always awkward with his son, recognizing his wife's prior claim.

"Not so bad. I liked the training; I guess I was about the only person in the camp who liked infantry training."

"Did you get plenty of sleep?"

"Usually, Mother."

"You'll be going overseas soon, won't you, William?"

"Charlotte!" Her mother was angry with her; even her father frowned. They were not to speak of this.

"Well . . . soon." William stretched his legs. Charlotte decided that he was very handsome in uniform. At boarding school the girls all had pictures of their boy-friends but Charlotte had a picture of William. She called him Clive Manners and he was going to marry her as soon as the war was over and she was seventeen; two events that would, naturally, coincide. Clive wrote her long, rather badly spelled letters but when she read them aloud to her jealous friends they sounded very romantic; Clive was a poet who was going to run for Congress. He was all things a man could be. Now Clive talked to them, rather prosaically, about how many hours he slept, what he ate and the company of which he was administrative officer.

"Do they seem anxious to go overseas?" asked the Vice-President, filling his son's glass.

"I really don't know. Some of them are and some of them aren't."

"Are you?" asked Charlotte. Clive would be.

"Oh yes; I think it might be fun. Paris and so on. Besides I don't mind being in the Army."

"Fun!" His mother withdrew from him, from his unreality, withdrew into a vision of death, the death of her son. "I don't see how it could be fun."

"Well, maybe that's the wrong word but everybody I knew at school is over there now, or else, like me, on their way. We can all have a pretty good time."

"I see what you mean," said his father who, though older and illusionless, still had a certain vision of young men dying together; Leonidas at Thermopylae.

Clara Hawkins said nothing. She was a woman and like all women forever excluded from the romanticism of men. Besides she knew the future and these two men did not.

"I hear you're going to run for Governor," said William, changing the subject to everyone's relief except Charlotte's: she wanted to hear more about soldiers.

"Where'd you hear that?"

"Oh, it was in the papers."

"Never believe the papers," said his mother, without thinking.

"Is it true?"

His father shrugged, bored suddenly at having to dispel a momentary illusion of youth and the battlefield. "I haven't made up my mind yet."

He went on talking and Charlotte was bored; her father sounded as if he were talking to the press. The only difference was that he was usually very witty with the press. She stretched out on the hearth rug. Her mother coughed warningly and Charlotte sat up and straightened her dress demurely over her breasts. William, she noticed, was watching her.

"I've been considering going back into politics and the party wants me to run for Governor. But for one reason and another I don't think I'd like to be Governor at this time."

"Why not go to the Senate again?"

"Well, that's a couple of years away yet and besides I'd hate to unseat a friend. I'm just debating these days; that's all."

"I hear some of my officers talking about what a good President you'd make."

His father smiled, "It's easy to be a good President but the opportunity seldom comes twice in a lifetime. I missed mine a few years ago."

"And just as well, too," said his wife. "The White House would've killed you. Your father's so conscientious. He'd insist on doing everything himself and that can be an extremely wearing job. No, I'm just as glad we never got into *that* place."

Charlotte loathed her mother then; it seemed impossible that any woman could be so lacking in ambition. The man *she* married would most certainly be President.

They talked on. Evening came. The light ceased to come through the window and her father turned on his desk lamp; William and his mother were no longer dark outlines but shadowy figures now, mysterious in the light of a single shaded bulb. Her father's face was white and sharp in the light.

George announced dinner. They went to their rooms, washed and arrived at the table late. They sat by candlelight and Charlotte said little; she watched Clive Manners and daydreamed of the White House. They talked of family, of relations, of friends, of politics, of everything but war.

After dinner they sat by the fire and they talked until, finally, there seemed nothing else to talk about; then they were silent, watching the fire, not thinking, a part of firelight.

"You'd better go up to bed, Charlotte."

"Oh, Mother; I wanted to talk with William."

"You can talk to him all you like tomorrow."

Everyone said good-night and Charlotte, defeated, went up to bed. She went into the bathroom and, on an impulse, she opened the other door which went into her brother's room. She almost never went into this room but now that it was William's again, for a short while, she wanted to be in it, to be aware of William. His pajamas were on the bed; his clothes, what few he had brought, were hung in the closet. His cap was on the bureau and she picked it up and put it on. It was too large for her. She felt very strange wearing it. She seemed, for an instant, to be someone else and yet, at the same time, herself. She was excited. Then she put the hat back on the bureau; she returned to her room. She left the doors of the bathroom partly open. Then she turned out her light and went to bed. She could not sleep, though.

"Charlotte! I haven't seen you in years."

"Emily! How are you?"

"Couldn't be better. I'm divorced now, you know."

"No, I hadn't heard. I'm sorry."

"Don't be sorry; best thing that ever happened to me." Emily was thirty and with a careful use of make-up managed to look several years older.

"It's so difficult to tell whether one should congratulate or console; I expect congratulate is the safest."

"And usually the most accurate. No woman would ever want to be consoled; it'd look as if she'd been deserted."

"Impossible situation," said Charlotte drily, knowing exactly why Emily's husband had divorced her. Emily was a bad girl; it would have been quite all right if she'd been a bad girl privately but she always insisted on making a public display of her badness which, when she was eighteen, was rather charming but now that she was thirty was less so; in fact she was something of a nuisance. But Charlotte was fond of her. Emily had, incidentally, been in love with William.

Emily glanced at the last picture taken of William. It was on the mantelpiece; he was in uniform in this picture. The picture had been taken during his last week home.

"How beautiful he was!" exclaimed Emily. "I loved him madly."

"Yes, I remember."

"How could you? You were only a child then. You were much too young to appreciate him. He was such a saint."

"I remember him very well, Emily; now wouldn't you like . . ." she tried to get away, to stop this talk of William.

"How thoughtful he looks," remarked Emily, squinting at the picture (she was nearsighted).

"Yes, it was taken just before he went overseas."

"I know but he used to be always smiling. He looks quite sad here; just as if he knew what was going to happen . . ."

"Wouldn't you like a drink, Emily?" Charlotte spoke quickly. "Let's join Stephen at the punchbowl."

"Oh certainly; you know I haven't spoken to him yet. You'd better watch out, Charlotte; I'm a free woman now."

Charlotte smiled and led Emily over to the punchbowl, like a horse to a trough, she thought grimly.

"Hello, Emily, Charlotte; want some punch?" They took some from him and Emily told Stephen all about the divorce.

"Have you met the Canon yet?" asked Stephen, turning to Charlotte when Emily had, for a moment, stopped talking.

"What Canon?"

"Oh you know: Canon Southey. He's doing the christening."

"No, and I suppose I'd better meet him. Who discovered him?"

"He's an old friend of your mother's."

"Of course, I don't regard marriage lightly, Stephen; quite the contrary." And Emily told Stephen what she thought of marriage.

Charlotte crossed the room. The Canon was obviously the short fat man with a white clerical collar. He was talking to her mother. Her mother liked churchmen and they, grateful souls, responded warmly to her. Stephen's uncle had been a Catholic priest. She'd met him once; he was dark like all Stephen's family. Stephen himself was dark and yet light at the same time; his hair was black, his eyes dark and his skin fair.

48

When he was suntanned, though, he looked extremely Latin.

5

He was suntanned the first time they met. She had left her finishing school and gone on the stage in New York. This phase lasted for two years. At twenty she decided that her stage career had run its course and she retired, to her family's relief. In later years she was to speak of this period as a brilliant and dazzling life, a stardom which she'd given up for marriage. Her family and Stephen, of course, knew better. She had said three lines in her penultimate show; in her last vehicle she'd said nothing although she crossed the stage twice.

"Mr Giraud, I want you to meet Miss Hawkins. She's from the South, too. I think all Southerners should get together." Their hostess left them.

Charlotte tried to look like a lady of the theater. This was a "bohemian" party and someone said that Noël Coward would be there but, unfortunately, as it later developed, Mr Coward was in London at that moment. Still it gave the party a certain air to think that he might have come had he been in New York and unengaged that evening.

There were two rooms in which the party was allowed to gather: they were both small and the walls were painted different colors which made Charlotte a little dizzy. She drank gin gaily, though. Delighted to be among these people, to be accepted by them. It was always so difficult to be accepted by the group one wants to be accepted by; Charlotte had felt her lack of background two years before when she'd come to New York. Now she belonged. Her family would not have approved of this group and this thought gave her considerable satisfaction. There were several unpublished writers here, several unproduced playwrights, one rather famous poet and his friend and, of course, a quantity of painters and actors. Now, out of all these fabulous beings, these admirable witty people, she was introduced to a young Southerner (fortunately handsome) who was, very likely, from a good family: it was too depressing. She was not quite sure which rôle to play: the

Southern aristocrat who has chosen, in the face of almost insurmountable social disapproval a bohemian life; or a young girl visiting in Babylon, visiting naively; or a cynical woman of the stage with a vague and probably disreputable past. She had almost decided upon this last rôle when Mr Giraud said, "You're the Vice-President's daughter, aren't you?"

She tried to recast her rôle but she was completely offguard now. She stammered, "Yes . . . how . . . how did you know?"

"I knew your brother at college, the one who was killed."

"Shall we sit down?" said Charlotte. They found a couch with gin on it; no one would sit here because the couch was wet and so Mr Giraud, a resourceful young man, took the wet cushion off the couch and, amid congratulations from the more drunken guests, they sat down and looked at one another solemnly.

"Were you in the Army with William?"

"No, I only knew him at college. I was a little younger than he was. I knew him pretty well though. I knew he had a younger sister."

"Yes, I was only a child then."

"It seems like a long time ago."

"Were you in the war?"

"I never went overseas."

"William did."

"I know. I'm sorry; I was very sorry at the time."

"Sometimes those things . . ." began Charlotte but, no, she could never say what she really thought about William. She preferred to forget him completely. It was so silly discussing him now when he'd been dead five years. Mr Giraud was almost his complete opposite. He was dark and quick, not light and slow, his smile was brilliant, not warm, and there was no light in his dark curling hair, no light at all.

"What's your first name?"

"Stephen, call me that; and you're Charlotte?"

"Yes. What do you do? Are you an actor?"

"Lord, no!"

"What's wrong with actors? I happen to be an actress." She was dignified.

"Sorry. I guess I spoke out of turn. I just couldn't think of myself as an actor. I've had all kinds of jobs lately. I left home when I got back from the war (I lived in New Orleans). I came up here to be a painter."

"How wonderful! Then you're an artist?"

"I don't think so," he said humorously, sadly (was it Clive Manners who'd been both sad and humorous at the same time?). "I don't think I'm very good. Besides I can't make a living at it and I'll have to make a living one day."

"How awful! Can't your family . . . I mean . . ."

"No, they can't. We're poor as only Southerners can be poor."

"I'm so sorry. What will you do then . . . for a career?"

He sighed. "I'm going into the State Department next month; my family still have a little influence."

Charlotte frowned: the State Department was not particularly popular with her father. "I suppose that's something; will it give you time to paint?"

"I don't think I'm going to paint any more."

"And why not?" Poet and politician; one without the other?

"I'm thinking of burning my paintings next week, all my work." They were both quiet, faced with the awfulness, the significance of this final gesture.

"I'd like to see them before you do."

He showed her the paintings a few nights later and she marveled at them, not knowing whether they were good or bad; it was enough that he'd painted them. Already she liked everything connected with Stephen Giraud. The paintings were not destroyed after all but put in storage and she helped him move out of his studio (a small room in the Village). She saw him off to Washington. Two weeks later she retired from the stage and went back home where her mother received her severely and her father received her with delight, glad to have her back. Yet both were soon a little disturbed by her frequent visits to Washington where, though she stayed with unimpeachable friends, her activities were unknown. Her mother insisted that she go to college. In the South going to college still meant the difference between being educated and not being educated; Charlotte, however, didn't listen to her mother who had grown, gradually, used to her daughter's independence; mechanically, though, she pulled strings that were no longer attached. Since William died it made no difference to her what Charlotte or anyone else did. This Charlotte knew. Her father had grown closer to her since William's death, not that he had ever been really close to his son but his son's death had made him aware of death and perpetuation: his daughter was his only projection into the future. He knew he would not live much longer and, fortunately, his seed was in Charlotte. She realized this, realized that he felt this way and, in turn, drew closer to him.

To her surprise Stephen liked the State Department and he had much hope for the future. She saw him as often as possible. They went to the Zoo together every Sunday and, though he had little money, he insisted on taking her out to dinner. They danced together and they talked. Their talks were long, sentimental and rather incoherent. They disagreed about politics, art and her friends for they were now invited out together everywhere; Charlotte spoke of her "affair" to her most intimate friends, pledging them to the secrecy she herself couldn't maintain. Soon all Washington was interested in Stephen Giraud and Charlotte's friends believed her when she called it an affair. Actually Stephen was rather proper and Charlotte herself had no desire to have a real affair, to go through that again. But still she told everyone just what she felt about Stephen; all her life she had had a great difficulty in keeping secrets for the simple reason that no secret she told could ever be as secret as the one she did keep, would always keep as long as she lived. There were times when she wondered if anything *had* really happened and then she would look at the picture on the mantel and her hands would grow cold and she would remember and be afraid.

Finally Stephen discussed marriage. She had already told

her closest friends that they were going to be married. It was a relief when he finally got around to it himself.

They were in Rock Creek Park. It was midsummer but here in the Park everything was cool and green. The thin stream, Rock Creek, wound noisily over rocks between the steep low hills; hills covered with short trees and laurel bushes. They left the car and crossed a wooden bridge, pausing a moment in the middle of the bridge to watch the water swirling. They climbed one of the hills and sat down under a large tree. They were far from the city and even farther from reality. Their movements were, at least to Charlotte, all part of a dream for which there'd never be an awakening, only a continuation, without climaxes, only beginnings.

Casually he asked her to marry him and, casually, she accepted. He complained that he was sitting on some sharp stones. He got up and it took him several minutes to clear the ground of sharp stones. By this time any climax that might have been developing was destroyed.

"I expect," said Charlotte thoughtfully, "that you'd better meet the family next. That's always done about this time."

"I wish now I'd met them before, when I first came to Washington. It wouldn't look so sudden if they'd known me all along."

"I suppose so but . . . I don't know; I wanted to keep apart from them I guess. I wanted this to be different; you know what I mean."

Yes, he knew what she meant.

"And you're from New Orleans, Mr Giraud?" Mrs. Hawkins was inquiring. The young man had refused a drink and then, when the Vice-President insisted, took one drink; this could be extremely indicative or it could be meaningless.

"Yes; my family's been there for a long time. They came from France."

"No relation to Georges Giraud, are you?"

"Yes sir; he's my uncle."

This simple declaration eased the tension considerably, removed all doubt as to acceptability and got the conversation on that familiar Southern plane: what relation one is to whom. Dinner was announced and all through dinner families were discussed and Charlotte learned after several hours that she and Stephen were distantly related. The question of acceptable family mattered greatly to Clara Hawkins and, once it was firmly established, Stephen became, in her eyes, eligible. She had already decided that Charlotte was seriously interested in him; now all that had to be determined was his character and whether his family had money. It was quite possible that he was a fortune-hunter and even though he came of good family he was, after all, French which is not at all the same as being Anglo-Saxon. Everyone knew the French were unpredictable.

"What sort of work do you do, Mr Giraud?" Charlotte had already told her father that Stephen was in the State Department but her father, after many years of questioning people, insisted on hearing everything from the subject; nothing was accepted second-hand.

"I'm in the State Department . . . sir."

"Do you like it?"

"Have some more beef, Mr Giraud. Is it too rare? We like rare meat in this house, you know."

"I'll have some more, thank you. It's just fine this way. Yes, I like the State Department. Someday I'd like to get in the foreign end of it."

"I suppose it can be an agreeable life," said the Vice-President, unconvinced. "I, of course, never got along too well with the boys in your outfit. They always had such a holier-than-thou attitude about everything connected with foreign affairs (I was on that committee in the Senate for years). I always claimed that it took a minimum of brains and a maximum of starch to make a diplomat. I may be prejudiced, though; things may be different now."

"Well, of course, I haven't seen much of that side yet but I expect diplomats have always disliked politicians."

The Vice-President was about to put a piece of beef in his mouth; then he decided not to and he put his fork back on the plate. For the first time Stephen interested him. It took a

54

great deal of courage to suggest to his face that Bill Hawkins was a politician and not a statesman. He himself was somewhat undecided as to which he was. The newspapers called him an elder statesman.

"You might add, Mr Giraud, that the converse is also true; politicians have always disliked and mistrusted diplomats. Tell me some more, though, about your work there."

Charlotte allowed Stephen to talk about himself (naturally, no mention was made of his career as an artist). And finally, with regret that he had no money, her family arranged the wedding with taste and at considerable cost.

"Charlotte, this is Canon Southey. He christened *you* when you were just a baby."

"Is that so?"

"I must say you've grown," said the Canon giggling.

"It was inevitable," said Charlotte a little flatly.

The Canon decided that he'd been, perhaps, too flippant. "One really feels one's age," he said seriously, turning to Mrs Hawkins. "Just think it was practically only yesterday that I christened your daughter and now I'm christening her son. Time," he remarked, "flies."

"It certainly does," said Mrs Hawkins.

"Will the young man be down soon, Mrs Giraud?"

"I expect him down any minute."

"Ah, good. I expect the piano will be the best place to put the font. I think I put it there last time. The godparents are here, I presume?"

"Yes, one of each."

"Good. I wish you'd have them step over here; there're certain things they'll have to read aloud during the ceremony."

"Certainly, Canon. Will you excuse me?"

She would get Stephen to find the godparents. One was Florence Nail, her best friend at the finishing school; Florence was talking to her father. Herbert Moore, an Assistant Secretary of State, was to be godfather; he was Stephen's immediate superior. She couldn't see him anywhere. He was known to be a heavy drinker and it was more than likely that he was in the bathroom or outside in his car, drinking his own liquor.

She must tell Stephen to find him; she crossed the large room, stopping at different groups on her way: stations of the cross.

But Stephen was not Golgotha; or was he? Such a difficult question. He was exasperating anyway. She had grown more irritable in the last year or so; she was less able to accept his casualness, his forgetfulness, his habit (and a most unflattering one) of going to sleep right after dinner. But above all she was tired of living with her family and having no money. Every time she thought of it, which was often, she prayed that their party would get back in office. The Embassy at Rome was terribly desirable and not, she had heard, too expensive.

Stephen was surrounded by women. She approached him.

The wedding and the wedding night were both successes. Since it was then spring, the time of Mardi Gras, they went to New Orleans to visit *his* family.

The Girauds' house was in the French Quarter. It was old, much older than the Hawkins' house, for instance; its plumbing was not adequate and the electric lighting looked as if it were only on trial and would, very soon, be substituted by gas. But the place was also magnificent. There was a patio in the center of the two-storied house; in the middle of the patio was a rococo Versailles fountain from only one of whose innumerable spouts trickled a single dirty stream of water. Gardenias grew on bushes in the garden and several tall magnolias grew on either side of the door, their flowers like bad wax imitations of something else. A second-storey iron balcony ran all the way around the house; it was very ornate and graceful still, in spite of the rust. A Negro servant showed them into the dark damp drawing room. Spots of damp showed on the wallpaper and the furniture (shabby reminders of the beheaded French King) looked brittle and old.

Stephen waited patiently here with Charlotte, as though this was not his home but a stranger's. She was depressed.

"Is it always so dark?" She gestured at the closed blinds.

He nodded. "Ever since Father died Mother's insisted on keeping the downstairs rooms in mourning. The rest of the house is more cheerful."

"Stephen!"

"Hello there, Jeanette." He embraced a large woman dressed quite stylishly. He introduced Charlotte to his sister. She was in her thirties and, at the moment, pregnant. She had been pregnant several times before, Charlotte knew, but for one reason or another she'd never had a living child. She was trying for the fourth time now; she was an optimist.

"I've heard so much about you, Charlotte. We loved your pictures in the papers. New Orleans has made quite a to-do about it all. Here let's sit down; now tell me everything."

"Where's Mother?"

"She's with the doctor now." Jeanette frowned. "Her liver's been acting up. I've told her a thousand times she should've gone to a specialist years ago but she pays no attention to me. Lately she's been . . ." and Jeanette described in considerable detail her mother's symptoms. Jeanette was a good-looking woman, Charlotte thought, trying to discover a likeness between Stephen and his sister; there wasn't much. She was very dark (with a dark skin unlike Stephen) and her nose was larger than his and her eyes were a startling gray. She talked incessantly. Stephen had three sisters. Jeanette, his favorite, was the eldest. She and her husband, a broker named Smith, lived in the house with her mother. The other two sisters were married, too. One lived in Michigan and the other in California. Their mother had never forgiven them for leaving New Orleans; until this generation no Giraud had ever thought of leaving Louisiana.

"How long can you stay?" asked Jeanette when she'd finished describing her mother's liver.

"Two weeks, that's all."

"Oh, what a shame! Well, Ralph and I've arranged all sorts of things for you. I'll talk them over with Charlotte later to see if she agrees. You've nothing to say about them and . . . by the way, you'll have to go up to Baton Rouge and see Uncle Georges; he knew Charlotte's father."

A servant told them that Mrs Giraud could see them now.

She was small and old with white hair, a brown wrinkled face and hands with grotesquely knotted fingers; on one of these fingers was a gold ring, fashioned like a water lily with a large diamond in the center. The ring was striking and Charlotte, glancing at it, wondered how the old woman ever got it off her finger, if she did.

Mrs Giraud was in bed; a four-poster bed in a room that was surprisingly feminine and cheerful in this house. She kissed her son and then Charlotte.

"So you finally got married, Stephen," she said and she looked at Charlotte appraisingly; she spoke, Charlotte noticed, with a French accent.

"You know," said the old woman, "this generation, my children, were the first to marry outside of Louisiana. Perhaps it's a good thing; what do you think?"

"In this case," said Charlotte, "I think it was a very good idea."

Mrs Giraud smiled. She had large white false teeth. "Sit down," she said. "Did you talk to the doctor, Jeanette?"

"No, Mother, he got out of the house before I could catch him."

Her mother grunted and crossed her hands. "I'm not in bed all the time, Stephen," she explained. "In fact I'll be up for dinner tonight. The doctor thinks something is wrong with my liver. Are you Catholic, my dear?"

The transition was abrupt.

"No . . . no," said Charlotte helplessly, wondering what else she would say.

"I didn't think so," said Madame Giraud (from that moment Charlotte always thought of her as Madame Giraud;

58

in New Orleans many people did call her that). "My son isn't either . . . now." She looked at Stephen.

"Let's not talk about that, Mother. Not now, anyway."

She paid no attention to him. "No member of our family, until this generation, ever left the Church." She looked at Charlotte who noticed how black her eyes were. Then Charlotte who'd been daydreaming became aware of the statement about the Church and she wondered whether she was expected to answer or not. Stephen helped her.

"We've all discussed that many times," he said gently. "We went through it when I was in college."

"I know," said Madame Giraud sweetly. "I merely wanted Charlotte to understand how things were . . . are in our family. The Girauds came originally from Grenoble, Charlotte. The first one, a Chevalier Eugéne de Giraud, came to America, to Louisiana in the last part of the seventeenth century. He was, Charlotte, the first cousin of a Cardinal, a Prince of our Church." The old woman stopped dramatically. She was gathering strength from these old names and, except by her, forgotten ones. Charlotte was bored although not for a moment did she show it. In the South she was accustomed to all this talk of families; it didn't seem very important whether Stephen was a Catholic or not. She herself was, like her father, a pious pagan; her father at election time could be seen entering many churches to pray for victory, an expression of sanctity on his face.

"In New Orleans we take our religion seriously. Renegades are regarded seriously." She smiled to show that hers was not, actually, an Inquisitional nature. "What denomination are you, my dear?"

Charlotte thought a minute; she was not quite sure herself but she pretended to be: "Episcopalian."

"How nice," said Madame Giraud. "Your children, and I'm sure you'll have many children, will be brought up as Protestants, won't they?"

Now she was coming to the point, thought Charlotte; she

wondered why Stephen let her do all the talking. She looked at him but he looked away and examined, carefully, the medicine bottle on the table. Jeanette was watching two birds chattering on the window sill.

"I suppose so," said Charlotte.

"They will be the only male Girauds, if you have sons," said Madame. "Stephen's Uncle Georges is a widower with no children and his Uncle Raoul is a priest. I had always hoped that my grandchildren . . ."

"Couldn't we talk about this some other time, Mother?" Stephen was abrupt.

"Of course," said his mother indulgently. "It's only that when one gets to be my age there aren't many days left to discuss things in; one becomes conscious of the hours even." Madame sighed, a little pathetically, Charlotte thought, and yellow wrinkled lids covered the black, almost fierce eyes.

"We don't mean to tire you, Mother," said Jeanette, standing up: the others did the same.

The black eyes stared at them again. "Your wife, Stephen, is lovely," she said. "Tonight I'll join you at dinner, turn the radio on for me, will you? There's a program that comes on at this time; I always listen to it: 'The Second Mrs Arbuthnot'; it's really so much like life. Thank you, dear; yes, that's the station."

The radio was on very loud when they left the room.

"Mother's at it again," said Jeanette, leading them into a small bright little room, the family sitting-room on the second floor. "She used to bother Ralph to death; finally we promised her that our children will be Catholic. She'll keep on bothering you, I suppose."

"Oh, that's all right," said Charlotte, taken aback by all this ridiculous religious talk. It was, of course, impossible for her children to be Catholic; her father would never hear of it since most of his support was in the Protestant South.

"Mother takes her religion very seriously," explained Stephen, explaining as he often did the obvious.

New Orleans was gay and Charlotte had never realized that

food could be so well-cooked. One Sunday, after Mardi Gras, they drove up to Baton Rouge to see Uncle Georges, a retired lawyer and the only prosperous member of the family.

Charlotte was glad that Uncle Georges was such a good talker; she could relax for the first time in a week. She thought of Stephen. He was so different from what she had expected; externally he seemed quiet and rather passive, but as a lover he was just the opposite and she considered this phenomenon g avely. He sat opposite her in another armchair to the left of his uncle. His dark hair was tangled from the open drive but his face was serene: enigmatic, that was the word. And Charlotte having found the word which described him found him less mysterious. But now, already, the physical was less important to her (and probably to him) and she had begun to think of money, a home, his career. She was ambitious for him and for herself. She wanted him to be a great man. Not, perhaps, as great as her father but great enough. She hoped the State Department was the right place . . . if only the party was in office; he might be too young for Rome but there was always Brussels or the Hague. Of course they would have several children; dark handsome boys like Stephen; she daydreamed happily.

"Do you, Charlotte?"

She was panic-stricken; she'd not been listening and she had no idea whether she did or did not. "Well," she said uncertainly, waiting for some sign.

"Good," said Uncle Georges; "we'll all have a drink."

"How is your father?" said Uncle Georges when the bourbon had been distributed.

"Very well, thank you. He wanted to be remembered to you."

"Fine, fine. Delightful fellow. I hear he may be running for the Senate soon." She talked to Uncle Georges and she thought of Stephen and the future.

The next day they drove back to New Orleans and Charlotte, as they came closer to the city, was nervous at the thought of Madame Giraud, of more discussions about unborn children.

"We won't have to stay much longer, will we, Stephen? I mean I love your home but I think it'd be nice if we could have some time to ourselves." She was anxious not to hurt Stephen's feelings. He understood.

"I know it's difficult," he said. "We'll try to get away as soon as we can."

But it was not necessary to escape for Madame Giraud that morning had (just after "The Second Mrs Arbuthnot" program), with all the ceremony of her Church, died; she now awaited burial.

6

Charlotte glanced at the gold water lily ring on her finger; it was loose; it had always been loose and she reminded herself to have it fixed. When she looked up Stephen had left the room and the group of women stood, leaderless, by the punchbowl. Fortunately, as Stephen left the room, Mr Moore, the godfather (he'd been in the bathroom he said) returned.

"I've been looking all over for you," she said. "You have to do some work now."

"My godchild's already in trouble? Must be a woman this time." He was a hearty man, red in the face, stocky and generally considered a good fellow, a good mixer, and an excellent politician. He was a Republican from Duluth.

"No, you're going to have to read some sort of incantation over the child's head."

"Fine, fine; you won't mind if I have a short drink first? Even Republicans drink you know." He laughed noisily and went toward the punchbowl; Charlotte felt a vague frustration: he couldn't go far, though. She wondered when Stephen would return.

Florence Nail was still talking to her father.

"Florence, dear, we're going to put you to work."

"Anything, Charlotte; you know I love work." Florence's manner was sardonic and this manner very often gave even her most casual remarks a sinister significance which they did not, rightly, have.

"How's your party, Charlotte?" Her father looked up at her. He moved as little as possible these days. He was far from old but the thought of age and of his death had made him something of a hypochondriac.

"Very well. You found anybody interesting to talk to here?"

"Miss Nail, of course," said her father with a perfunctory gallantry. "But that's about all. People don't seem very interested in politics or anything else any more."

"They're interested in horses," said Florence significantly; the perfunctory compliment had secretly pleased her.

"Yes, the county people have always been interested in horses," said Charlotte. "Even when you were young they were interested in them." This was the wrong thing to say; her father frowned at any reference to his age. She was talking absently, though. She was looking around the room for Herbert Moore. Then she saw him, in back of the punchbowl. Her father grumbled something and then a young couple came over to speak to him. Charlotte took Florence by the hand, led her to Herbert, took Herbert by the hand and led them both to her mother and the Canon.

"Here they are," she said.

"Ah, excellent, excellent," said the Canon. "Now if you'll take these prayerbooks here; yes, that's right. Now I've underlined the parts . . ."

Stephen came back into the room. The noise of the people irritated him slightly; he hated the sound of women laughing in high-pitched voices. He saw Charlotte with Herbert and Florence; Charlotte was leading them to the clergyman in the corner. She was frowning and he wished she would not frown because she was already getting a line like her father's. He looked earnest with a line between his brows; she looked merely peevish. She had grown irritable and impatient in the last year. There had been quarrels: the first serious ones they had ever had. She had reproached him for being incapable of making a home, of making money, of getting ahead. She was almost too ambitious and now, most absurd of all, she told friends that she'd given up a brilliant stage career to marry him and, absurder still, they believed her. Charlotte lied with such inner conviction that she was always believed. Of course, he could not really blame her: she had wanted to escape from her parents, to be independent and she wasn't. Soon, though, they would have a house in Washington.

Then she *was* quite happy with the baby. She had refused until a few months ago to hire a nurse. She had done everything for the child herself. He had complained once that she cared more for the child than she did for him; she had said that it was not her fault. Charlotte very often called on unseen forces to justify and explain her actions. But she had grown a little less interested in the child when she discovered that, after too long a nursing period, her breasts had begun to sag alarmingly. The baby had promptly been bottle-fed and Charlotte found more time to go to parties.

In a few years Stephen was sure that he'd be appointed Minister to some small, probably undesirable country; it would be a beginning, though. Herbert Moore had practically promised him this. Herbert was now talking very seriously to the clergyman. He was something of a buffoon (Herbert was; though, for that matter, so was the clergyman).

Charlotte looked pretty, he thought. She would take a long time to get old and lose her figure. He was body-conscious, a habit from his days as a college athlete, a middleweight boxer. He pulled in his own flat stomach as he thought of bodies and for a second, held his breath.

"Why, Stephen, you're quite red in the face," said Emily, approaching him from the left.

There were shrieks of delight in the room and Charlotte turned from the Canon and saw, near the door, the nurse, a thin woman in a white uniform, leading the baby by the hand. She went over to the door. Someone had picked the child up and it looked rather nervous.

64

"Here, Billy," she said and she took the child in her arms; he was fair and plump and looked, at this minute, rather upset. He didn't talk very well yet, and, fortunately, he almost never cried. He walked well.

"How's he been, Miss Clayton?"

"Perfectly perfect,' said the nurse who tended to be overenthusiastic, given an opportunity. Charlotte seldom gave her an opportunity.

The guests fussed over the child and Charlotte put him down and led him to the corner where his grandmother, godparents and christener were.

"What a fine little man," said the Canon and he put his hand uneasily on the child's head; he disliked children and women and delicately but firmly he had avoided marriage and its inevitable product. Now, of course, at his age, there was no longer any reason to be seriously afraid of children or women and so the Canon treated them more cordially, though he was still both delicate and firm in his relationships with them.

The godparents kissed the baby and his grandmother discovered that his hands were dirty.

"Really, Charlotte, you should have Miss Clayton take better care of him."

"It's not important," said Charlotte, trying to dismiss the subject, to avoid a discussion.

"Not important that your child be kept clean? Why, Charlotte . . ."

"For God's sake, Mother!" snapped Charlotte and the others grew embarrassed as outsiders always do when manners wear thin and the hidden dislike of two people is made suddenly open.

"How old is he?" asked the Canon hurriedly, answering this call to his profession, spreading Christian charity like a syrup.

"What? Oh, he's two, a little over two." Charlotte was still angry. Her mother stood silently beside her, martyred: the serpent's tooth.

"He's certainly a big boy. What's your name, young man?"

The child regarded him interestedly but didn't answer.

"He doesn't talk yet," said Mrs Hawkins, as though scoring a considerable victory against her daughter.

"I see."

The child succumbed to a massive ennui and yawned.

"I expect we bore him," said the Canon, giggling again.

"Let's give him some champagne," said Herbert, the godfather, in need of champagne himself and wishing now that he'd never accepted the job of godfather. He had enough trouble with his own children; especially one son at college who wore his hair unpleasantly long and claimed to be a poet: children were such a nuisance. His wife, dull woman, had thoughtlessly died when the children were quite young. Herbert felt sorry for himself and he wanted to give this child champagne.

"What a terrible idea, Herbert; and *so* like you," said Florence Nail in a suggestive voice; Herbert was upset for a moment, wondering how much this dark sarcastic young woman knew about him. Then, since he'd only met her once or twice before, he decided she knew nothing; still there *was* something in the tone of her voice.

"Now, Miss Nail, you will also read the part of Sponsor. Do you think you can find the place? Here, let me show it to you. It's the first paper clip; I've clipped all the pages where you'll have to read. Yes, here's the first place; it's marked in pencil."

Florence Nail studied the page seriously; she took this godparent business seriously. Of course it was actually just a formality, a social event to these people, even to Charlotte who looked perfectly stunning. Charlotte had been the most stunning girl in school; Florence had had a "crush" on her. They had exchanged pieces of green grass once, years ago (it had been quite the rage to go in "greens" with another girl; an eternal friendship) ; no one knew that in the gold locket Florence always wore about her neck was a piece of grass. She had asked Charlotte recently if she remembered the day they'd gone in "greens" together and Charlotte had quite forgotten. Charlotte forgot everything that happened to her.

Clara Spotsleigh Hawkins regarded her grandchild fondly as he stood between his mother and the Canon. He was so much like William, so very much like him.

Charlotte was talking to the Canon, Charlotte speaking with assurance of matters of which, her mother knew, she understood nothing: christenings, the Church, education. She liked her daughter less and less each year. She loved her still, of course, but she disliked her. She had thought that marriage, having a child, the sharing of similar experiences would draw them closer to one another . . . but it hadn't. There was the same distance between them. Charlotte's vicious temper, her selfishness: if there were better qualities (she is my daughter and there *are* better qualities) her mother was no longer able to recognize them although she tried. It seemed as though her daughter was separated from her by a great distance, a vast expanse of desert. But perhaps this was her fault. Clara Hawkins started an examination of herself, started it dutifully for she was still shaken by the exchange with Charlotte, her breath was still coming in short gasps and, most maddening of all, Charlotte appeared quite cool now, appeared to have forgotten what she had said. Charlotte was always that way. Even when, years ago, that terrible scene had taken place Charlotte had, through some evil magic known only to herself, remained cool and at ease afterwards, after the fit of crying. That was over ten years ago and yet Clara Hawkins, recalling it, still felt a little sick.

How had she known?

She had asked herself this for twelve years. She had never even admitted her drinking to herself, so secret was it. In fact until Charlotte spoke that terrible sentence she had never once thought about her drinking or worried about it. Her daughter made her aware of it, made her feel guilt and with the years the drinking had increased.

But Bill never knew; he would never know. Charlotte wouldn't dare tell him. And he wasn't sufficiently aware of his wife (or anyone else) to discover it for himself. That was Bill's only fault and rather a large one at that; he never noticed things that did not directly concern himself. Bill was selfish. For years Clara Hawkins had thought this about her husband, about all the Hawkins, except her son; he had been a Spotsleigh. He had been like her own charming kindly father who had lived without ever hurting anyone's feelings and, when he died, took so long about it that he managed not to cause too much sadness by his death. He had been placed in the family burial plot where she herself would be buried. She preferred to lie near her father rather than her husband. William, of course, was far away; his golden body rotting in the fields of France. She felt cold and detached, thinking of this, removed from this christening, from everyone. She could only think of all that beauty, her future, in the earth, and she pitied herself as she had pitied herself ever since that day when, suddenly, she had known what was going to happen. She had, at least, been prepared; poor Bill hadn't been, though. Her husband had broken down completely that night when he heard his son was dead; he had wept for the only time in his life and she had been so moved by the violence, the primitiveness of his grief that she had, for once, pitied him more than herself. But now he had forgotten William; they had all forgotten William.

Now the Canon was placing the font on top of the piano. He was wearing his robes and he looked solemn, aware of the Divine power which would soon pass through his hand to her grandson.

People were pulling up chairs, laughing people; everyone laughed nowadays at what was sacred. She hated the smiling people with their insensitive faces and expressionless eyes: people without tragedy and, therefore, incomplete.

Then Charlotte, the child, the godparents all went over to the piano, leaving Clara Hawkins alone. She went over to where her husband sat.

"Does this seem familiar, Bill?"

"What's that, Clara? Familiar?" He had been talking to a group of politicians.

"I said doesn't this seem familiar?"

68

"The christening or the party?"

"The christening, both."

"Well . . . no, I can't say that it does."

She was impatient now; sorry that she'd spoken. The politicians began to withdraw. "William and Charlotte were both christened in here, years ago. Remember?"

"William. . . . Yes, that's right, it was like this. Same preacher, too. Funny, isn't it? everything's just the same. He put the jar in the same place on the piano."

He was old, she thought, looking at him. She hoped he wouldn't get sentimental.

"Will you all take your seats, please?" The Canon's rich sure voice filled the room and there was an obedient silence.

The Vice-President listened. As he grew older he found himself emotionally moved by things that had never moved him before: silly things, romantic things. He had been particularly moved when he discovered in his desk recently a letter from his mother written to him fifty years before when he was in school, written in her elegant spidery handwriting which made the misspellings appear, somehow, right. Now Clara was making him remember his dead son but he could not react to anything but spontaneous memories; when they were forced, the way Clara liked to force things, he felt nothing at all. He felt nothing at all now except, perhaps, a sense of futility, a vista of christenings, one succeeding another endlessly, the same jar on the same piano, the same words being said long after one was gone just as they'd been said a long time before one was born; he was old enough now to see and realize the rise and fall of generations, childhood, manhood, and death. Death.

He moved in his chair, as though by motion to prove to himself he was still alive.

The Canon was still talking; he was explaining the ceremony and making a speech . . . no, a sermon of it.

Clara seemed rather old to him. She was standing beside his chair, her eyes on the Canon; she appeared to be listening intently. Clara had grown more and more silent with the years. She had been rather quiet when she was younger and he thought it a delightful and unusual quality in a woman but now that he was older and had less to say, or, rather, wanted to say less, he would like to have had her talk to him more. But she did not. She ran the house with an uninspired efficiency. She played bridge with several ladies of the county twice a week; she was active on welfare committees and, occasionally, she visited Washington with him for important functions. Sometimes they entertained but usually only small groups. Their lives were slowly ending, it appeared, in inertia.

He wondered whether she'd been drinking today. For years he had known about her drinking and he'd been sorry for her, had wondered what to do. Finally, he had decided that there was nothing to do and, having decided this, he ignored the entire situation; he allowed his wife to maintain her legend. And he wanted, naturally, to keep this a secret from everyone else, Charlotte especially. He looked at Charlotte.

She was sitting in front of the Canon. She wore a white dress today and she looked striking; she was a beautiful woman and, oddly enough, he never felt related to her. She didn't seem to belong to him; she was independent of everyone including Stephen. Yet he was fond of her; they understood one another.

He had forgotten her christening but he remembered his son's clearly. The President had been godfather. Now both William and the President were dead and Charlotte and this child had not been born at that first christening; they were born later, one out of the other. It was a chain, that was the usual image, and one man, one old man, could see the links behind him and the ones ahead of him with a greater clarity than younger people, with a chilling clarity for this was a large thing, impersonal; he shuddered thinking of it.

Now the most recent extension of the chain was before him, a placid blond child, held by its mother in a room of politicians, exposed to the facsimile pomp of the Episcopal Church.

That was the trouble; the church. For the church, which

should be able to comfort him now as it had his father ("I die confident of entering an everlasting life": his father's words), did nothing of the sort for him. He was confident of nothing, of Nothing. It seemed like such a conceit to feel that there was a personal guardian for each of the many human beings born, creatures who move about the earth like ants in an ant hill and are, actually, less numerous than ants. The whole business was absurd. He had read about most of the religions and he was, at last, aware that the basis of every religion was political not mystical, regardless of the apparent and perhaps genuine mysticism of the ostensible founders. The churches were almost always formed as political instruments to frighten people into the obedience of temporal customs ("Slaves, obey thy masters."). It was so convenient to keep people from killing one another by maintaining that they, when their bodies ceased to function, would, had they disobeyed certain laws, spend eternity in a place of torture. And if there were contradictions one, if one had faith, ignored them for there was a constant confusion in all sects about good and evil. Why, for instance, did the Christian God go to all the trouble of making a world (the center of the universe until recently) to test people, to tell whether they were good or bad, when he had created them in the first place and, being omnipotent, had known whether they were to be, ultimately, good or evil? It all seemed rather complicated and a little insane. Why not make them all "good" and put them in Heaven to begin with? Logic and the functioning of the human mind had nothing to do with these fantasies; to attack them merely meant that one was doomed and lacked faith. If one succeeded in an argument with a religious man one was accused of dialectics and submitted to the final, the crushing argument, of the God-worshippers: "Then how did life start?" As if the unknown beginnings of origin on this plane of being (and there were doubtless countless other planes) had anything to do with this examiner God of theirs. It was enough to admit that there was reality. The origins of reality were not yet explored but there was very little reason to suppose that this unusually human Christian God had had much to do with the making of existence.

But as a politician he appreciated the value of religion; its power in maintaining a certain amount of order. Individual mystical revelations he found tiresome and not of much interest to an adult. He had, also, been interested to note that once churches were divorced from the actual exercise of temporal power, they tended to wither.

The Canon spoke of life everlasting.

Clara Hawkins felt relaxed as the melodious familiar words flowed in her ears; she was transfigured by the sound of the Canon's voice, by the soothing promises of eternal happiness. It would be complete happiness to spend eternity with William in the Carolina house which, in Heaven, would be theirs again.

Stephen tried not to yawn. He hadn't slept well the night before. Emily was standing on his left and Charlotte on his right. Emily was standing much too close to him, her right hand barely touching his leg. This was very entertaining; he wondered if he should move closer to her. Emily, though a fool, was an attractive woman and he suspected that he was the only reasonably attractive man in the room who hadn't had her. He tried to make up his mind what to do.

Charlotte listened carefully. She concentrated hard on the words, ignoring the sentences and their combined meaning. She had always had a difficult time with Shakespeare and the Bible. They sounded almost exactly alike to her and had the Canon suddenly said: "I am dying, Egypt, dying," she would have thought it the Old Testament. Billy moved restlessly; she tightened her hold on him. He tried to distract her from the words she was concentrating on but she would not be distracted. She would listen to these words, utterly oblivious of the people in the room; people who were still drinking she could hear, for, behind the mysteriously vague words of the Bible, she heard ice clicking against glass. But this was a solemn moment and she would be solemn, too. She had a gift for surrendering herself to the moment if the moment was not too long. If she were with a General for five minutes she would find herself speaking easily in military clichés. With novelists she spoke knowingly of publishers, galleys, reprints. Now in the presence of the Church and the Christian God she thought in terms of "verily," "thou," and "life everlasting."

"I am dying, Egypt, dying."

"Will the sponsors for the child step forward?"

How pretty Charlotte is, thought Florence Nail, who had always thought this; she always looked at Charlotte when she was with her. White is so becoming to her. Did we wear white when we graduated from school . . . yes, we did wear white. But then Charlotte left school before graduation. That was when she went on the stage. It was a pity she gave up her career for Stephen. He isn't right for her. Is any man right for Charlotte, for Charlotte?

Stephen decided to move closer to Emily. He did and her hand felt very cold. He let his own hand drop near hers. The blood rushed to his head. He looked at Charlotte beside him. She was frowning slightly, listening to the sermon; it was a sermon now. He wondered how the old fool had had the nerve to give a sermon to this particular group of indifferent slightly drunk people. Emily would be pleasant but she'd talk about it; he would have to be faithful because he couldn't afford to be talked about. With an effort of will he stopped the pulse in his throat that was beginning to flutter. He moved away. Emily sighed.

The Vice-President decided that this was the last christening the Canon would ever do in his house; he was giving a sermon and, from the sound of it, a much-used one. He looked about the room and saw that the guests were uncomfortable and this pleased him so that he was almost glad the Canon had decided to sermonize. He disliked these people, suspecting their motives. People were so eager when they were with him. It was not so much that they wanted something specific (though often they did); rather they wanted to *be* something and he must help them; he must touch them with the glamour of history. Through contact with him they became more important, more glamorous to themselves. "You look like a Saint," said the women who met him during a campaign. He grinned as he thought of this. He looked at his wife who, he knew, wanted to look like a Saint but succeeded, after much effort, in looking only pained. But perhaps the Saints also looked pained. They were a pretty queer lot anyway.

Clara Hawkins was mesmerized by the promise of Heaven which the Canon was now extending to her as a reward for a difficult life well-done. She was carried upon his words, a leaf on a river with no rapids, no visible whirlpools or waterfalls. She didn't hear the sounds of drinking nor did she smell the smoke of many cigars. She listened instead to the many comforting words. She would be rewarded.

The Canon was afraid now that he'd spoken too long. It had happened quite without premeditation. He had slipped into one of his favorite sermons which he'd not given for some time. He had slipped into it effortlessly and the familiar cadences had sounded so good to him that he wasn't able to stop. The expression on the Vice-President's face *did* stop him, though. He disliked the great William Hawkins almost as much as his audience professed to admire him. The Canon sensed that the great man thought his Church amusing and the Canon hated him most uncharitably, aware also that the great man had a good-humored contempt for himself and, further, had once expressed a doubt that he, Canon Southey, believed what he preached. I do believe, though, he said to himself, motioning the godparents to step forward and speak. I must believe.

At last he's stopped. The Vice-President sat back in his chair. It would soon be over. Already he wanted to talk again. He was so used to talking that an enforced silence, when there was an audience near by, upset him. He would tell that story about Hoover. He smiled as he prepared it in his mind, got the sentences right.

The hand, with drops of water on the fingers, was raised

high, dominating the room. An incantation was said. The hand descended slowly toward the head of the child.

"I christen you William Hawkins . . . ," and Charlotte, listening, looked at the fair hair, the blue eyes of her son: terror rose in her, engulfed her.

A single drop of water fell on his face.

the white flowers

ONE THING: he would not have to go to school this week. The school had been very understanding: they consoled him for his loss as well as for the nation's, for William Hawkins died in the early spring of 1940 and his grandson mourned with the rest of the family in the old home.

It had been a shock to the family, especially to Bill. He had seen his grandfather at New Year's and he had seemed well, not at all like a man who, three months later, would be dead. Bill had always thought that a man about to die would show it, would have a certain expression in his eyes: like an El Greco perhaps. But his grandfather had been cheerful and almost agile (in the last few years he moved very little). As recently as last fall Bill had escorted him to the Senate chamber where he had made his famous speech against the President who, he maintained, was maneuvering the country into war, just as another President had done over two decades before. Now the Capitol was in mourning and the President had made a surprisingly nice statement about the passing of an elder statesman. Tonight the house was crowded with relatives, political friends, newspapermen; almost anyone who wanted to get in the house got in. At the moment Bill was hungry, for, with the death of the center of the house, all the outlying parts of the house, including the kitchen, had ceased to function. Well, he would go out to the kitchen later on. He was really quite hungry. Neither he nor his mother had had lunch when they left Washington around noon. His grandfather had died several hours earlier though no one had been notified until noon. He'd died of a cerebral hemorrhage while dictating a speech; he had fainted and, a few minutes later, died; everyone commented on how quick, how easy death had been. A delegation had been selected from the Senate and the House and they would come officially tomorrow for the burial at Arlington. A few were in the house now, consoling Mrs Hawkins and drinking bourbon sadly.

The Vice-President lay, pale and handsome in his coffin in the drawing room. Here candles were lit and the shades pulled down, curtains drawn, as people silently passed through the room to look at William Hawkins.

Bill Giraud had been impressed by the whole business. Death, it appeared, was an incredibly solemn business and not, basically, unattractive. It definitely had its aesthetic side and certainly it provided drama and interest for people who, looking at the dead, envisioned themselves cold and lifeless: ridiculous thought; when one was alive death was abstract. One would never be aware that one had ceased to be aware, had begun to decompose. It was a fascinating subject to explore and, mentally, he explored it.

His grandmother was pale and her eyes and the end of her nose were rather red; she had, no doubt, cried a great deal in private. When Bill and his mother arrived from Washington they found that the embalming had already been done, that the Vice-President would lie in state this evening and would, in the morning, be buried at Arlington. Bishop Southey officiating.

His mother's reaction to all this interested him. He always watched her when he was with her, trying to discover what she felt, how she would react to things; she was not at all consistent and he watched her, almost hypnotized. She was beautiful. He never really thought she was beautiful because he knew her features, her expressions too well but because everyone else thought she was, he did, too.

He watched her in the car as they drove out to the house. She was greatly moved, he knew, but she didn't weep; her face was set and she wore a black dress (not as attractive as a dress she'd worn once, years ago; a white dress with silver stars on it: Titania).

She had kissed his grandmother warmly when they got out of the car. The two embraced for a longer time than usual. Then newspapermen took pictures and asked for statements. The members of Congress were grave, troubled; several were drunk but solemnly so. They spoke to Bill kindly, recognizing him, and he tried to look serious and (as much as possible) like his grandfather, although his dark suit was too small for him and he had to keep pulling the trousers down.

Two of the politicians were off in a corner of the hall talking and Bill, who liked listening to private conversations, listened to this one while he appeared to be listening to a fat man who was telling him what a great man his grandfather had been. It was a curious effect listening to two conversations at once. He managed to hear most of the private one, though.

"Who in the name of God's going to be appointed?"

"Damned if I know. No one had any idea the old devil would go off like this."

"The Governor isn't here yet, is he?"

"No, he isn't coming till tomorrow; he'll be at the funeral, I suppose."

"You haven't any idea who he's going to appoint?"

"No, not much. As you know he's a great friend of mine and I did chalk up the largest Congressional vote in the last election." The man who said this laughed jovially to show that he was joking if necessary, or serious if necessary; it was an ambiguous laugh.

"He could do a lot worse," said the other, nodding. "Atkins and Mason will both expect the appointment, too, and . . . Good Lord!"

"What?"

"You don't think the Governor'd appoint that battle-ax?"

"What battle-ax?"

"The widow. Clara Hawkins."

The other man grunted, considering. "I never thought of that. I don't think he will. Still, he *was* a protégé of old Hawkins and he's pretty sentimental. Yes, it might be a smart move politically . . . for the Governor anyway. We'll have to stop that."

"If he tries it."

"Yes, if he tries it. Let's find a drink. Someone in this morgue must have a bottle."

Bill finished his conversation with the fat man. Then he went into the library. His mother was there. She looked tired, wilted. She was alone and sitting at the Vice-President's desk.

"Are you tired?" asked Bill, wanting to help her. She didn't answer, though. She sat in the chair, daydreaming, one hand resting in a rather curious position on the desk. Finally she said, "Get me water, Bill."

He went back to the kitchen. There were newspapermen here, too. They were laughing and telling stories and, he noticed, eating. The servants were nowhere in sight. He poured a glass of water and then, after a moment's hesitation, he went to the icebox and took out a slab of cold beef in his fingers. He ate it quickly, greedily; he was very hungry.

"You took a long time," said his mother. She took a swallow of water and then put the glass on the desk in front of her. He sat down on the couch and looked at her. Lately her hair had begun to turn gray around her face but, except for her hereditary frown, her face was an unlined as ever.

His stepfather came into the room.

"You're late," she said; she sounded weary, martyred.

"I'm sorry, dear." He bent down and kissed her cheek. "I was busy at the bank until late. It was all so sudden. Where's your mother?"

"Upstairs, I think. I don't know why she's let all these people in; it's like a madhouse. It's so undignified this way, so . . . cheap."

"You must remember," said her husband gently, "that your father was public property." He paused and then said in a hushed, reverent tone, "What time did he die?"

"Around eight-thirty, I think."

"Your mother's certainly managed everything well. She must be terribly upset, too."

"Oh . . . yes, I expect she is; naturally she is. It happened so quickly."

"It was a cerebral hemorrhage, wasn't it?"

She nodded, not answering.

"Well, then it was quick." Everyone seemed to be so glad that *it* was sudden; Bill wondered if it might not be better slow, a gradual death. Not painful, of course; just gradual. Everyone was impressed by the suddenness, though.

"The papers are full of it this evening; even got the war down at the bottom of the page." His stepfather sounded pleased; he was a wealthy man, a bank president and he'd admired the Vice-President. He had been thrilled to marry his daughter. Bill suspected that he liked publicity although he, like his wife, maintained that nothing in the newspapers was ever true.

Clara Hawkins entered the study. She walked unsteadily and Bill decided that grief had upset her equilibrium which was, he had often noticed before, never very good. He and his stepfather stood up. His stepfather, looking solemn, went up to Clara Hawkins and said, "I'm sorry I couldn't get here earlier. If there's anything I can do . . . anything . . ." he mumbled earnestly.

"Nothing, thank you, Roger."

"They'll soon be out of the house," said her son-in-law comfortingly.

They were still a moment.

"The Governor called me tonight," said Mrs Hawkins at last.

"Is he coming tomorrow?" Charlotte asked in a voice to show that, though she was willing to converse automatically, she could not be expected to concentrate.

"Yes," said Mrs Hawkins. "He also told me that he's appointed me to the rest of Bill's term in the Senate."

"What?" Charlotte sat up very straight, alert and concentrating. "You didn't accept the appointment did you?"

"Oh yes; I told him I'd accept." Clara Hawkins was calm, even triumphant. "It's only for two years more anyway."

"But what on earth would you do in the Senate? My Lord, you've never paid any attention to politics. Father always said you knew less about politics than any politician's wife he'd ever known."

Bill couldn't understand why his mother was so excited. He thought it very nice that his grandmother was to be a Senator.

"That isn't true," said Clara Hawkins evenly. "I've lived in politics for forty years and I've learned quite a bit. Roger, would you get me a drink, please? I'm so tired."

Roger grinned. "Certainly, Clara." He left the room.

"I think you're being very foolish, Mother," began Charlotte.

"I don't think it's really any of your business, dear."

Charlotte sat back suddenly as if she'd been struck. Bill tried to hide himself as much as possible in the couch. He had never heard his grandmother speak like this to his mother. In fact he'd always thought of his grandmother as a helpless figure, a foil for his mother's occasionally unkind humor.

"What do you mean it isn't any of my business?" Charlotte's face was red now and her eyes glittered. Her voice sounded angry and harsh, the sound that Bill had always feared, that once meant a beating and now, even worse, meant reproaches. "It's a very important matter to me what happens to the Hawkins name. It *is* my business what my father's widow does. After all you were only married to a Hawkins."

"I have been," said Clara Hawkins, "a Hawkins for forty years and I must say I've never disgraced the name. And, speaking of disgracing a name, *you* were the first Hawkins ever to be divorced."

"Bill, go get the white flowers you left in the car; put them

81

in with Grandfather." Charlotte's voice was sharp and barely controlled.

He left the room quickly. He could hear the voices of the two women arguing as he crossed the hall and went out the front door to the driveway. There were many cars parked here. He would have trouble finding theirs.

In the old days, many many years before, when he was seven, six years ago, he came often to this house to visit his grandparents. He liked staying in the house even better than the place where he'd lived with his father and mother in Washington; at least he lived with his mother for his father was almost never home. He traveled for the Government and once he brought Bill a small Eiffel Tower and another time a copper camel from Egypt. Bill had quite a collection of things like this. He also had two castles made of wood and hundreds of English soldiers (they were only made in England; they represented all nationalities and periods in history). It was possible with blocks to build fortifications between the two castles where, one in each, the two kings lived. One was Napoleon and the other was Thutmose of Egypt. Bill had read a long book with small type and interesting pictures about this Pharaoh; some of the words confused him but the impression was glamorous and he always gave one castle to Thutmose. He had to have Napoleon because he had a Napoleon-figure, with one hand in vest. When he grew bored with Napoleon he would demote him to a company commander and have him killed at the beginning of a campaign.

School interrupted his days.

School had started without reason two years before when, at five, he'd been sent to a kindergarten. He had already forgotten most of that year. He'd been sick to his stomach the first day and all of his memories after that were a confusion; noise, paper, paste, sandboxes and someone playing the Grand March from Aïda as they trooped downstairs at recess time.

The first grade (last year) was still vivid in his memory, though. He had played quite a bit in the playground. There was an interesting jungle of iron bars which he could climb around in. There was also a sandbox which he found dull (not at all like the sand beach beside his grandfather's river). His clearest memory outside of the classroom was of a small boy named Sidney. He had dark hair and wore a beret which meant, as everyone knew, that he was a sissy. The only way to cope with Sidney was to hit him quite hard in the face. Unfortunately Sidney's nose, which had been very small and frail to begin with, broke and there was a frightening amount of bright red blood. Bill was known then as a troublemaker and this was, in a way, fortunate for he disliked fighting and now everyone was afraid of him; also, he was large for his age.

The classroom itself was pleasant, though a little tedious. His teacher was a woman with gray hair who preferred the girls in the class to the boys; a situation which was, obviously, resented by the boys. She taught everyone to read, however. Everyone except Bill who had learned how at home the year before. First came the alphabet. For each letter she'd put an apple, a toy bear, any object that corresponded with the letter, on the window sill. She did several letters a day. Bill tolerated this. He found it extremely dull sitting in the classroom but he accepted the fact that he had to sit there; when he was younger he would've run away. He ran away from home several times and each time the police brought him back and his mother had whipped him. He remembered once standing at the window watching her outside in the garden, tearing off a switch from a dogwood tree. It was spring and the dogwood was green and she had trouble in breaking the branch off but she did finally. Then she came upstairs. It was late afternoon and the room was almost dark and the light of her cigarette burned red in the dark. She whipped him with the stick until blood came, until his bare legs bled and when he tried to hold the stick she burned one of his hands with the lighted cigarette. This happened often. Now that he was in the second grade he could be sure of a whipping once a month. Sometimes the whippings were just and sometimes they weren't but in either case he regarded them as inevitable. His father never whipped him, though; he loved his mother the most, of course, but he liked being with his father more.

Then, just this year, soon after the second grade started, a mysterious thing happened. His mother asked him if he ever touched himself there which was certainly an unusual question since it was impossible not to and he said, of course. They were in the bathroom; she said that wasn't what she meant and he had no way of knowing what she did mean. She was severe and she asked him to tell her the truth and then he started to cry and she took him in her arms and everything was all right again, safe and secure.

Then the doctor came and asked him the same questions. He said no this time. Finally he discovered that an unpleasant fat boy who lived next door (he barely knew him) had been caught doing something rather mysterious to himself and when his mother had caught him said that Bill had shown him. The whole thing was confusing and, though, after a few days, he stopped consciously thinking about it, he never really forgot.

Now, at seven, there were a great many interesting things in books; he read all the books he could get. When he visited his grandfather he was allowed to sit for hours reading in his grandfather's large library. He enjoyed reading adult books in spite of the difficult, often impossible, words. His mother would come in, of course, and tell him he should be outside playing; she always wanted him outside. His grandmother would rescue him, though. She would say that his reading did no harm and then the two women would go into another room and argue, leaving him in peace. It seemed that his mother was always arguing with someone though she said she hated arguments and only liked "discussions". She was wonderful; she smelt better than roses and when she took him in her arms he was happy and he could almost forget the beatings.

He read a lot: the *Arabian Nights* especially, even though the letters were terribly small. He played with his soldiers and, when he was home in the city, he wandered around the streets of the neighborhood and played with a few boys, but they were all rather stupid, even the ones who were eight or nine years old. A boy named Tommy was his best friend for a year, then something or other happened and they stopped being friends; they didn't see each other for a long time.

The second grade was in a new school. This was much the best school of the three he'd been to. It had two acres around it, right in the city. Best of all there was a tremendous pile of lumber at one end of the playground; it had once been a wooden house that had been pulled down. The lumber pile was very high and it was full of tunnels and secret rooms where no large person could go. Many of the boys explored the lumber pile; none of the girls did because they were afraid they'd ruin their dresses. The boys wore corduroy knickers which were impossible to ruin.

Bill soon became the king of the lumber pile. He ordered passages built and rooms made and because he was strong *and* knew all the secret passages he was the acknowledged King and he wore a gold crown which had formerly encircled a furnace pipe at home. He hated five o'clock when he had to go home, to abdicate. Often as not his mother had something to scold him about, something she had been thinking about all day. He was not, she claimed, "considerate" and he knew she was right. Every day when he got up he'd make up his mind to be considerate but when he offered to do something for her she would tell him not to bother her and so, since it was impossible to be considerate, he accepted her reproaches seriously, knowing that to appear serious and contrite would save him from a beating. There were times when he wished he was a man, fourteen at least. But that age seemed far away.

His allowance was twenty-five cents a week after he got in the second grade. It was a great deal and he invested it mostly in chocolate, rock candy and artillery for his armies. Sometimes he would save a dime and when he had ten dimes he would buy an Oz book; these books were quite wonderful and there were, fortunately, so many of them that he could always find a new one in the bookstore.

One day, however, he went through his mother's pocketbook and found a silver piece twice as large as a quarter. He went to the drugstore and found he could buy ten chocolate bars with it. His mother discovered this and he was beaten and called a thief; in the future he took only nickels or dimes from her pocketbook: it was an adventure and as important as the money.

She could surprise him pleasantly, though. Once he had been playing in the vacant lot near their house. There were many big bushes that he could hide under and make houses of. One day in the fall he built a fire in the stone stove of the bush house and the dry branches caught on fire; he ran home. All the bushes in the vacant lot were in flame. A policeman came to their house and his mother told him how sorry she was, told him who she was, was polite but positive and the policeman left, charmed. She was very nice to Bill and told him not to play with matches again. He was surprised and relieved.

In the summer they went to the seashore and stayed in a thin-walled house among a number of thin-walled houses, all surrounded by pine trees. The pines smelt wonderful, like Christmas, but it was painful to step on a pine cone barefoot. Twice he swam out too far and almost drowned. Each time his mother had saved him. The second time it happened she lost her car keys in the sand and he was beaten for this. It was a strange lonely sensation to be out beyond the line of swimmers, to feel himself being pulled farther and farther away from shore. He had trod water but somehow, strangely, he was too embarrassed to call for help, too proud. He would not call for help even if he drowned and it was lonely, swallowing salt water and floating farther away from the white beach. His mother, watching him from the shore, saw he was out too far and she brought him back.

His father was usually with them during the summers at the beach. His father liked to bury him up to his neck in sand; this was fun though sometimes the sand felt very heavy, packed all around him. When his father was not at the beach he played by himself, building cities out of sand. First he would build a great sea-wall against which the waves battered futilely and

86

then, behind this wall, he would build an Arabian Nights city with domes and minarets. Sometimes he would destroy these cities himself, pretending to be a djinn; other times the sea would attack the city, coming up over the wall, flooding the streets, and buildings would crack and towers crumble most realistically. It was marvelous how, within a few minutes, an elaborate city would vanish into a level stretch of sand.

The days when he stayed with his grandparents were the best. He spent the summer with them in the big house although his mother had wanted him to go away to camp. "To learn to be self-reliant." Whatever that meant. His grandfather had insisted, however, that he stay with him that summer and his grandfather was always obeyed, even by his mother. On weekends his mother would come see him and, occasionally, his father.

He had finished with the second grade and he looked forward to the third grade which he would start the next fall. He would return to the woodpile school and he was glad; his mother had sent him to different schools every year because he "wasn't developing properly." She seemed to like this one, though. Since Bill disliked athletics the school said that he showed no leadership and his mother talked to him gravely about this. No one knew of his kingdom or of his underground leadership.

One day Bill fell off the top of the lumber pile (he seldom went up to the top, preferring the familiar labyrinth beneath); he cut his head badly and blood streamed down into his face. He was carried to the school nurse who was too frightened to do much of anything. They called a doctor and his father. His father arrived first, very pale; he had been in an important conference. Then Bill fainted. He came to in his father's car; they were driving home. The back of his head had been shaved and plastered.

He was a figure of heroic proportions in the school afterwards, for almost two weeks.

Unfortunately, the lumber pile was consequently made illegal and so it was necessary for the kingdom to become even more mysterious and undeclared. It was like, as Bill suggested one day in the most secret room, the early Christians in the catacombs.

He'd liked the second-grade teacher very much. She taught them all about Greek mythology and Hawaii; all of his life he was to confuse Mauna Loa with Mount Olympus. Each person in the class was made a Greek god and, by general consent, Bill was Apollo, the Sun-god, because he was so blond. This pleased him since Apollo was the most attractive of the gods.

The second grade ended in June with the inevitable pageant. One of the school's older girls (seventeen years old and practically married it was rumored) was Queen of the Spring Pageant. All the younger children were elves and fairies and they wore costumes. The Queen was the loveliest of all for she wore a flowing pale dress and flowers in her hair and, as the little girls in Bill's class noticed enviously, high-heeled shoes. Bill found being an elf hot and very boring. The principal of the school, a thin woman with white hair, presided at the Maypole about which everyone was supposed to dance. It was, as the pessimistic second graders had predicted, a dismal failure for several inscrutable first-graders had decided, at the last moment, to go the wrong way around the Maypole. The Maypole was finally deserted and the thousands and thousands of parents watching the pageant thought this was funny. But the Principal was upset. The Queen was crowned quickly then and the elves and fairies were free to join their parents.

This was also the spring of the locusts. The trees and bushes were full of them and Bill and his best friend, a boy named George, made a small guillotine with a razor blade and pieces of weed and they beheaded hundreds of locusts in imitation of the French Revolution. Bill had just been reading Carlyle and he found the French Revolution extraordinarily entertaining; he especially liked the man who was both green and incorruptible.

School ended with the pageant and there was the now familiar discussion about camp. His grandparents won; he was to stay with them. His father would be on a mission to Denmark and his mother was planning to visit friends on Long Island.

"What've you been reading, Bill?" his grandfather, who approved of reading, would always ask him this when he got back from the Hill in the afternoon. He worked on the Hill almost every day. *His* vacation hadn't started yet.

"All about Egypt." Bill climbed into his grandfather's lap. His grandmother went to get the drink; his grandfather always had liquor when he got back from work. They were on the porch overlooking the green lawns which fell away from the house and turned into gardens, then into woods and, finally, descended steeply into the river. It was warm this afternoon. The sun was already behind the trees and the tree toads were making noises; far away the river roared.

"Who were you reading about?" His grandfather undid his vest and sat back with a sigh. Bill examined his gold watch which, when a button was pressed, made chimes.

"About Ikhnaton mostly."

"Did you understand it?"

"Oh, some I did. There weren't many battles but there were some pictures of him and his wife."

"Did you read about monotheism?"

"Oh, yes. That was in there, too. It was pretty dull." Bill was vague.

"It's very interesting," said his grandfather. "He was the first Egyptian Pharaoh to say that there was one god. Quite an interesting concept for Egypt; naturally the priests didn't like him."

"But he was right, wasn't he?"

His grandfather was vague then. "Who knows what's right, Bill? In church you're supposed to think yes. But you'll have to decide all that for yourself. Do you go to church in Washington, with your mother?"

Bill shook his head. "I've never been in a church yet." He

liked to look at them from the outside, though; his mother's cook went every Sunday and she told him about the music and singing.

"Good," said his grandfather. "Don't ever go if you can help it and don't tell anybody I told you that . . . not even your grandmother. She goes to church herself but it's different with women."

Bill promised he wouldn't tell anyone.

His grandmother came in and gave his grandfather his liquor. "Run get us some grapes, Bill," she said. "But wash them before you bring them out."

Bill was always pleased to be sent to the vineyard. Just before the last garden became woods there was a long row of grapevines. Sometimes in the evening Bill was allowed to pick grapes for his grandfather. He took a pair of scissors and half a coconut shell with him. He had grown very fond of coconuts lately since he'd read the *Swiss Family Robinson*. Grapes looked rustic in a coconut shell.

He cut several clusters of the dark purple grapes. He ate a few himself; there was an art to eating them: first the skin cracked and then the grape, skinless, slipped into one's mouth. He chewed the seeds because if he swallowed them whole he'd get appendicitis and it was too much trouble to spit them out. He washed the grapes in the kitchen and took them out on the porch. He and his grandfather ate most of them.

Bill was comfortable here; he wore only a pair of short pants, no shirt, no shoes. Once when the chauffeur drove into Washington to pick up his grandfather he went with him and, barefoot, Bill walked down the halls of the Capitol to his grandfather's committee room. The policeman wouldn't let him go in, wouldn't believe that he was Senator Hawkins' grandson. Finally the committee of Senators came out of the room and his grandfather introduced him to all of them. They laughed and said the Hawkins family was just ordinary "white trash" after all. It became one of his grandfather's favorite stories.

Bill sat in his lap and ate grapes. "Did you pass the bill?" he asked.

"Which bill is that?"

"Oh, you know: *the* bill." All his life he'd heard his grandfather and the other Senators talk about passing the bill. It seemed quite foolish to him that grown men should spend all day in the Capitol passing a dollar bill (perhaps it was more) from one to another.

"No, it won't come to the floor for a vote until next week. It's still in committee." That was part of the game: the bill had to be put on the floor before it could be passed.

"Did they postpone adjournment again?" asked his grandmother.

"No, it's still the same date. Unless the New Dealers give us some new crisis." His grandfather was sarcastic. He didn't like the New Deal which, Bill understood, had something to do with the new President who couldn't walk.

2

"He and Roosevelt hated each other like poison," said one newspaperman to another; they were standing in the driveway talking.

"F.D.R. sent a nice note to the widow, though."

"Politics. The old boy was a great figure in the South. Doesn't hurt to say nice things about him now he's dead."

"Who gives a damn about the South?" said the other man who was, Bill decided, from the North, probably New York.

Tree frogs made rusty noises and a piece of the white moon shone in the cloudy sky. Last night his grandfather had seen the moon. Where *was* the car? More cars were driving in all the time and parking. He would have a difficult time finding the flowers.

A bowl of yellow chrysanthemums was in the center of the table. The table was very gay with birthday decorations. Earlier he'd received many presents, now there was a party:

he was ten and in four years he'd be fourteen and grown. Time had, at last, after a slow start, begun to move. Twenty-one was still a century away but fourteen was nearer.

The boys started coming at noon; this was Saturday; much the best day to have a birthday party.

There had been, earlier, some discussion as to whether it would be good form to invite girls or not; there were, of course, both boys and girls in his class. His mother thought he should have both but when she learned that the girls in his class never invited boys to *their* parties she left the problem up to him. He invited one girl named Virginia. She had long blond hair which he had, when he was younger and in the third grade, often pulled. Now they were on more dignified terms; they exchanged valentines. Ten boys, remnants of the kingdom of the now vanished woodpile, were invited.

Now they were coming.

Bill and his mother welcomed them. Each one brought a present. Everybody was subdued and cleaned; conversation was neutral, polite. Virginia arrived looking pretty, valiant as well, for there was a discouraged sigh from the boys when they saw that a girl had arrived. Bill was nice to her, though, since they were lovers. Two years ago, when they were younger and more depraved, Virginia had suggested that they go out into the bushes together. During recess time they did. They had gravely examined one another and Bill, especially, was surprised at the difference between them; then the bell rang and they went back to class. It had been very instructive for Bill and when the boys talked about girls, which was, admittedly, seldom, Bill was accepted as the authority. Actually he found procreation rather baffling. He had an idea that when a woman had a child her navel opened up and the child crawled out of her stomach. Then the navel closed up again. She could only have a child if she was married so the ceremony had more to do with it than anything else.

His mother, looking beautiful in a pale yellow dress, took them to the table and then she left. It was a wonderful party. Lewis, their Negro houseboy and part-time cook, served. There was a loud cheer when the chocolate birthday cake was finally brought in and only a few pieces of it were thrown about the room.

That evening as he was going to bed he heard his mother in the next room say to his father, with a sigh, "Well, he's ten years old now. It's been quite a job but I think I've done it well." His father agreed with her and Bill, pleased to be thought a good job, went to sleep.

His grandfather gave him a watch two weeks later, just before he went to camp.

"You're ten now, Bill," he said. "You're in the two-digit class and you'll never get out of it. You're getting old at last." This last pleased him; he asked his grandfather for an explanation of two digits and when his grandfather told him he asked, "Suppose I live to be a hundred?"

"No one in our family lives to be a hundred," said his grandfather, sadly he thought. His grandfather was over seventy now.

His mother gave him a gold signet ring and he regarded his advancing age as both pleasant and materially profitable.

School would soon be over. The Spring Pageant (he had experienced several of them now and he was quite cynical) would take place next week and he had a warrior role this time, a considerable advance over the elf and fairy days.

This summer he would go to a camp in New England. It would be his second summer at camp. This year it had been said that he was lazy and not self-reliant and, worst of all, not a "good mixer": it was extremely important to be a "good mixer" and he appreciated the difficult time his mother had in making him one. She only scolded and lectured now. He had grown quite large and the beatings had, at last, ceased. After dinner at night, when she was home, she would almost invariably talk to him about his turning over a new leaf, making a success of himself. His bad marks in school and his laziness at home had convinced her that he would never succeed and this worried her. Once he had heard her tell a teacher of his that he had absolutely no money sense at all. "I don't care

93

what you do as long as you do it well." He had heard this many times. One had to be a success. He wondered just how one went about it for his mother's advice was usually more general than specific.

His father he saw very little. When he was home from Europe he would take Bill to the movies and sometimes to Glen Echo, an amusement park near Washington. They got on very well and they didn't take one another too seriously.

The camp was casual; the food was bad and everything was handled inefficiently. The camp was near a large New Hampshire lake. The boys lived in cabins named, inspiringly, after American Presidents, Republican Presidents. Twelve boys to a cabin and a councilor. The councilors were young college men, tall and strong, handsome and infinitely wise. They were admired by all the boys.

For two years Bill had the same councilor, a man named Fisherman. He was, unlike the others, neither tall nor handsome but he was infinitely wise and because Bill read more than any of the other boys he took an interest in him. It was at this time that Bill had decided that, next to history, Horatio Alger was the most exciting writer he'd ever read. The camp had a few Tarzan books, some books about religion in unpleasant black bindings and a complete (if there could be a complete) set of Mr Alger's work. Bill read all of them. They were simultaneously exciting and relaxing. One loathed the arrogant Squire's son and one admired the strong boy hero. One feared for the hero when he left the farm and came to the city after receiving his deceased uncle's legacy of twenty-five dollars (which the Squire had tried to keep from him). And one was overjoyed, if not surprised, when the hero, after some unpleasant events which tested his honesty and pluck, got a secure job in American Business and married his employer's daughter and was able to give the Squire's son a job as a clerk (the Squire had speculated with capital and lost). Our hero's last act was to pay off the mortgage of his mother's farm. Part of Bill's satisfaction in reading these books came from the fact that all these marvelous boys became successful. He wondered if he ever could be like them. Probably not, because as his mother said he was spoiled; he had everything. He couldn't become a bootblack like Bob and, alas, he couldn't play the fiddle like Phil; he knew nothing about farms and most of these boys came from farms. He was discouraged. His background was all wrong and he could never succeed because he was lazy. He would take out a long hair of his mother which he kept enclosed in tinfoil inside a match box: this was his totem. Tears would come to his eyes when he looked at this hair and he knew he could not fail its owner although he was already, he was sure, a failure in her eyes. He made up his mind to make something of himself, to be like a Horatio Alger boy; then, his mind made up, he re-enclosed the sacred hair and made an effort, usually a futile one, to be a good mixer.

He never liked people in groups much. He always had one very good friend and usually a gang, a group of disciples. He had a liking and a gift for organizing secret societies.

Fisherman, that pale young man, a divinity student, told him that the Alger books were bad. This was something of a sacrilege and his admiration of Fisherman was severely tested.

"What do you mean they're bad?"

"Don't you think they're too materialistic?"

"Well. . . ." he wasn't sure what this meant.

"Don't you think there's something in life more important than making money?"

"Sure." He knew the answer to that one. "Being famous is."

"And there's nothing more important than these things?"

"I don't know what," said Bill with great conviction.

"What about the soul?"

Every evening Fisherman gave the boys a sermon while the sun was setting. The whole camp would stand around him on the baseball diamond, near the flagpole, where, a few minutes earlier the flag had been lowered and he would exhort them earnestly about not swearing, godliness, cleanliness and other serious matters. Fisherman also gave the boys in his cabin a mystifying talk about a certain sort of dream which he, rather

95

crazily, expected them all to be having. This talk was discussed for several days and it was decided that he was superstitious and believed in dreams. But the soul; he was telling Bill about the soul now. They were at the beach, waterfront, rather; there was no beach, only rocks. It was late afternoon and, in spite of the shouting boys, peaceful. A sailboat with a red sail moved slowly across the lake.

"Well, what about the soul?" Bill was a little truculent. They were playing "King of the castle" out on the floating raft and this was his favorite game.

"Some things, spiritual things, cause an inner peace which is more important than worldly affairs."

"Why?" asked Bill and Fisherman, though he talked a great deal and kept Bill from swimming, never did explain satisfactorily.

Bill was made chief of his tribe (there were four tribes in the camp); he wrote his mother this, hoping she would be pleased but when she answered him she never mentioned it.

He was twelve and he stopped going to camp.

His mother told him one spring: "Bill, you know that your father and I haven't been getting along." He said that he knew this and she asked him if he knew what divorce was and he said yes for he had seen enough movies about it.

"Your father and I are getting divorced." It was dramatic; it was like the movies only much more exciting since it was partly his own drama. He was surprised and yet, when he thought about it, he wasn't really surprised at all. His mother always fought with his father when he was home, which was less and less. One evening he had gone into the bathroom and, hearing sounds, he opened the door into his mother's room. She was sitting on the bed sobbing and his father sat in a chair watching; his father looked angry. This was in his grandparents' house. His father was supposed to take him into the village to see *Frankenstein*. Furiously his mother ordered him out of the room; upset and almost crying himself he went into his grandmother's room. She asked him what had happened and he told her. Then they were both quiet and they could hear his mother's voice angry now and clear. Without a word his grandmother went to her daughter's room.

"Stop that, Charlotte," she said. The voice inside the room went on. "Stop it, Charlotte . . . this minute." The voice inside stopped and his father came out of the room.

"What's the matter with Charlotte, Stephen?"

"You ask her," he said. "Come on, Bill." As they left to go to the movies Bill saw his grandmother go into the room, shutting the door behind her. The voice began again.

Now in different tones, in different mood, it asked, "Does this . . . upset you very much? Do you think we should do it?" She had never asked him about anything before. He was thrilled.

"I don't know," he said.

"Would it hurt you very much not to live with your father?"

"No," he said truthfully.

"You'd be able to see him whenever he likes."

"Yes." He didn't know what to say.

"Would you like to go with me to Reno or stay here with Grandfather?"

It was exactly like a movie. He wondered if he might not be dreaming. Reno. "I want to go with you," he said, thinking of Reno and pleasing her.

His father drove them to the station. They said good-by formally. Then he and his mother got on the train. To his astonishment she started to cry; when he tried to comfort her she pushed him away. Finally she went to the ladies' room. When she came back she was all right. The trip across the country took a long time but the desert was interesting.

When they got to Reno they went to a dude ranch. Here there were many women like his mother, getting divorces. There were also a number of cowboys, tall slim men who were nice to the women getting divorces. Everyone lived in little cabins and they gathered in the Big House dining room for meals. This was a gloomy dark wood room with cowhides tacked to the walls. They always had tomato salad with mayonnaise which Bill thought was very good but his mother complained about the food.

There were other children on the ranch, several were Bill's age and they played together.

The ranch was in a small and fertile valley. Tall trees, lawns and flowers grew in the valley but beyond its narrow radius was white sand with sagebrush and juniper growing out of it. In these hills of sand the cattle lived.

Bill learned how to ride. His mother insisted that he ride bareback. She had been told by someone that that was the only way to become a good rider and so Bill was assigned an old horse named Two Bits who had a very high backbone. He learned to ride.

The other children were pleasant. There were four altogether. Two boys and a girl in one family and a girl who was the niece of the ranchowner. They were all about Bill's age and soon he was their leader. His particular friend was the ranchowner's niece, a blond thin girl his own age. She was quiet and obedient and cried occasionally at the oddest times. There were also some children belonging to a wealthy Spanish lady who owned the nearest house to the ranch, three miles away in a smaller valley. She was married to a cowboy and her home, done all in white, was considered extremely fashionable by everyone at the ranch except Bill's mother who thought it rather cheap. The Spanish lady's children were, unfortunately for them, sissies who kicked and spat in fights; they were, consequently, ignored by Bill's gang.

Bill practiced magic this summer. The Oz books supplied most of the incantations and the results were often marvelous. There were certain spells that froze people and other spells made one invisible. It was a magic summer.

He rode often with Joyce, the owner's niece. They would ride out far beyond the ranch, into the sand hills and then dismount near some old arroyo and look for arrowheads and flints and fossils. He told her stories about the East and his

98

grandfather, camp and the school, and she, who had never left the ranch except to go to Reno, listened to him gravely. Sometimes she told him about rodeos but that was all she knew about. In the winters she went to school in Reno but she didn't know very much. She was really dumb but he liked her because she listened to him.

She knew where to find river clay, gray river clay, and she watched him with awe when he modeled heads and once, shocking enough, a grown woman with nothing on: his mother. He was really a good sculptor and he worked hard at his heads and figures and, once, when he had an especially good figure he buried it in the sand; two weeks later he dug it up and it looked old. He showed it to everyone in the ranch; finally he gave it to the ranchowner's wife who thought it might be old Spanish though certainly not Indian.

The riding, the magic, the sculpting continued through the summer. He grew tanned but not as tan as his mother who had turned dark brown and looked like an Indian. His mother was popular at the ranch. Every evening she went into Reno or to another ranch for parties. He didn't see her very much. When he did she criticized his riding and if he complained about anything, the food, for instance, in imitation of her, she would tell him to stop his "beefing"; she used many Western phrases now and she swore a great deal.

Once he went with his mother and a beautiful woman named Jane, his mother's best friend, on a picnic and he enjoyed this more than anything else he'd ever done with his mother. They sang as they rode and finally they camped in a group of tall glacier-deposited rocks. Here the two women took off their shirts and blue jeans and wore only their long underwear. It was funny and they all laughed a great deal. But this happened only once.

His serious trouble with his mother all started because of a woman named Rosemarie. She was a good-looking woman with white skin and dark hair. She had been married to an Englishman and now she was divorcing him. Though she was an American she spoke with an English accent and she talked a great deal about England and the Court (she had been presented to the King and Queen). His mother, for some reason, disliked her and she told people that she thought Rosemarie had no breeding. No one else liked her then because people usually followed his mother's lead; they did on the ranch, certainly, because his mother was the most important person there. No one paid much attention to Rosemarie except Bill.

She gave him chocolate candy and she talked to him, told him stories about England, the Court. And often they worked the Ouija board together. Once his mother was gone for a week. He had no idea where she was and no one else did either. It was supposed that she was in Reno. Since Bill could take care of himself everything was all right. He missed her dutifully but since he'd seen little of her that summer he was not particularly upset. He performed magic, made statues, idols, and he talked with Rosemarie.

She told him about her wedding. It had been a grand affair. The cake was over two feet high and was, as he understood her, made of almonds. He never actually listened to what she said as much as he did to her soft melodic voice. Her accent fascinated him and she was really very kind. They took long walks together around the ranch and she told him about lords, told him that they were being made even now. He asked if he were English would he be able to be made a lord and she told him yes. He made up his mind to go to England when he was grown.

The second day after his mother had gone into Reno Bill, bored by magic and Joyce, went into the Big House and here he found Rosemarie. She was sitting by the window in the gloomy wood-paneled room. Over her head was the head of a moth-eaten buffalo. She was reading a book and eating candy; she ate a great deal of candy, a habit Bill found appealing.

"Sit down, Bill," she invited. He sat down in the chair opposite her. They had a view of the corral from the window; a heifer was being killed. It was an interesting thing to watch. Bill often watched them kill heifers. He watched now from the window; first, the animal was shot through the head. Then, almost before it fell to the ground, two men jumped into the corral and skinned it. This they did very quickly. Then the calf was beheaded, hung up and disemboweled. The stomach was a lovely pale shiny blue color and when it was opened usually had hay inside it. Bill watched this spectacle and Rosemarie did not.

"I guess we'll have steak tonight," said Bill. It was both a joke and a fact that heifers were eaten here the same day they were killed.

Rosemarie shuddered. "How unpleasant! Where's your mother?"

"I don't really know," he said. "She told me she was going into town yesterday. I guess she'll be back soon."

"Does she often go off like that? Leaving you?"

"Oh no; this is the first time really." His mother usually had a strong sense of duty which she occasionally mentioned.

"Perhaps she's going to be married again," said Rosemarie smiling, offering him candy.

"I don't think so," said Bill.

"What about Roger Gilray?"

"Do you know him?" Bill was surprised. Mr Gilray had been in Reno last week and for some reason no one was supposed to know that he was there. Mr Gilray was a large amiable man with a great deal of money. He lived in Washington and was one of his mother's friends.

"No, but I've read about him and your mother in the papers."

"Did they write about them? I wonder why?" Bill could never understand why newspapers wrote the things they did about his family: so many things they said were untrue: you can't believe anything. . . .

"Because they think your mother's going to marry him."

The idea was a new one to Bill. "I don't think so," he said. "Mr Gilray was here last week and my mother didn't say anything about marrying him."

"So Gilray's in Reno." Rosemarie seemed interested but Bill was much more interested in hearing about England.

"Now everyone's talking about it and all because you told that Rosemarie woman Roger was in Reno."

"No, I didn't, I said . . ."

"Then how did she know? How could she know? Answer me that."

"I don't know. She said she read about it in the papers . . . not about his being in town at least but . . ."

"You told her that. You let your own mother down. It's all part of your selfishness and disloyalty. Telling that awful woman everything about me. Now everybody in the world knows about Roger's being here. Well, this is the last time I ever take you any place with me. Perhaps you'd prefer living with your father, although even *he* thinks you're completely self-centered."

"But I only told her . . ."

"Don't alibi to me," and his mother hit him very hard in the face and left the cabin. For the last time in his life he cried.

3

They lived now in a small Washington apartment. His mother went to many parties but she was always home in the early evenings and they got along fairly well. Many men came to see her: a Polish Count, an Argentine, an Army officer and Roger Gilray. Bill liked most of them, especially the Pole who laughed a lot and told Bill all about the Battle of Waterloo . . . with soldiers. The soldiers, now grown to an immense army, were set up in Bill's room; no matter where he lived the soldiers were always with him.

His mother decided that he should go to a Washington boarding school that fall. He would come home during weekends but during the week he would board. And so, with misgivings, he left the pleasant school.

The new school was, at first, harsh and masculine. All the teachers were men and all the students boys. The youngest were ten or eleven and the oldest were men of seventeen or eighteen. The school was a church one and it had imitation

Gothic buildings and an ugly chapel where the headmaster gave a daily sermon.

Bill was received into the dormitory coldly. It was a long room with a linoleum floor, freshly waxed, and lined on both sides with doorless cubicles. Each cubicle was furnished with an iron cot, a battered bureau and an upright coffin for hanging clothes in. It was all ugly and uncomfortable and would, Bill knew, mold character.

The master in charge of the dormitory was a young man who taught manual training. He came from the Midwest and had a curious accent which was much mimicked behind his back. His name was Mister Owens and like all the masters he was called "sir." Bill disliked calling people "sir" instinctively; slowly he got used to it.

Mr Owens ruled the dormitory humorously and vigorously. He had a slipper with which he slapped the buttocks of disobedient boys. He swore occasionally and always said "ain't" and the boys admired him greatly and imitated him. He treated the younger boys contemptuously. He was quite distant with Bill, though. He showed him his cubicle, gave him a list of rules. Then he left him. Tomorrow classes would begin.

The other boys came over to look at Bill. Most of them were older and had been in the dormitory two or three years. They watched him unpack and they talked to him, asking him where he was from and what his father did. The fact that his parents were divorced interested them very much. They said unpleasant things about the school he'd been to last; they said that it was a girls' school. Then, seeing another boy unpacking, they went over and began to make fun of him. Bill was glad that he was large for his age, that not many boys ever picked fights with him. The oldest boys in this dormitory were fourteen. For boys over fourteen there was another dormitory. Most of the students in the school, however, were day boys.

Bill was frightened the first evening and on his guard the first week. He was not homesick, having been away from home before, and, besides, there was no real home to be sick for. The first night in the dormitory was frightening. There was ominous talk of initiating the new boys. They did go so far as to lock one boy in one of the upright coffins but he made so much noise that Mr Owens, appearing suddenly, suggested they let him out. There was no more talk of initiating after that.

Some of the boys Bill liked and most of them he disliked. He had one fight with an older boy two days after school started. He won this fight and was, thereafter, accepted. He hated fighting, however; he hated the idea of hurting people. When someone wanted to fight him he was usually strong enough to hold them off without hurting them or being himself hurt.

The classroom work was not easy and Bill, besides, had trouble in getting sufficiently interested in any of the subjects to get good marks; only fear of what his mother would say made him pass. When his marks were bad she would reproach him for being lazy, for not working harder for her. After the first term she decided he'd work harder if he stayed in school all week and not come home on weekends. He was pleased though he would never have admitted it to himself; he liked being away from his mother.

The dormitory was split, roughly, into two groups: those who had pubic hair and those who did not. Bill because he was large for his age and strong was, though young, included in the ruling class. The duties of the pubescent ones (they were in numbers a minority) were to tyrannize and control the others. This they did, being stronger. Bill didn't particularly like this persecution of younger boys but he took part in the tyranny because if he didn't he'd be thought different and odd and it was wrong, he knew, to be different. "Don't think you're a special case or different from anyone else." His mother had said this to him often.

Bill's particular friend was a boy named Jess McGuire. He was a year older than Bill but not as well-developed. He was a terrible fighter, though. Because of a furious initial attack he was almost never defeated. He was one of the two important dormitory leaders. The other was a boy of fourteen with a man's body and vices. He smoked, drank and he took girls out in the woods behind the school. Jess was less advanced in extracurricular matters but he was a natural leader and he was the actual tyrant in this group of fifty boys. The boys who were older than he resented him but no one wanted to fight him. The only boy who could and had beaten him was his co-leader and this young man was indifferent to dormitory affairs.

Jess took a liking to Bill and Bill became his protégé.

"You got to be tough," said Jess one day. They were in the dormitory after the final afternoon class. No one else was there yet. They were eating doughnuts bought from the drugstore across the street.

"I know," said Bill, looking tough. "Why don't we form a gang?" Bill suggested.

"What for? We already run things." Jess was a leader but no organizer.

"Oh, to run things even better. Something that'd be secret, that Owens wouldn't know about."

"But I . . . we already run things," Jess repeated.

"Well, there's still Dick." Dick was the fourteen-year-old.

Jess nodded, thinking; he disliked his co-ruler but he never dared say anything against him. And so the gang came into being. Bill organized and Jess commanded. They enrolled the half-dozen strongest boys in the dormitory and Jess and Bill ruled the dormitory. When Dick, the man, objected, six of them beat him up and that ended his power. A week later he moved into the dormitory for older boys.

Bill was pleased with the way his organization was working. Jess was, of course, the leader but Bill managed the organization. It pleased him that in only two months he had become so powerful in the dormitory. He wrote his mother about this but she wrote him only about his marks which were, as usual, bad.

Sure of himself he now questioned the power of Mr Owens whom he disliked. One afternoon when everyone was taking showers before dinner Mr Owens told Bill to do something and Bill refused and Owens threw his slipper at him; Bill caught it and threw the slipper out the window.

"You have shown a great lack of discipline and judgment, Giraud. I am surprised and shocked. What would your family say to this? I'm sure they wouldn't approve of your disobedience, would they?"

"No, sir."

The headmaster looked at him sternly. He was a tall lean man with a gold-rimmed pince-nez. His voice was richly clerical: he *was* a cleric. He had received Bill in his study, an austere room with the arms of the school over his desk. The school, though only a few decades old, already had an old and permanent air about it, like a bank.

"What possessed you to disobey Mr Owens? It's a very serious thing, disobedience. I also understand that you threw his slipper out the window. I am shocked, Giraud, to find that a boy of your intelligence and background would do a thing like this. If it had been someone else, some boy who'd had less advantages than you I might have understood but from you . . . a Hawkins. . . ." His voice trailed away sadly.

"I'm afraid I shall have to tell your mother about this," said the headmaster at last.

"Please don't, sir," said Bill, suddenly afraid.

The headmaster was quick to notice this; he was glad to have discovered, so quickly, a weapon, an insurance of future good behavior.

"Very well, Giraud; I shall overlook your disobedience this time. But if it happens again I'll be forced to take it up with your parents . . . your mother, if anything of this nature happens again."

After this Bill and Mr Owens treated one another with respect.

The year finally came to an end. The graduation ceremonies were conducted on the lawn in front of the chapel and they were both moving and virile, not like the pageants at the other school.

They ate ice cream and listened and listened to the headmaster speak about boys becoming men. Then the sixth formers, powerful demigods whose exploits were discussed by the younger boys as the doings of legendary figures, got their diplomas and it was very beautiful. Then Bill went home to see his mother. They still lived in the small apartment. It was decided that he spend the summer with his father in Canada. His father was on an important mission there and he would, when the mission was finished, spend the rest of the summer near Quebec.

4

"You like the new school?" An awkward beginning but they had to begin somewhere.

"Oh yes; it's a lot of fun."

"I don't suppose you have much time for reading now?"

"No, I still read a lot."

"Have you thought about what you want to do when you're grown?"

"Oh yes."

"Do you know?"

"No."

"Well, that's pretty clear. People almost never end up by doing what they start out to do."

"Didn't you always work in the State Department?"

"No, I was a painter first."

"You painted pictures?" The dark man with the streaks of gray in his dark hair nodded.

"Why did you stop?"

"No money; I had to earn a living."

"Well, the State Department's probably more sensible." He knew he sounded like his mother then. She always made certain answers to certain statements. She would have said what he said.

His father smiled, "Perhaps it's more sensible."

They came to a small town, a New England town with a white church and steeple and box-shaped white houses with green shutters, a few stores and a filling station where they stopped for gas. Bill got out of the car and walked around the station. He watched a group of local boys in red-checked shirts and blue jeans; they watched him. He thought of their lives in this small town whose name he didn't know; they would live here, most of them, all their lives. All sorts of things would happen to them; each of them had problems but he would never know about them; he would never see this town again and he would forget and they would forget that, for a few minutes one spring day, he had come into their vision for an instant and then moved on. As they drove away he was aware suddenly of isolation, of sentences spoken and answered: he was aware of the island and the remoteness of the sea.

They went on talking, though, as they drove. "It was like Mother, I guess, when she quit the stage to have me."

His father chuckled. "She quit a long time before that. She quit before she married me."

"But she said . . ." Bill stopped; this was one of those times when his father said something that was just the opposite of what his mother had said.

They drove awhile without speaking. They passed farms and villages and many fences made of stone.

Then Bill said that he would like to be a painter.

"Have you ever tried it?"

"Oh yes. In school I've painted some. I also worked a lot in clay, making heads mostly. They say my clay things are pretty good but I like the painting better."

"Then why don't you take it up seriously?"

"But I couldn't make any money out of it." What was it his mother had said: "There's no money in art; the field's over-crowded." Yes, she had said that once and he had always remembered it.

"Why make money? You'll inherit the Hawkins money one

day. Your mother and I could support you until then. You should do just what you want to do." His father was sounding less and less like a parent all the time: it was strange.

"But . . . well you have to be successful at something and suppose I wasn't; suppose I wasn't any good?"

"That's a chance you take but what difference does it make if you're doing what you want to do? Being a success doesn't make you particularly happy."

There was no answer to this. His father sounded like Fisherman. He could understand a failure like Fisherman talking that way but his father was extremely important; everything his father said contradicted what his mother had told him; he was confused.

"You'll find," his father continued, "that pleasing yourself in the important things is much more important than pleasing other people."

"Yes, but that's selfish," said Bill; he was on safe ground now; some people, his mother, for instance, were unselfish and they expected the people they loved to be unselfish and do what was expected of them: it was so clear. To not do what was expected of you, to be selfish was almost the worst thing one could be: almost as bad as being lazy.

"What if it is? You'll find that people who want *you* to be unselfish are usually quite selfish themselves; they want *you* to do things for them."

This was almost blasphemy. He resisted his father in silence.

The house near Quebec was small but cheerful. It was near a country club and he played tennis with his father almost every afternoon. He got to be quite good. When his father wasn't home he played with some Canadian boys at the club. It was a serene, an easy summer; his father, he noticed, never criticized him.

His stepfather came out of the house and stood beside him in the driveway.

"Do you see it?"

109

Bill shook his head. "I've forgotten just where we parked it."

"Probably over there, under the trees."

"I was about to look there."

"This is a sad day," said his stepfather. "Your grandfather was a great man, one of the greatest this country ever produced."

"Why?" asked Bill; he had been told all his life that his grandfather was a great man; he thought so himself but he wondered just why other people did.

"What do you mean why? After all he was Vice-President . . ."

"Lots of people have been Vice-Presidents. I can't even remember the names of more than a couple."

"He was a great statesman; his . . . his agrarian laws were revolutionary."

"But they were all changed ten years ago; he told me that himself."

His stepfather looked at him angrily. "He ran this country for several years and it takes a great man to do that."

"That's true," said Bill, "but Wilson ran it longer and he never thought Wilson was a great man."

"I'm surprised at you," said his stepfather, moving to more tenuous but safer grounds. "I thought you admired your grandfather."

"I do . . . I did. I just wonder sometimes why people thought he was so great. Grandmother's just as important now as he was; she's a Senator."

His stepfather laughed, remembering his wife's fury at the elevation of Clara Hawkins. "Let's go find those flowers." They walked across the crowded driveway to a clump of trees among which cars were parked; perhaps the flowers were there.

In the early fall they drove back. The mountains, old and smooth, peakless, with pine trees and evergreens at the summits, and the leaves of the trees that lined the road were red; they passed all these. They drove south across New England. The fields were brown and stubbled now, contrasting with the leaves which were red as fire but cold. They passed the stone fences, boulders shaped by the Ice Age, gray and pitted now. Everything was settled, tranquil and old; not warm and graceful like the South but, rather, strong; granite and iron and a cold wind.

"And how was your father?"

"Very well. He's going to become an Ambassador soon he thinks."

"Well, it's about time; he's been trying for it long enough. Did you like Canada?"

"A whole lot. It's pretty there and we played a lot of tennis; I wrote you about that."

"That's right you did. That must've been nice." She seemed pleased but, more important, she was calm and loving. Of course, he had only been back a day. But still she was unusually gentle. In two days he would go back to school. She maintained her calm for these two days and not once did they have one of those almost inevitable evenings when she would scold and reproach him and say terrible things. Perhaps she had changed, perhaps the unemotional mood of the summer would continue forever; he hoped this and, for a while at least, it seemed so.

His grandfather seemed rather frail when he went to see him the day before school started. He had been delivering a series of speeches against the President and it was rumored that the President would throw the full weight of his office against Grandfather in the coming elections. The old man was tired; his voice shook when he was angry or recalling anger and the lid of his left eye twitched nervously. Clara Hawkins was concerned about him and continually told him to relax but he would not. By violent activity (mental; he still moved very little physically) he hoped to obscure a premonition of his death; he was shortening his life by a few years but he was also disguising the appearance of death for he was never alone now except when, exhausted, he finally slept, late at night, slept without dreaming.

"How was Canada, young man?"

"Just fine, Grandfather."

"You've grown at least a foot, hasn't he, Clara?"

"He looks like William did," said Clara Hawkins.

"No, he doesn't, Mother," said Charlotte suddenly. "I don't think he looks anything like William."

"Nonsense," said the Vice-President, "of course he does."

No one could contradict him and, safe behind his power, Clara Hawkins added without fear of her daughter, "He has William's coloring, too; and his eyes."

Bill saw his mother frown and look at her hand where she still wore the gold lily and diamond ring of Grandmother Giraud. Then she smiled; her moods shifted quickly.

"Well, Daddy, how's the war with the Administration?"

Her father looked grim. "If I live long enough I'll impeach the bastard. How any man can dare to trample on the Constitution the way that man does is beyond me. I said last week in the Senate . . ." and his voice, harsh and angry, repeated what he'd said.

Bill watched him admiringly. His grandfather was awe-inspiring. Not even the teachers or the sixth-formers were as magnificent. He would be like him. His mother wanted him to be like this, strong, self-assured . . . but how did one go about being William Hawkins when one was, actually, only William H. Giraud and quite a different person? It would take a lot of work but what kind? No one could tell him.

His grandfather spoke and they listened to him and Bill wished that he could be like this man; be what his mother most admired. But how?

"He is so like our William," said his grandmother staring at him.

5

Jimmy Wesson was the idol of the school. He was, at fourteen, an important baseball player and he was considered the best athlete in the school. He was tall for fourteen and muscular; he was, everyone admitted, charming; no one disliked him. He moved easily through this world, his short sand-colored hair curling and uncombed. He accepted admiration naturally, pleasantly. Bill, though only thirteen, was now in Jimmy's class where all the boys were older; he had done well in his studies the year before and he'd been, to his family's surprise, promoted.

The dormitory assumed new importance for him. He was, of course, used to it, an old resident, a man of power. This was, also, the first year that sex interested him. He had listened the year before, without much interest, to the boys discuss women. Their discussions and descriptions of the act he found disgusting and dubious. He doubted whether his mother and father had ever done such unpleasant things to one another. But this year everything was different. What they had told him seemed quite possible. He also discovered that the boys in the dormitory all knew more about these things than he did; at least they appeared to know more and they certainly practiced things that he did not. He discovered that almost without exception they did things with one another at night; this year he was aware and it seemed to him that everyone else was aware, too. Before he had never paid much attention to the noises at night but now he was interested though somewhat repelled. Jess McGuire tried to get Bill to join him one night but Bill refused, more because of shyness than anything else, and Jess never forgave him. But now Bill listened at night and wondered what to think, what was right; it all seemed innocent enough and there were times when he wished he had the courage to join the others.

In the middle of the term Jimmy Wesson became a boarder. It made a great deal of difference in everyone's life. First of all the balance of power shifted; it was now a triumvirate with Bill in much the weakest position since Jess quickly made Jimmy his friend. They were daytime friends but not at night for once one night Bill heard a loud "hell, no" from Jimmy's cubicle and a nervous "O.K." from Jess. Everyone wanted Jimmy for a friend, in one way or another, but no one could get beyond his amiability, the vagueness of his charm. Bill was shy with him and they didn't speak for almost a month.

But one day after class Jimmy came up to Bill; they were walking back to the dormitory.

"You read a lot, don't you?" Jimmy began this way.

Bill, surprised and pleased, embarrassed, said gruffly, "Quite a bit."

"Gosh, I wish I could. I can't ever seem to get interested in anything except baseball stories; I got a lot of those at home but I can't seem to read real books; how do you do it?"

"I don't know; I just guess I like to, that's all."

"Well I wish you could teach me how."

"If you want to." He tried to sound bored, to disguise his excitement.

"Sure I want to. What do I do first?"

Jess was upset by this new friendship. The balance of power had shifted again and now he was the weakest member of the triumvirate; in fact, so far had Jimmy withdrawn his friendship that the triumvirate had become, essentially, a duumvirate. Jess now hated Bill and he split the dormitory into two factions: his followers and the duumvirate's. Jess's group was the minority and Bill, unworried, ignored him. He was much too busy with Jimmy to have time for a feud. They were reading Zweig's *Marie Antoinette*. Bill had become interested in the French Revolution recently and he was reading all the biographies he could find: Danton, Mirabeau, Necker. His favorite daydream now was a revolution in the United States; he would be a leader and he'd make speeches that would send people to the guillotine. Jimmy liked a few of the books though he had trouble understanding them. This mystified Bill because Jimmy's marks in school were much better than his.

Jimmy liked *Marie Antoinette* and he thought the story of the Dauphin's masturbation very funny. They became so involved in reading that they didn't notice there was trouble developing in the dormitory; their power was threatened. Jess was organizing a final bid for power. The declaration of war came when Jess, one afternoon in the dormitory, suggested in a loud voice to several of his followers that Bill would like to start a revolution in the United States. This brought Bill and Jimmy out of their cubicles.

"What do you mean?" asked Bill, his stomach contracting; he was afraid and angry both; he knew now that he would have to fight.

"Just what I said. I heard you two goons talking about it once. You two sure think you're a lot better than the rest of us." This pleased his followers who were now surrounding them in a circle. The duumvirate's support was scattered about the dormitory, uncertain and disorganized. Bill looked at Jimmy and saw that he was grinning; his mouth was set in a grin: he knew, too, that there'd be a fight.

"Better watch what you're saying, McGuire," said Bill in as ominous a tone as possible. His voice had changed this fall and he wasn't completely certain of it yet.

"I'll say what I damn well please," said Jess. "I been in this dorm a hell of a lot longer than either of you two goons."

"Yeah? What about Dick? He was here longer'n you and we took care of him." Bill wanted to fight now; anything to stop this tension. His heart beat rapidly and when he looked at Jimmy he saw that he was still grinning.

"You think maybe you can get me out of this dorm? I can knock hell out of any guy in here." This was his cue; Jess swung at Bill and hit him sharply in the shoulder. Four boys jumped on Jimmy holding him tight. Jess went into his whirlwind attack. Bill was thrown off balance. They fell to the floor together; Bill on the bottom. Wrestling, Bill was sure of himself, though. He was stronger than Jess. Gradually he pinned him down. Jess struggled violently. None of the other boys helped him, though. It would have been unethical. They stood in a circle watching. Four of them still held Jimmy. Then, as Jess was almost pinned, he managed to wrench free, he kicked Bill as hard as he could in the stomach and Bill collapsed, breathless, on the floor. The pain and shock was terrible; he gagged and tried to breathe. Slowly he got his breath back. He sat up in time to see Jimmy shake free of the four boys and rush at Jess; he grabbed him by an arm and a leg and with a strength that amazed even Jimmy's admirers, lifted him up over his head and threw him against the wall. Screaming, Jess was taken to the infirmary. His arm was broken and when, finally, he returned to the dormitory a few days later he was completely changed. He spoke very little; what popularity he'd had was gone and he made no further attempt to regain power. Next year he went to another school, another exile.

Bill and Jimmy were even closer after this. Jimmy was now, though young, the school's leading athlete and he had as many friends as he wanted, most of them were athletes, but he was closest to Bill who, though he played basketball well enough, disliked games and was frank about it. They continued to read the same books.

One weekend they both got permission to leave the school and spend a weekend with Bill's grandparents. His mother was in New York this month. She wrote him regularly though he had no idea what she was doing there.

Jimmy enjoyed the Hawkins estate and the Hawkins family enjoyed him as, of course, everyone did. He and Bill climbed about the cliffs above the river and they even swam in the rapids.

His grandfather was much thinner, Bill noticed, but he talked as much as ever and his memory was as good as it had always been. He remembered having met Jimmy's father in Kentucky. He recalled in great detail that meeting.

On Sunday afternoon they burned ant hills. It was very amusing. Some of these hills were over a foot high and Bill, who understood ants, having watched them for years, was sorry for them as he poured kerosene down into their corridors; it was necessary, though. They set fire to the ant hill and they got almost as black as the hill did. Then, the hill destroyed, they went back to the house to wash and there it began.

"I don't think this is like the others," said Bill.

"No, I don't think so either. They're . . . so dirty."

"It isn't the same what we did."

"No, it's not the same thing."

"I guess you always ought to try everything once."

"Yes."

"It's O.K. I guess."

"Yes but . . ."

"Never again?"

"I don't think it'd be a good idea, do you?"

"I guess not again."

But it happened again, many times, and the other boys in the dormitory never knew and publicly Bill and Jimmy stood strongly against that sort of thing and they would not allow it in the dormitory. But they themselves continued and it changed, subtly, and gradually; when they began to know girls, it ended altogether, slowly, easily, without violent emotion. But it was important, though; it was important for both of them to begin to learn the need and the boundaries of love.

6

His mother returned from New York one day, married to Roger Gilray, a bank president who had been married once before.

The event was sudden and Bill, now out of school for the summer and living with his grandparents, was surprised and not displeased.

Roger Gilray said, "Well, young man, I seem to be a member of the family now," and he laughed. He seemed happy and he treated Bill's mother with the same respect that almost everyone did and, for this reason, he pleased Bill who was most anxious for his mother to be respected and obeyed.

Roger Gilray was in his middle forties and he was stout. His face was full and amiable though not at all handsome. He was not bald as most bankers are but he was heavy; he moved heavily; he spoke weightily and his manners were massive. He was incredibly wealthy. He did not work hard now; he had worked hard once but now he devoted most of his time to his Maryland estate, outside of Washington. Here he kept horses and a large collection of paintings. He collected things in a businesslike manner and he now had one of the best collections of Blakes in America. He was not as simple a man as he appeared. There were days when he wouldn't speak at all. He would look at his wife, at everyone, as though they were strangers. He seemed to Bill like a poet at such times (Bill himself was a poet this summer).

He and Bill got along together very well. Gilray, though a banker, read books and thought about them and he discussed books with Bill.

Once at the table, Charlotte said angrily, "Roger, all you do is quote books, other people's ideas. You don't have any of your own."

Although this might have been true Bill thought it cruel of his mother to say so; his mother had said the same things to him and he felt sorry for his stepfather, knowing how he felt.

They moved into the Maryland house and, immediately, his mother wanted him to go to camp for the summer again: "to be with other boys; to learn to be a good mixer." This time, though, Bill complained and to his surprise and pleasure his stepfather took his side and Bill spent the summer in Maryland. He rode a lot and he swam every day in his stepfather's pool. The house was not so beautiful nor so large as his grandfather's but it was more modern and there was a swimming pool as well as stables on the estate. It was nice to be rich, Bill learned, and he wondered how his mother had managed to live as long as she did in the small Washington apartment. She liked being rich; he knew that. He also knew that she didn't love Roger Gilray but he knew she would never marry anyone for their money. She had told him that herself. But later, much later, it was to be: "I married him only for you; so that you could have everything." She was fond of Roger, of course; she told everyone she was.

"I think Roger is one of the sweetest people I've ever known." She was dressing and the sight of her naked body always made Bill uneasy; but she was never self-conscious. "Damn this sleeve; it's still torn. Ring the bell for Maria. No, people say things about me, women especially, because they're jealous but just remember it was Roger who wanted to get married. You remember when he came out to Reno that summer and you told that woman all about his being in town? Of course, you remember and I was furious with you. Well, he wanted me to marry him then and I wouldn't. I finally did, though, because I think he's one of the kindest men I've ever known *and* he'll live up to his obligations which is more than your father would do . . . God damn it, Maria, didn't I tell you to fix this sleeve? How many times do I have to tell you?"

Jimmy spent a month with him that summer and Bill had never been so happy before. He even wondered at the time if he'd ever be as happy again. His mother was nice to Jimmy, charming him completely, but she told Bill she didn't like him very much and he, with a sudden insight, realized that she disliked charm in others. Jimmy thought she was wonderful, however.

On hot nights, and this summer was a hot one, they went swimming in the pool after everyone was asleep in the house; it was strange swimming in the dark; sometimes it was so dark that they couldn't see the water around them: it was like a dream, a dream of darkness and dissolution; they were detached, floating effortlessly in a cool element. Bill wondered if death was like this.

Then he and Jimmy would sit by the side of the pool and watch the stars and they talked about everything and everyone. They talked of the books they were reading. Jimmy, though still not a good reader, enjoyed the books more.

They talked of everything.

They made plans for school, for the administration of the dormitory, and for Jimmy's athletic career. He had already made up his mind to be a professional baseball player and Bill thought he should do this if he wanted to.

They talked these dark nights by the pool; they talked of girls. They both wanted to have them but they didn't know how to go about it. All the girls they met at dancing school or school dances were "nice" and, unfortunately too, rather silly. It was impossible to do anything more with them than an occasional kiss because they didn't know anything more or if they *did* know anything more they pretended they didn't which was just as bad.

And Bill knew, vaguely, even while they talked of all this, that he and Jimmy were in love; although not even to himself would he use that word. He would far rather die than admit such a thing. But in spite of this, gradually, insidiously, the bodies of women appeared in his dreams and he knew that soon these dreams and their eventual reality would destroy the relationship.

After they had talked and watched the stars they would go back to the dark house and climb the stairs silently to their room.

His mother was more agreeable this summer than usual. He hoped (as he had hoped vainly after the Canadian trip) that she had come to the end of a cycle but she had not. She had merely turned from "correcting" and "guiding" him to "correcting" and "guiding" her husband.

Roger Gilray, though a genial man in spite of occasional periods of brooding, did not like parties or organized society and his wife did. She felt that it was her duty to draw him out; she told Bill about this one morning while she was having breakfast in bed (she always had breakfast in bed now). "The trouble with Roger is that he makes no effort with people. Of course, he's unpopular. Almost all the people that come to the house are my friends not his. They're the sort of people he should know but he refuses to make *any effort* to be nice to them. He'd enjoy life so much more if he learned to discipline himself, to do what was difficult." She yawned and stretched and drank her orange juice. She looked handsome even in the morning without make-up, her face covered with shining cold cream. She had got into the habit of talking with him in the morning. She didn't find too much to criticize this summer since Roger's faults occupied most of her time. She did mention, though, that she was not sure she liked his attitude and he *was* rude to people. "You must change your attitude, Bill." This was her favorite word this year. His attitude was wrong; he was too critical; he would have to turn over a new leaf.

But there were other times when she would suddenly kiss him or hold his hand and at these times he was happy; there was nothing in the world, no happiness, to compare with this. When she was affectionate he almost forgot the times of anger. He knew that she had forgotten them and he almost did, too.

It didn't take him long to discover that her marriage to Roger Gilray was a failure. Roger was generous with her and he allowed her to change his home and the external pattern of his life but he was not changed. Charlotte was never happy now if there weren't people in the house: preferably house guests; she was always surrounded by people and Bill knew she was happy then for he could hear her deep laugh when she was at the center of a group; she laughed only when she was contented.

"Your mother's a very remarkable woman," said one man, slightly drunk. Bill was serving canapés. His mother smiled proudly, hearing this. "Very remarkable indeed. Most beautiful woman in Washington."

Bill agreed that she was remarkable.

Then everyone talked about the war in Europe. The war was Bill's principal interest outside himself until, in the late summer, his mother announced she was going to have a child.

Gilray was happy. He no longer sulked and Charlotte, for that matter, was better-tempered and if there was still trouble between them it no longer was obvious. Fascinated Bill watched his mother's stomach enlarge: ugly yet moving.

"I can't get anything to fit any more. God, but it's awful being so huge. Still I'm glad it won't be until fall. I can't stand being pregnant in the summer again. I had you in the summer and I thought I'd die of the heat."

7

"I've always wanted a child. Poor Mabel, my first wife, couldn't have one; high blood pressure but now . . . at last.

It's a great feeling, Bill, a great feeling. Every man wants to have his name carried on. It's the only immortality there is."

"You must get plenty of rest, Charlotte. I don't see how you expect to keep healthy going out to parties every night of the week. You'll have a miscarriage if you're not careful. I wish you'd relax and . . ."

"For God's sake, Mother!"

"Good idea to have a big family. I've always wished I had had a large one. You know I get the most terrible headaches lately. Arteries must be hardening, I suppose. You have no idea what an awful feeling it is to grow old, to be wearing out. One feels so helpless. There's still a lot of life ahead, though."

Yet he died before his second grandchild was born.

"I can't believe it; I can't believe it. Not now." She seemed furious, disbelieving; there was no helping her, though: there never was a way to help her. Bill was with her now. He'd been called out of class by the headmaster who had told him the news. She'd recovered quickly, however, and she telephoned her husband and called for her car. On the way they bought a wreath of calla lilies.

They found the wreath in the car. The car had been parked on the lawn at a distance from the other cars. Bill took the wreath out and his stepfather helped him carry it back to the house.

"I hope your mother won't be sick."

"Sick? Why should she be?"

"All this excitement and being pregnant. I read of a woman just the other day who had a miscarriage because she was emotionally upset."

"I don't think she's so excited now. She's gotten over the shock she had this morning."

"I think she's probably excited all over again," said his

122

stepfather chuckling. "Your grandmother's appointment has certainly upset her."

"I can't understand why that bothers her so; after all it keeps everything in the family."

"Maybe that's why." He didn't explain.

Bill understood, though; he had always understood about his mother and his grandmother. "It has always been a sad thing to me that Charlotte has never been able to understand her mother." His grandfather told him this once and Bill had been surprised, surprised that his grandfather, who lived so importantly, so much apart, should be aware of these things.

"Mother's never understood *me;* never. William was her pet; it was always William this and William that. Everything she ever did was for him. Then, of course, she always resented how close Daddy and I were. She was jealous of us, of me. Then she used to have an insane temper when I was a child. She was quite violent. And: I was always ashamed of her, ashamed of how badly she dressed, how stupidly she talked. She used to humiliate me in front of people. I hated to have people visit me because of that."

"Your mother has never tried to control herself and that's why she's so unhappy now. Mr Hawkins was that way years ago but he learned to control himself. You should always remember that, too; you can't be indifferent to other people's feelings."

He had heard all these words many times and, naturally, he took his mother's side. He knew she was right and, besides, she was the most convincing. There were times when he disliked his grandmother, thinking of how unkind she'd been to his mother; it was, in a way, difficult to understand since she was always so good to him; he enjoyed staying with her. But his mother was right.

Charlotte thought that, too. She was still in the study. Her mother now sat at the Vice-President's desk, the light shining on her white lined face, her mouth a rigid line, a glass of bourbon and water beside her on the desk. This was an unusual sight; Bill thought his grandmother didn't drink.

Charlotte sat on the couch, almost in darkness, her hands resting upon the large curve of her stomach.

"Anything I can do, Mrs Hawkins?"

"Nothing, thank you, Roger. Do sit down though; over there by Charlotte; I don't think she's feeling well."

From the darkness Charlotte said, "I'm perfectly all right." Her voice sounded tired Bill thought. He sat down in a chair opposite the couch, a copy of the most recent *Congressional Record* was on the table beside his chair. He saw that it contained his grandfather's last speech.

". . . nor do I see the need for a European or for a Pacific war. We have not so much national treasure that we can forever maintain a stable home economy while, at the same time, giving huge sums to maintain Europe's wars. I suspect collusion, Mr President. I suspect certain of our national leaders of a desire for war and, incidentally, for a continual state of crisis here at home which will keep them in power. I will oppose every measure calculated to drive us into the European war and I defy this Administration to promote a Second World War!" The voice was harsh and clear and when it was heard in the Senate the crowds in the gallery were quiet and most of the Senators came out of the cloakrooms to hear. There was no applause when he finished speaking; there was a respectful curious silence as the people listened to a legend, a figure from an earlier time. They did not like William Hawkins any longer but they still respected him; Bill was puzzled that his grandfather should suddenly become so unpopular. There were times when he thought that his grandfather had been puzzled, too.

"Could we have a picture Mrs . . . Senator Hawkins?"

"If you like."

A blinding light filled the room for an instant. "Thank you." The newsmen left.

"You're making a mistake." The voice was weary and insistent.

"However, it's my concern, Charlotte. I knew that Bill would have wanted this."

"You know he didn't." The voice was defiant now.

"My dear, how would *you* know? I realize, Charlotte, that he was very fond of you but I'm sure he didn't talk politics with you. Politics, you know, is different from political personalities. He always respected *my* judgment when it came to politics."

"How on earth can you say that, Mother?" Irritation, the weariness gone.

"Because it's true; because I lived with your father a long time before you were born. I was close to him all his life no matter how fond he was of you. I think he would have wanted me to accept the appointment and so I have."

"Suit yourself." Defeat; her anger turned inward. She turned to Bill. "Did you take the flowers into . . . the room?"

"No, I left them in the hall."

"Well, take them there now. I wish you'd show a little more consideration. I asked you especially . . ." It was turned upon him now. He left the room.

Newspapermen were in the hall talking to George who would not talk to them. There were fewer people in the house than there had been. Many were leaving now. All the photographs that could be taken had been taken. Tomorrow they would all be at Arlington and then William Hawkins would cease to interest them, after forty years.

He took the wreath of white calla lilies.

The room was lit only by candles, the curtains were drawn and there was no suggestion that outside the moon was shining, white and dead.

The old man lay in his coffin. Flowers were banked against the expensive metal casket. Everything had been arranged well; Bill admired his grandmother. He approached the coffin.

"I could never accept the Christian slave philosophy. Perhaps I am too much a product of Western civilization, too unoriental to appreciate it. I cannot accept miracles. I cannot believe in the vast and particular importance of this one race on this one planet. I know we shall merely retrace our steps back into the womb. It was dark then; it will be dark again when we are dead, when I am dead."

He had said that a year ago and he had said it sadly, without his usual harshness, his speechmaker's voice.

He was very white, his features sharp as though they were modeled in ice. His hair was carefully, unnaturally brushed. He was still; the entire room was still, a vacuum. There was no motion in it, no sound, almost, it seemed, no air though the flowers created a certain illusion of life, of decay. Their odor was sickening, sweetly rotting. He was nauseated for a moment. He felt as if he could not breathe, could never breathe again. With an effort he remembered that outside this room people moved and the moon shone on the river and the river roared as it rushed upon rocks and the rocks were constant: in one shape or another they would endure. Only this room was dead.

He placed the white flowers beside the coffin.

"Well, did you take them in?"
"I took them in."

the king

IT MADE a difference in their lives: the King was coming.

Some of them had met him before the war, had known him as a person and, as a person, had not thought much of him but when he came to the Hawkins' house he would come as a King. His country had been conquered by the Germans and it would be, everyone said, free again, soon. Now he was in Washington and he would come to their house for tea and a reception and, like fragments of metal drawn to a magnet, they were all drawn to him, fascinated, hypnotized for a short time by this symbol, this central man. He was related to all the other central men, the Kings, for a thousand years. Oh, it would be good to have the King in the house since the center of this house was dead. The two women needed it, mother and daughter, needed the central man. Here, for an hour or so, they would have the King to talk to, and they would move about him as they had once moved about William Hawkins. The King was a man, of course, and, some said, a disagreeable one but today he would not be accepted as human. Today he was to be their symbol, and they were no longer aimless fragments but, for a time, satellites, with a path to follow. Silently, without reason they had faith in him. It was difficult for the two women to have faith in an idea, an abstraction, but in a man, in a crown, they *could* have faith. He would, for a while, reduce the burden of their freedom. He would assume their responsibilities; he would free them. They wanted the King.

To Charlotte he was, in a sense, a man as well as a center point; she thought vaguely of seduction, of becoming a royal mistress although he was not particularly handsome. It would be amusing; he would give her a house in Antibes or, perhaps, Cannes; Antibes would be pleasanter, though. She thought of this with one part of her mind while the rest of her consciousness was concentrated upon the idea of the King personified; it was so long since she'd seen a man climb the steps to a throne. So long ago.

To Senator Clara Hawkins the King was clearly a symbol. She had never allowed herself to contemplate seduction, even when she was young and it might have been, on several occasions, possible. She had venerated William Hawkins too much; she had a romantic conception of the central man and she loved, romantically, Kings. Now this King was coming to their house. He would remind her, she knew, of her husband and she would like that. No man had reminded her of him since he died almost two years ago; almost two years, as short a time as that.

Charlotte opened her eyes. She was home. She was never able to think of her other houses, the one with Roger especially, as home. Home was always this house of her father's. She felt at ease here.

The morning was misty. She could smell leaves burning; it was an acrid smell, not pleasant the way it would be late in the fall. The leaves were still rather green. She looked at her clock: nine-thirty. She stretched. Roger would probably arrive for lunch; he hadn't come to the house for the weekend.

"I've got some conferences at the bank: quite special."

"That's too bad, dear."

"I'll see you for lunch."

"That'll be fine; I'll take Bill with me and we'll spend the night with Mother. I'll have to fix things for the reception anyway."

They both tried very hard to be civilized now. But he bored her, made her angry. She wondered why she'd ever married him. Of course, he had wanted to marry her and that had had a great deal to do with it. Then there was the money; it was important to have money and she had had very little after the divorce. And Roger *was* sweet. That was why. She had grown tired of excitement and Stephen had been exciting. She had wanted something unemotional and now that she had it she wished, she wished.

What *did* the King look like? She had never met him. Her mother had but her mother never remembered how people looked.

"He's not very large."

"Is he as tall as I am?"

"Well . . . perhaps."

"I'm quite tall for a woman; a man as tall as I am wouldn't really be small."

"Perhaps he's shorter. He wears a rather pretty uniform as I remember: white and gold."

She had seen newspaper pictures of him when he came to Washington but they told her nothing. She would have to wait and she was excited; she would not admit it to anyone, though. This was the sort of thing one should be above and yet one wasn't. Why was this King so important to her? She had known many men that were more important, better known. He was not supposed to be handsome and he was definitely middle-aged and, further, it was said that he was a fairy which would, of course, be tiresome if it was true. Yet he had assumed a tremendous importance in her life. Two weeks ago she'd read in the papers that he was in Washington. Then her mother had met him at an official reception. Charlotte persuaded her mother to invite him for tea, to give a social rather than an official reception for him. She was surprised when her mother agreed to this. Her mother had sent the King an invitation. His aide-de-camp sent her a date and the reception was planned: this was the day. Charlotte arranged everything. She invited almost a hundred of her friends (her mother knew no unofficial people) and, hearing that Stephen Giraud, now an Ambassador, was in Washington she invited him, too. She was curious to see if he'd changed. She had an explanation, of course, for inviting him: he had been the last Minister to the King's country before the war. He would naturally like to see the King. But she had another reason for inviting Stephen.

The maid, a new one, brought her breakfast on a tray.

"Is Mrs Hawkins up yet?"

"Yes, ma'am; the Senator had her breakfast an hour ago. She's arranging flowers now."

It still made Charlotte angry to hear her mother called by her father's title. The maid left and Charlotte ate her breakfast slowly. The sausage had too much sage in it. Neither she nor her mother liked sage but the Vice-President had liked it. Her mother still had sausage made for him.

She was on better terms with Clara Hawkins now. There had been a terrible fight with her mother, over money; but that had been, for the time, resolved. The Vice-President had left everything outright to his wife with no provision for his daughter at all.

"But it's ridiculous, Mother. I don't see how Father could have made such a will."

"But he did."

"I don't understand it. I've got less money than anyone in the family."

"But, Charlotte, after all you're married to Roger Gilray and he has a great deal of money."

"I know but I dislike being dependent on him; I'd like to be independent and I haven't a cent to my name."

"I'm surprised you even think of independence when you're married to a man . . . a man who's quite generous with you. I had no money when I married your father and I had none when he died."

"It's different now."

"I can't see why. You have *some* obligations to your husband, you know."

"Certainly I do but that hasn't a damn thing to do with having one's own money . . . just in case."

"Please don't use that tone with me, Charlotte."

"For God's sake!"

A few minutes of dialogue, all in anger, and then:

"I see no reason why I should turn over any part of your father's money to you. It'll all go to Bill when I die and you'll be his trustee, although I'm not even sure of that now. I haven't made up my mind yet."

"I think you're being unfair. I'm sure Father would never have left you the money if he'd known you were going to act like this."

"And I'm sure your father knew what he was doing. He was indulgent, too indulgent with you when he was alive. I think he lived long enough to regret it when he saw how spoiled and self-centered you'd become."

It broke, her control broke. "How can *you* say such a thing to me? He had nothing but contempt for you. He knew you drank. He knew he was tied to a stupid woman for the rest of his life. You used to bore him to death. Many times he told me he was bored being with you. That's why he always had so many people around him; but he pitied you. Everyone pitied you: even Mrs Lang, his mistress, pitied you . . ."

"You won't say another word to me, Charlotte. Ever. Let me tell you that I'm making Roger Gilray Bill's trustee and I'm putting a provision in my will that you're never to touch one cent of the Hawkins money. You'll have to depend on your alimony like any other loose woman. I never want to see you again, Charlotte."

After this they had become better friends. The dislike was still there but now, having said everything they had always wanted to say to one another, they were on better terms. After a month of separation they drifted back into a relationship. Clara Hawkins was busy being a Senator. For some reason peo-

ple took her seriously and she made long speeches in favor of
a League of Nations, an organization that her husband had
regarded with considerable and, to him, justifiable cynicism.

The orange juice was uncommonly sour. She hated orange
juice anyway. In fact, this morning, nothing tasted good.
Perhaps it was the excitement of the King's coming.

She drank the orange juice quickly. She always saved it for
last. Then she put the tray down beside her bed. She would get
up but, for a moment longer, she would relax. She stretched.

The telephone rang and she picked up the receiver.

"Charlotte? This is Stephen."

"Oh, how are you, Stephen?" She remembered; yes, she
remembered.

"Fine, thanks. I just called up to ask about that invitation
I got. You really want me to come?"

"Certainly I do. I sent it out myself."

"But Roger will be there."

"That doesn't make any difference. He wants to see you, I'm
sure. He hasn't seen you in years."

"Well, I hope he's interested in seeing his predecessor."

"*You* don't mind meeting him, do you?"

"No, I don't mind."

"You don't sound very cheerful."

"I'm just tired. I've been traveling too much lately."

"Are you going abroad again, soon?"

"Depends on the situation. Probably. How's your mother?"

"The same as ever."

"How does she like her job?"

"Adores it."

"You sound rather flat. Don't tell me you disapprove of her
still."

"I don't know what you mean." An instant of silence. Why
was a telephone silence always so noticeable, so ominous?
Then, "What's this I hear about your getting married again,
Stephen."

"I don't know what you mean."

"Don't be funny; is it true?"

"I haven't decided yet. I might get married."

"It's Janet Hamilton, isn't it?"

"Yes."

"But, darling, she's such a witch. She has no breeding at all and her morals! Why, she's slept with everyone. She's much worse than Emily even."

"That isn't true."

"Well, perhaps she's missed the Supreme Court though I understand Justice . . ."

"I don't think that's very funny, Charlotte."

"I'm not trying to be funny; I'm quite serious."

"I don't see that it's any of your business anyway."

"No, not really but I'm still concerned about you. Besides if anything happened to me she'd raise Bill."

"That's unlikely. Besides Bill's almost grown."

"At fifteen? Don't be ridiculous!"

"Well, we'll talk about it this afternoon. By the way, can I bring her? I think you should meet her . . . again."

"Bring anybody you damned please."

"Well, don't get that way about it or I won't come at all."

"I'm sorry; I'm a little upset, that's all."

"I understand." He was so casual. He had no respect for her as a person and even less for her feelings; he wanted to court Janet Hamilton in front of her. Charlotte was hurt. Yet there was no reason, absolutely no reason, why she should care what he did. But she did care still. She had never seriously considered his remarrying and now it was rumored that he'd be married almost any day. Janet Hamilton had been married twice before; she was wealthy, an excellent horsewoman and a woman of phenomenally easy virtue. Women loathed her because of her money, her looks, and the fact that she'd had affairs with almost every desirable man of her generation and class (not counting, of course, the ones that were out of her class and generation). Charlotte sympathized with her somewhat, for other women usually disliked Charlotte for comparable reasons and she disliked most women but pretended not to. Janet Hamilton pretended nothing and Charlotte envied her her ease and independence. Now she was going to marry Stephen. It was well known that she was very much in love with him.

Charlotte, herself, had not been scrupulously faithful to Roger. She had been, up until her miscarriage after her father's funeral. Then she was told that she could never have children again; a fact which pleased her but hurt Roger. He was cold with her after the miscarriage and she in turn didn't bother to control her temper which had, as she got older, grown more uncertain. She believed vaguely, however, in having principles and she refused the first group of interested men. But then one day, one afternoon when Roger was still in the city, she had an affair with a charming young Romanian. It had all happened quite naturally: the logical result of boredom and marital unhappiness, she told herself. They met several times after that afternoon. One day he asked her for money and the affair ended. Ungenerous words were spoken on both sides. But that was the beginning and there were more lovers. She was very discreet and only a hundred or so people knew about her affairs. No one, however, knew the full extent. She still managed to give the impression of a great but unhappy lady. No one blamed her because she seemed to take the whole thing rather desperately and, besides, no one liked Roger much. She acted a great deal. She wasn't like Janet Hamilton who made no pretense about anything and, further, appeared to live quite happily in spite of the censure of women.

The conversation with Stephen ended for lack of words.

She began to dress. She wouldn't put on her tea-gown until after lunch. There was work to be done and she looked forward to it. She liked working with her hands. She was the only one in her family who did. She would try to get her mother and Bill to help her but neither would. They were so helpless, so inconsiderate.

Clara Hawkins, though thrilled at the thought of the King, was somewhat suspicious of him. Her love of Kings was real and nothing the King could do as a man would disquiet her.

But she, after all, was a public official and as one she could and did suspect his motives. Just recently she had been made the chairman of a Senate subcommittee to study loans to foreign powers as well as Lend-Lease aid. The King had, this week, requested a large loan and the White House was behind it. Clara Hawkins, however, for reasons mostly ideological, should oppose this loan. Because she was chairman the King had accepted her invitation. But then perhaps it would not be her responsibility. Very likely *the* committee of which she was only a member would, as usual, obey the Administration and her dissent would not matter.

She could not remember him clearly. She hadn't felt well the night of the official reception and she had, though no one guessed it she was sure, drunk too much. But generally she drank less now that she was busy with the Senate.

Clara Hawkins drank her grapefruit juice aware of each of the vitamins she was drinking. Now that she drank whiskey in public she found that she drank less and the habit, further, endeared her to her fellow politicians. They found it remarkable in a woman politician (a twentieth-century phenomenon they'd never much liked) and they discussed, admiringly, the amounts she could drink without getting drunk.

"George, we'll use the New York Champagne for the reception."

"Not the French? Not even for the King?" George was the most impressed of them all; he expected to see a man seven feet tall, wearing a crown.

"No, we wouldn't have enough French anyway."

Miss Whey, Clara Hawkins' secretary, came in with the morning mail. She lived in the house.

"Sit down, Miss Whey. What've we got today?" Familiar jingle.

"One questionnaire, three letters asking for money, three asking for Federal jobs, one woman demanding a pension because her husband was killed by a mail truck, two invitations for parties at the State Capitol, five for Washington, a speaking date at Bennington, a letter from Higgins trying to find how you stand on the Higgins-Wescott Bill and a proposal of marriage from a constituent." Miss Whey sat back and cleared her throat.

"Let's see the proposal." Smiling, she read a serious, insane letter from a person who had long since left reality. When she finished she said, "Answer the ones you can; I'll get to the others this afternoon, after the reception."

"Yes, Senator."

Clara still felt like an impostor when people called her by her husband's title. But, and she smiled to herself, she wouldn't be a substitute soon. She had decided to run for office when her husband's term expired and the Governor would support her. No one knew that yet. They wouldn't know it until the last minute, until the State Convention. And she would be elected; she had a great sentimental appeal, she knew. Then, of course, the Governor would support her and, besides, no Hawkins had ever been defeated in the state. She thought of her daughter with greater kindness than she usually did. It was possible to ignore her daughter's contemptuous estimate of her once she'd proved she was something more than a prominent man's wife. She did not have, she knew, her daughter's gift with people, her daughter's surface warmth and charm. Everyone was attracted to Charlotte but, on the other hand, Clara Hawkins impressed people with her sincerity, her dignity; she had presence and in the South, when she was young, it was important for a person to have presence. So few people had it now, though; even the word was almost never used. Yet it was more important than charm. But she no longer cared what her daughter thought. She grew angry if her daughter was rude to her, offended her dignity. She had a great sense of dignity which she'd got from her father . . . and from Bill, too. He had a sense of dignity. Strange how suddenly, how abruptly he died. I wonder what he'd say about my running again. He never thought of me as being intelligent: Charlotte is right there, but he loved me and she will never know or understand how much. I wonder if we've got enough cake.

"Yes, Mrs Hawkins, I made plenty."

The kitchen was busy; extra maids wandered about, carrying things, preparing. She saw one of them take Charlotte's tray up to her room. Well, Charlotte would soon organize things; Charlotte was a wonderful organizer. She would have made a good wife if she'd liked men, thought Clara Hawkins, who was the only person who understood this about her daughter. Charlotte envied men, especially when she loved them and she always competed with them; tried to be more popular, to be known as responsible for their success.

"Good morning, Grandmother."

"Good morning, dear."

He looked like William; she was glad that he was not dark like his father. He sat at the end of the table in the dining room, his grandfather's seat.

"You've had your breakfast, Grandmother?"

"Oh yes; quite a while ago. You're up early for a change."

"The birds make so much racket outside my window."

"Yes, I suppose they do." She paused in the doorway wondering whether she should enter the dining room or not. She had nothing to do here and she should be in the living room arranging flowers. She watched her grandson, undecided. He had grown in the last year; he was almost six feet and this was probably his full growth; he was almost as muscular as William had been. His hair which had once been silver was now darker but still blond. It would stay blond now; the way William's had.

"Brush your cowlick down, William."

"I did, Mother; look where I put water . . ."

"I know perfectly well you didn't try. Here, let me."

"See? It won't stay flat."

"Well, you should try to do something about it."

"All right, Mother, all right."

"And William . . ."

"Did you say something, Grandmother?"

Have I said something? I've been dreaming. "No, dear, I didn't say anything."

"I like the pepper in this sausage."

"I know you do. You always have."

"But I didn't use to like it."

"Why, when you were a child and old Annie used to bring you into the dining room in the morning . . ."

"Annie? Who was Annie?"

She was confused; time, the years, were running together. She sat down at the table and listened a moment to the uneven beating of her heart.

"Are you all right, Grandmother?"

"Oh yes; I'm perfectly well, William." Which was he? Where was she? Her heart was fluttering; perhaps she was going to have a heart attack. That would be something real at least. She had been overworking lately. Where was her husband? But it was morning and, of course, he'd be down on the Hill. Charlotte and William were both away at school. A foolish idea sending children away to school just when they were becoming people. Babies were nicer but people, even if they were one's children, were interesting. She turned to William to ask him why he wasn't in college today, why he was sitting in his father's place at the head of the table. She could say nothing, though.

"Would you like some water, Grandmother? Some brandy maybe? You look awfully pale." Grandmother. So she was here after all. Time moved so quickly; it had, in an instant, killed both her husband and William and she was alone; Charlotte upstairs having breakfast in bed and this boy, this ghost of William, across from her. Why had she been left so far behind? Why had the other two left her here like this; they had left her alone, completely alone among strangers. She must defend herself against these others. . . . Perhaps she was dying. Her heart still beat rapidly. She touched the smooth mahogany surface of the table: this was real and firm; she would keep her hand on it until she was sure where she was, had erected her defenses.

Distantly: "Are you sure you don't want anything?"

With a great effort: "Some brandy, please."

138

"Mother, do you think you ought to?"

"Of course, William. The only reason I drink it is to stimulate my heart; my heart isn't good, you know."

"Well, if you think so."

"I don't see why you want to get into the Army. I don't understand why you want to go and . . ." He will be killed. I know what is going to happen. I can't forget what's happened but when . . . when?

"Thank you, dear."

And the brandy brought her back. The confusion of time was ended. She was alive and this was her grandson. She kissed him lightly on the cheek. "Now finish your breakfast." She touched the top of the table with her hand; it was real and as smooth as polished marble. She had lived so long. It was natural that she should be, sometimes, confused.

3

His grandmother was acting strangely. He wondered if she'd been drinking; no, it was too early in the morning. Last year his mother had told him that his grandmother drank too much and, further, had been drinking for years. He'd found that almost impossible to believe but he believed his mother. Then he read things in the papers: kindly jokes about his grandmother's ability to hold her liquor. Then, once, he'd seen her after a political rally; her usually pale face red and her eyes bloodshot. Except for this and an untypical gaiety she didn't show that she was drunk.

But she had not been drinking. Perhaps she was going to have a stroke. This frightened him; her lips were trembling; it was almost as if she were carrying on a conversation with a ghost.

"Are you sure you don't want anything?"

"Some brandy, please." He went to the sideboard and got the bottle of brandy out. He poured her half a glass and took it to her.

"Thank you, dear." Her voice was stronger and she swallowed the brandy quickly. Color began to come back into her face. She kissed him, much to his surprise. She was usually undemonstrative.

"I feel much better now. I think my heart's beginning to wear out, though. I really should see the doctor soon. It's so uncomfortable getting old, Will . . . Bill. You know I feel just as young as ever when I'm sitting down. I can remember my wedding day party, over forty years ago. And I don't really feel different, sitting down. Moving about's when you feel old." She sighed and pushed the brandy glass from her. She stood up and, with her usual quick step, left the room.

She had changed since his grandfather died. He thought she was much more human now. His mother, of course, didn't approve of the change. She was as calm as ever but she smiled more often now. She seemed to enjoy her work though it was hard being a Senator. She liked to have Bill come and sit in her office in the Senate Office Building: the large high-ceilinged room, old-fashioned, Senatorial. It had been her husband's. There were pictures of politicians on the walls of the waiting room where Miss Whey and her secretary sat; then, off to the left, was his office (they still called it *his* office) ; nothing had been changed since William Hawkins died. There were still the same Indian relics on the mantelpiece, the flattened bullet which had killed *his* uncle during the siege of Atlanta. The office was furnished with large black leather chairs and a long couch. He had often stretched out on this couch after one of those long and violent debates on the floor. Bill enjoyed visiting his grandmother almost as much as he'd enjoyed visiting his grandfather. There were less people in the waiting room than there'd been when his grandfather was alive, fewer Senators dropped in to talk. He had always been thrilled to walk down the corridors of the Capitol with his grandfather, aware of people whispering and pointing. Oh, the old man had been a great one even if some of his history teachers called him a reactionary and blamed him for opposing the two wars. It was always clear to Bill why he had: no one likes wars and his grandfather had merely said what most of the people thought. It was very simple, basic, but the New England history teachers couldn't understand it.

He finished breakfast. Today was an important day, he remembered. The King was coming. He would be able to tell the people in school about that; none of them had known a King. As he left the dining room he wondered what Kings were like. Probably dull: just like any other politicians. He would go to the Encyclopedia and find out about this King's family. He was supposed to be one of the most royal Kings in Europe; if it was possible to be more royal than someone else.

The sunlight shone pale yellow on the carpet of the hall. He paused and daydreamed, watching the dust floating in the sunlight. As a child he had sat for hours daydreaming, watching the shafts of light in the hall and the dust swirling hypnotically in the light.

"Why don't you go outside and play? You're always hanging around the house."

"Yes, Mother."

She couldn't say that to him any more. Thank God he was almost grown. In two years he would be in the Army. The idea of the war both pleased and frightened him. She, of course, didn't want him to go. And, strangely, as he got older she found more instead of fewer things to criticize in him. The outbreaks were more violent and they were directed not only at him but his stepfather; she was displeased with both of them: their "attitudes" were wrong. He pitied his stepfather who had to live with her; Bill, at least, was away at school most of the time. He no longer spent his summers with her. She had decided that it would be a good idea for him to work (to learn the value of money; to be self-reliant and not to be so damned spoiled and critical) ; and so he had worked this last summer in a factory. It had been dull and not at all difficult; he wondered why people like his mother who had never worked made such a fuss about working when anybody could do it and most people did. He tried to tell her about the factory now that he was home, preparing to go back to his New England school (he'd changed schools again). She hadn't been very interested in the factory, though; she was much too busy with problems of her own. He wished sometimes that he could help her, could keep her from frowning. She could be pleasanter he knew if other people, his stepfather, his grandmother, himself, didn't make living so difficult for her. She told him frankly many of the things that made her unhappy. She was always frank.

She was phoning, her breakfast tray beside her. "Yes, Stephen's coming. Well, fairly large; a hundred people, perhaps. You know how it is. Yes, yes. Good-by, Claire."

They kissed. She still wore a triangular adhesive patch, which, when worn all night, was supposed to remove the line made by frowning; it *had* helped a little. The room smelt like her: perfume, stale cigarettes, and cold cream. It was a familiar smell; one he had known all his life. He looked at her as he sat down at the foot of her bed. She was very beautiful still. He was coming to believe it now since everyone said so. There were times when he actually thought her dazzling (when she wore her star rubies) . Though, to examine her closely, her nose was too large and her mouth, unpainted, was thin and tended to go down at the corners. But he believed what people said about her. One tends to accept things one hears regularly all one's life. For instance, at thirteen, Bill had decided he wanted to be a writer and Roger Gilray (or had it been his mother?) said that it was the most difficult job in the world and that, besides, the field was overcrowded. Since one of Roger's old college classmates was a successful novelist he knew what he was talking about. Bill had decided not to be a writer. Fortunately he preferred painting now. Color was important to him. He saw everything as color and line. He lost interest in words: they were too pallid, too inaccurate. Color was more satisfying, more real. He won a prize for painting at school and his mother had written him telling him that it was very nice but that if he'd put the same amount of energy into his schoolwork his marks would be better and grades were, after all, more important. She was worried about him, he knew. He must *not* be a failure. She told him this many times.

"Have you seen Mother?"

"Yes, she came to the dining room while I was having break-fast, she's been up a long time. She didn't look very good."

"She's probably been . . ."

"No, she just looked sick and her mind seemed to wander. It was very strange. I got her some brandy and then she was all right."

"Very likely," said his mother. He could tell now that this was going to be one of her tense days. "I wish we weren't hav-ing this damned party this afternoon; I've got a terrible head-ache."

Bill motioned at the phone. "Is my father coming?" he asked.

"Yes, he's coming."

Bill was glad; he hadn't seen his father for over a year. His father never stopped traveling. Of course, now that he was an Ambassador he *should* stay longer in one place but somehow he didn't. He was always moving about. Bill would have liked to be able to travel: his father must love it. Once, long ago, his father'd been a painter.

". . . bringing that woman, too." His mother had been talk-ing.

"What woman?"

"Janet Hamilton."

"Oh, I remember her. She has black hair and she's always riding in horse shows."

"Just where she belongs: with all the stable boys."

"Why, what's the matter with her?"

"She isn't a lady."

"Well . . ."

"She . . . it's a long story, Bill. When you're older I'll tell you." This was also familiar. He wondered when he'd be old enough to hear all these mysterious stories.

"I don't suppose Mother's doing anything about the decora-tions for the party?"

"She didn't seem to be doing much."

"Well, I'd better get up then. I want you to help, too. Close that window." He closed the window for her. She got undressed and he watched her, uneasily as always. She was completely unselfconscious. She was not as large as the Rubens women nor as slim as the Botticelli ones. The Medici Venus perhaps. He noticed that the female torso made a face; so, for that matter, did the male.

"Let's go down. As usual I'll probably have to do everything."

They sat for lunch at one end of the already extended dining-room table. The table was now almost as long as the room and it was piled with silver and plates. On the sideboard the heavy Georgian tea service was brightly polished. Clara Hawkins sat at the head of the table. Bill on her right; her daughter on her left. There was a place set for Roger Gilray who'd not yet arrived.

"I've invited Stephen."

"Really? George, will you pass the lamb chops again." Lamb had such a rank taste but *he* had liked lamb. "Do you think that's a good idea?"

"Yes, I think it is. Bill hasn't seen his father for a long time and . . . *I* should like to see Stephen again. It's been two years since I've seen him."

"No, thank you, George; I won't have any but Master Bill will. Well, I'm sure I'd like to see Stephen. I was thinking of Roger, though. Wouldn't he mind?"

"No, of course not. After all we're civilized people."

"That's the current illusion at least." How different her daughter was now; she had changed over the years. At least when she was younger she seemed to have principles but she had none now. The whole country was that way, too. The women, especially, had changed. The young girls in the streets, waiting, frightened her. She had lived too long. Of course, the war had something to do with it. The one before this was still vivid to her. She frowned; she would not allow herself to become confused again. I shall really have to take a rest soon.

"Where is Roger?" By asking a question about the present

she was able to place herself in time. She would not slip back. She concentrated.

"I don't know. He should be here any minute. He said he was coming to lunch."

"How's his bank?"

"The same as always, I suppose. He complains about taxes mostly."

"Poor Roger."

"*I* can't pity him." Charlotte really disliked her husband. Well, it was bound to happen. Charlotte always began relationships with great enthusiasm and then felt cheated if the other person did not obey her, did not live up to her expectations. Poor Charlotte.

"Have you any idea where Father's going to be sent next?"

"No, I haven't, Bill. Do you know, Charlotte?"

"No, I haven't heard. He's being mentioned for St James but everybody's mentioned for that."

"No, Stephen hasn't a chance. He hasn't got the money. You have to be a millionaire for that post. It's a shame we haven't Rome any more. That was much the best post. I remember when I was there before the last war; I loved Italy and now we're fighting those Italians: they're really the silliest people."

Charlotte liked Italians. There had been the most charming one in Washington a few years ago. He had completely charmed her. "You are one of the few great ladies I have ever known."

"Why, Nino! What a sweet thing to say!" There was really no adequate answer to such a compliment and so she had had an affair with him. He was too expensive, though, and soon he faded away, gracefully, with great charm, leaving behind, like the Cheshire cat, the shadow of a white-toothed Mediterranean smile.

"Roger, you're late. We started without you." Their faces touched an instant, conventionally, coldly.

"I was in a conference. Hello, Clara, Bill."

"Hello, Roger."

"Everybody ready for the royal majesty?"

"We're preparing," said Clara, smiling. Charlotte knew she liked Roger; not as much, perhaps, as she'd liked Stephen but still she liked him. It seemed to Charlotte a subtle revenge somehow. Her mother always took Roger's side. Her mother was always against her; ever since she'd been a child. That scene about the money, for instance; Charlotte knew she'd been a fool to get into an argument about that. She had lost her inheritance: she was sure of that and now she must try and get it back. She would not apologize. She would never do that but she would think of something. Already they were on better terms. She was careful not to get angry at her mother. And, of course, one day, it would all be Bill's. She looked at him. He was very quiet. He was almost always quiet, and watching. Sometimes he got on her nerves terribly because she hated to be watched, to be criticized. Sometimes when they talked of other people she found his comments sharp and knowing and she would tell him not to be so critical of other people. *She* was not.

"I hear the King's asked for a loan. Is that right, Clara?"

"Yes; he's talked to the President about it, I understand."

"Congress going to give it to him?"

"I suppose so. He'll get it from Lend-Lease anyway. Besides with all those emergency powers the President can do pretty much as he pleases."

"Thank you, George. Ah, charcoal-grilled, my favorite kind. Well, it'll be a bad loan from a banker's standpoint."

"The government isn't run like a business," said Charlotte; this was one of her favorite themes. It had been her father's and she had since adopted it. "That's been the trouble with this whole New Deal."

"Let's not talk politics," said Clara Hawkins. "I get so sick of them."

Roger thought she looked pale. She's getting old like the rest of us. He himself was fifty now and only recently he'd been young. Of course, he wasn't really old yet but he would be soon: it was too ghastly. He looked at Bill enviously. His muscles were hard and his skin tight and he was already old enough to make love as much as he liked. He wondered if Bill did, had discovered this world yet. He himself had started late and he'd married the wrong woman. He smiled grimly. He'd done it twice. One got no wiser after all. There was merely less time. If Bill was wise he'd start now, at fifteen, and be alive, enjoy himself and never marry. That would give him sixty years to make love; well, perhaps not the last ten though it was, in some cases, possible. But still to have sixty years of life ahead of him; Roger envied him. It was not that death was frightening; rather there was so much time wasted. He sighed and thought of the King.

The King, he had heard, was a charming man with a handsome mistress. There were, of course, rumors that he didn't care for women but it was also known that some woman lived with him. Kings were romantic, nostalgic.

"I wish I'd been able to have my hair done in town yesterday. I never seem able to get anything done now, the city's so crowded."

She looked well, he thought. The gray hair about her face softened the strong, too strong, Hawkins features. Her mouth was already beginning to droop and he knew that in a few years she would have to have her face lifted, her jowls smoothed out. Secretly he was pleased that she was beginning to show age, that she would, in a few years, be just another woman past forty, chic, well-preserved but no longer real.

Then he told the stories he had heard about the King.

Bill listened to him; he liked listening to Roger talk. He talked interminably, of course, once he got started. Many people, his mother among them, thought he was boring. But Bill knew that he was merely telling people what he had read and he'd read many excellent books and, also, he had a good memory. Bill usually listened to him; he did now because he was interested in the King.

It seemed that the King was over fifty but looked younger. He had been King for thirty years. The Queen was dead and some said she'd been poisoned. Now he had a mistress who was supposed to be with him in Washington; she never went to receptions, of course.

Then, after he'd heard almost as much as he wanted to know about the King, he stopped listening to Roger and he thought about his father. He wished sometimes that he might see him more often but actually he didn't much care. He barely knew him anyway. He thought it strange sometimes that he didn't know his own father as well as he knew Mr Forster, the art teacher at school. Still it was one of those things that must be accepted.

Now his father was going to marry Janet Hamilton. He had heard this rumor before. She was a striking woman as he remembered and his mother's women friends all said unpleasant things about her, which was, according to his mother, a good sign . . . usually. Women never liked other women who were successful. There were times when he wished that he had a woman of his own. He had never had sex with one but he would one day soon; he had made up his mind. Many of his schoolmates, older mostly, had had girls and they told him all about it. Now that he was in New England for school and had greater freedom than ever before he would be able to make the experiment. In the town where the school was located there was a girl known as the Beaver. She was quite popular and always available and Jimmy (Jimmy had gone north with him to school) claimed that he had been with her but Bill doubted this. He thought of Jimmy. Then his mind began to wander; he thought, finally, of the King.

4

The people were arriving.

Clara Hawkins stood in the hall. She stood very straight. She wore a dress of wine-colored velvet and her large old-fashioned diamonds were clipped, like medals, on her breast. Charlotte stood near her; Charlotte in black with a string of pearls. Roger and Bill, being male and of less importance, were in the dining room arranging things, giving people liquor and helping the servants move things about.

"Hello, Bishop."

"My dear Senator Hawkins, how are you?"

"Quite well." Southey was really very kind. He would have made a wonderful husband, Clara thought. She wondered why he'd never been married.

"And *you* look enchanting, Mrs Gilray."

"Thank you, Bishop. So glad you could come." Charlotte was being abrupt now; she's always rude to my friends, always. Well, it makes no difference now.

"This is the first time we've had a King, isn't it?" He ignored Charlotte. Charlotte was now talking with some young people; she was smiling and laughing. "Charlotte is such a warm person." How many times had she heard that? If they only knew.

"Yes, this is the first King we've ever had in the house."

"You must be quite thrilled. I mean, of course, many greater people have been here but a King is really something special, isn't he?"

"Oh, very special." She greeted some more people. The Bishop stayed at her side.

"Tell me," he said when she'd finished her greetings, "is the King Catholic or not? I've tried to find out in the Encyclopedia. Of course, his country is but so often the Royal families are Protestant."

"I'm sure I don't know."

"I hope he's Protestant," said the Bishop wistfully, rather naively, thought Clara who was religious herself but knew that most of the Kings and Presidents were not. It was all depressing. The things she had been taught as a child, decades ago, mere decades ago, were no longer accepted or practised. She was taught to believe in God and the practical inferiority of women (although they were finer, morally, than men) and now everything was changed. People did not believe in God; they didn't even bother to call themselves atheists. They did not think of God. At least, her husband had thought about death but these people didn't think: Charlotte never thought about anything except money and how extraordinarily badly people had treated her. What had happened to the world? To-day she was a Senator and she had always been taught that women knew nothing of politics. As if politics took anything more than an average intelligence and a certain instinctive sense of timing. This was not the world she'd been born into or taught to expect. She wished that she were dead, that she had never been born.

"I think it quite possible that our King is an Episcopalian. He went to school in England and he's related to Queen Victoria."

"It's possible; it's possible."

Florence Nail came into the hall. She was alone. She had never married. She was thinner now than ever before. Though not yet forty she looked like an old maid and what had once been only a significant expression was now downright sinister. She dressed badly. She wore green which made her look bilious and tired. She had been such a pretty girl once. Had she been afraid of men? of having children? Clara knew that no one really wanted to live alone yet this girl did. She had looked so nice the day of Bill's christening. That was the last time she'd seen Florence in this house. She had seen her at Charlotte's house several times, though. Florence was devoted to Charlotte and Charlotte seemed like her. But why had she, a pretty girl with money, never married? Such things never used to happen. Perhaps the end of the world was coming. There was every indication. This war, for instance: all the young men dying.

"How are you, Florence?"

She had visited Florence once, years ago. It was before Bill Hawkins was Vice-President. They had stayed in a small pension outside the city, in the Tuscan Hills . . . what a wonderful sound: the Tuscan Hills! But that was years ago.

"Very well, thank you. I read such exciting things about you in the papers these days." And as she spoke Clara noticed that she was looking at Charlotte whose back was turned. The expression in her eyes was oddly hopeless. Clara pitied her without knowing quite why.

"Really? You'll want to speak to Charlotte, of course. Charlotte!" Her daughter turned around and the two women embraced, socially.

"Florence, you look so pale! Have you been sick?"

"The same old liver trouble. Nothing serious but you look stunning, Charlotte, absolutely stunning." She always said that to Charlotte.

"Thanks, dear. Do go in and see your godchild."

"Oh yes, certainly I mean to . . . Is Roger here?" It seemed to Clara that she was thinking of an excuse not to leave but it was no use for Charlotte wanted her to leave and in a moment she went into the drawing room; Charlotte turned back to her group of "amusing" people. To Charlotte the world was divided between amusing and dull people. Clara pitied Florence Nail who was no longer in the amusing class yet wanted so desperately to be.

"Is this going to be a large affair, Senator?" The Bishop was still beside her. He was, with his calm presence, gently assisting her. She decided that *he* had never married because he wanted to serve the church unencumbered.

"Yes, it'll be fairly large; my daughter's arranged everything, you know."

Then Stephen and a handsome woman with black hair drawn severely off her face and gathered into a bun at the back, like a Roman matron, entered the hall. She was handsome, very aristocratic-looking. She wore pendant errings which pleased Clara; it was a face that would have been incomplete, unframed, without them.

"Hello, Clara," said Stephen and they embraced warmly. "How've you been?"

"Pretty well, Stephen, pretty well." She didn't know what to say. She was surprised at how glad she was to see him. He was as slim as ever but his hair was almost white, not gray, but white. He looked distinguished, much handsomer than he did when he was younger. Charlotte was not in the hall and Clara was pleased; she wanted a moment with Stephen before her daughter took him away.

"This is Janet Hamilton," said Stephen.

She shook hands with the younger woman. So this was Janet Hamilton. She had heard about her: she was supposed to be loose. Her husband, a wealthy man, had divorced her for adultery and she had not even bothered to defend herself. Clara would not have received her a few years ago but things were different now. It seemed of so little importance what people did. They did everything anyway; they were merely less cautious these days. Clara had learned to accept such things. They were all a part of the mystery: what had become of her world? One day she had been living quietly in it and then, suddenly, it was gone.

Janet Hamilton had a handshake like a man, thought Clara who had, over the years, shaken many thousands of hands.

"How do you do?"

They greeted one another. Then Clara, noticing Southey waiting beside her, said, "Stephen, you remember the Bishop, don't you?"

"Oh yes, of course, of course." They shook hands. Stephen obviously didn't remember him. Southey had christened his son and had, before that, married Stephen and Charlotte.

"A lot of water," said Southey gravely, "has gone under the bridge since we last met."

"Yes, I suppose it has," said Stephen vaguely.

"The christening," said Clara, as though musing; Stephen understood.

"Yes, a lot's happened to all of us in the last . . . thirteen years. This war . . ." he made the gesture everyone made when they mentioned the war.

"It *is* terrible," said the Bishop slowly, nodding.

"Well, let's hope it'll be over soon," said Janet Hamilton cheerfully.

She seemed to be an unaffected woman, thought Clara. Not very bright but so few people are bright. Besides, very intelligent people were almost never happy; on the other hand, of course, it was quite possible to be stupid and unhappy. There seemed to be no answer.

"You're quite successful now, Stephen," she said, clearing her mind of these thoughts.

"Finally," he grinned; he still smiled like a child. "Charlotte didn't wait long enough," he added.

"Well, you *haven't* made any money." They laughed together; laughed at Charlotte.

"Where are you going next?" asked the Bishop.

"I haven't the slightest idea. There aren't many countries left these days."

"Latin America?"

"I'm a European man. No, I haven't any idea. By the way, is the King here yet?"

Clara shook her head. "He'll be here at four-thirty. You knew him, of course?"

"Yes, before the war and then I saw him recently in London. His government's there now. He's quite a shrewd man, you know. He always ran his own country . . . something rather rare."

"Really? That's unusual nowadays."

"He's an unusual man."

". . . an unusual man." Charlotte heard this across the hall. She recognized Stephen's voice and she was aware, also, that she had stage fright. The palms of her hands were perspiring.

"Hello, Stephen." They shook hands formally, awkwardly. "And Janet! I'm so glad you could come."

"Hope I'm not in the way."

"Not at all. Come back to the drawing room and I'll get you a drink."

The drawing room was already crowded with people. They looked at Charlotte and Stephen curiously. Janet, she noticed, was looking very handsome; she envied her her figure. She had an almost perfect figure by contemporary standards; slim, but not masculine. But she was such a whore. Public opinion meant nothing to her. She would go and stay in a man's apartment and invite people to come visit her; she liked to shock them, of course. But strangely enough, though the very proper people would have nothing to do with her, everyone else received her gladly. She was regarded as someone unique, a phenomenon. It was this acceptance that made Charlotte envious and which, in turn, made her angry for she hated to be envious of anyone.

"I haven't seen you for a long time, Charlotte," drawled Janet. "Where've you been?"

"I've been around," said Charlotte, trying not to be abrupt. She glanced at Stephen and saw that he was examining the room, remembering. It pleased her that he should remember now. Yet he was probably not nostalgic; after all he was free and she was not. She was tied to Roger Gilray financially and to her mother for, indirectly, the same reason and, of course, to Bill because she was his mother.

"The house hasn't changed at all," Stephen sounded surprised.

"No, it hasn't been changed. I don't think anything's ever been changed here since it was built. Father put electricity in and that was all."

"Nice old house," said Janet Hamilton, jarring the mood but not destroying it.

"The old man died very suddenly, didn't he?"

"Yes, it was quite sudden. George, get them a drink please."

"I was abroad when it happened. I meant to write you but I never got around to it. We were so busy."

"Just as well; we didn't read half the mail."

"Good scotch," said Janet Hamilton.

"How's Bill?"

"He's well."

"Is he here now?"

"Yes, I think he's in the dining room."

"I think I'll go in and see him for a minute." And Stephen left them together. Charlotte wondered whether she should go after him. She decided she couldn't because Janet would fol-

154

low her. She turned to Janet then and said, "Are you showing any horses this year?"

"A few, just a few." She looked at the door through which Stephen had gone. "I've sold most of my horses. All my best grooms got drafted."

"What a pity," said Charlotte maliciously.

"Yes, it is." Either Janet was stupid or a good actress.

Florence Nail joined them and Charlotte introduced her.

"The party's delightful," said Florence; as usual she sounded much too grateful, too anxious to please. She was becoming a bit of a bore as she got older, thought Charlotte. Still she was goodhearted. "I just can't wait for the King to come. I do wish he'd hurry." Only Florence would admit that she was curious to see the King; the others pretended indifference and many *were* indifferent. The King was, ultimately, important only to the Hawkins family.

"He isn't very interesting," said Janet in her slow, maddening voice.

"You know him?" Florence looked at her in the same admiring way she usually looked at Charlotte and Charlotte resented this.

"Oh yes . . . very well." The "very well" told them everything; as it was meant to.

The King, too, thought Charlotte grimly. "I thought Stephen said he was charming."

"He probably was with Stephen. I think he prefers men anyway but he plays both sides."

"Really?" Florence was shocked and this put Charlotte in a better humor.

"And he takes himself so seriously."

"Well, he should," said Florence, looking at Charlotte for help.

"I don't see why. After all there're at least a dozen Kings and he isn't the most important one by a long shot."

"Where did you know him?" asked Charlotte.

"One summer at Cannes. He used to come down there incog . . . under a different name." Janet Hamilton was proud of the fact that she'd been unable to get into the fifth grade.

Then Charlotte left Florence and Janet together. She knew Florence would soon be rescued; all the men would gather about Janet; they did.

Charlotte went about the room from group to group, being a hostess. Finally Stephen came back, rescuing her from this.

"He's grown, hasn't he?"

"He's taller than I am. He's a grown man now."

"Oh, I don't think so. I hope not anyway."

"Why?"

"Well, he's so lazy. He gets terrible marks in school and they say he doesn't work. Then, of course, he's so selfish. He doesn't think of anyone except himself."

"Then he sounds like a pretty bad job and naturally that's your fault."

"What? Well, I don't think that at all. Don't be funny. He has *many* good traits but I think a parent should concentrate on the bad ones. He's much better now than he used to be, certainly."

"Thanks to your guidance."

"Don't be sarcastic, Stephen. It hasn't been easy guiding him. I've had to do it all alone, too."

"That's what you wanted."

"Only because you were away all the time. Someone had to raise him."

"He doesn't seem so selfish to me. And if he's self-centered that makes him like almost everyone else in his family including you and me."

"You know that isn't true. I think of him all the time. I've made sacrifices for him . . ."

"What sacrifices?"

"When he was a child I almost never went out until he was four years old."

"Two years old, Charlotte. One and a half to be exact."

He was maddening. "He was the main reason I agreed to marry Roger so that he could have everything."

"There was, of course, no self-interest in it at all. You weren't interested in rubies or a big house."

"No, I wasn't!" She tried to control her anger.

"Charlotte, you're wonderful. Well, I don't see much wrong with Bill."

"How could you? You barely know him."

"That's true but I think you should leave him alone. I understand he's won some prizes as a painter. That means he's outstanding in some way and that's what you want."

"Oh, that!" She'd never considered the painting important; she remembered how easily Stephen had given it up. She sighed and then she said, "I wonder if it was worth it?" She looked about her. They were standing alone between the piano and the window. Here Bill had been christened thirteen years before. She was tired now. Soon she would ask her question. She would have to ask it sooner or later.

"What was worth what?"

"My marrying Roger."

"Financially, I should say it was; you didn't expect anything else, did you?" He was being ironic now but she could ignore it; perhaps this wasn't the best time to ask. No, she would ask. She might not see him again. She prepared the way for her question.

"Of course I did. Roger seemed kind and gentle. I was prepared to accept a quiet unemotional relationship but he didn't want that. He sulks most of the time now. He's rude to people, to my friends. Really, it's unbearable. I never wanted to marry him in the first place, remember that. He wanted to marry me. I finally accepted him for Bill's sake."

"For Bill? But why?"

"Because I wanted him to have all the things, the opportunities I never had myself and, alone, I didn't have enough money."

"What do you mean *you* didn't have opportunities? I thought your family did a lot for you and they certainly had as much money as Roger. They might not have wanted you on the stage but at least they supported you while you tried."

"They did not!" She spoke too quickly; she had been building an image of those years in her mind. The image was, perhaps, a little distorted. Still, philosophically, it was true. "Well, at least they didn't help me to get started the way I can, the way I will, get Bill started. I want him to be a success."

"Yet you don't seem to take his painting seriously. You don't want him to be an artist."

"But how do we know he's any good? Perhaps he's just wasting his time the way you did. Besides it's so difficult being a success in that field; you have to be a genius."

"And you don't think he is?"

"No, I don't."

"Well, Charlotte, I don't see how you'd ever know. You know nothing about art. Even if he isn't marvellous he should be able to do what he wants to do; what difference does it make if he's successful or not? He won't have to earn a living with the Hawkins money."

"*If* he's successful it'll pay me back for all my sacrifices."

"Charlotte, what in God's name *have* you sacrificed for him?"

"I married Roger Gilray." She was angry now. She could never get the conversation where she wanted it now.

"Charlotte, try to be honest; you didn't marry Roger for Bill's sake any more than I'd marry Janet Hamilton for his sake. You wanted money and you didn't have it and a millionaire was in love with you and you married him. There's nothing particularly ignoble about that but don't go holding it over Bill's head. You're being unfair to him and you look ridiculous to everyone else."

"That's not true. God damn it, Stephen, I . . ." She began to sob. She turned her back to the room; fortunately no one saw her.

"Now what's the matter?" Stephen motioned helplessly.

"I'm so damned wretched," she said finally, when she'd controlled herself.

"I'm sorry."

"You don't think that we might ever . . . if I divorced

Roger—that we could ever live together again?" It was humiliating but she enjoyed the pain it gave her to ask him this.

"What?" He was surprised. She'd been too abrupt but there was no other way. She was even prepared for the pain of his refusal. She knew now that he hated her and it frightened and relieved her. She wondered how she could ever have caused such strong feeling in anyone even though she had loved him and still, in a certain sense, loved him. Yet she was aware of all this as he tried to answer, tried to be polite. It was no use. Well, she had tried. She wondered how much alimony she could get from Roger. Stephen was paying for Bill's school. She could live very comfortably until she found the right man. She knew so many men who wanted her but she had no respect for any of them. Until now she had never respected Stephen. There seemed to be no man in the world like her father.

"I . . . I don't really know," Stephen was saying. "I thought you were through with me. I thought we were absolutely finished with one another."

"I shouldn't have asked. I'm sorry."

"No, I don't mean that. It's just that it's been such a long time."

"Yes, it has been a long time. Perhaps we'd better discuss it later. You'll be in Washington this week, won't you? Yes? Well, we'll have lunch together. What's all that noise? If it's the King he's early. How do I look? My eyelashes didn't run, did they?" It was much too late.

5

Bill was glad to see his father.

"Hello, there." They shook hands beside the dining-room table. His father's hair was practically white, he noticed; he still looked young, though.

"You're about ready for the football team, aren't you?"

"I guess so."

"You must weigh as much as I do."

"Hundred and sixty."

"Just the same; how do you like New England?"

"I hate the climate; in the winter anyway. The summer's nice. Like the time we went to Canada."

His father nodded. "Your mother tells me your marks aren't very good."

"No, I guess they're not." Why did they always have to talk about marks?

"Well, I don't suppose it's very important," said his father, rather surprisingly. "But you ought to work at something just to keep busy."

"I do; I'm painting a lot now. I won the New England prep school prize last spring."

"No! Why, that's wonderful. Why didn't you write me about it?"

"I did. I wrote you in Stockholm."

"Well, not much mail gets through these days. You should've stuck it in the diplomatic pouch. So you won the prize. Are you going to stick at it, at painting?"

"I think so."

"Why 'think so'? Isn't that what you want to do?"

"Yes . . . yes, I want to do that more than anything else."

"I can't see what's stopping you then. If I'd had . . . what makes you doubt you'll be a painter?"

"Well, Mother doesn't seem to think much of it. She says it takes much more work than I think to be a success."

"Forget what your mother says," said his father and he seemed angry. "She doesn't know anything about art anyway. You do as you please; work at your painting. I'll see that your mother doesn't interfere. You should do as you please. And if you're talented you shouldn't let anybody stop you from doing what you know you have to do. If I'd had the money or the endurance *I* certainly would have been a painter."

"You'd really rather be an artist than an Ambassador?"

"Of course." Bill was aware that facades were collapsing. He was standing uneasily in a world that was rapidly becoming unfamiliar, larger.

"You don't think there's anything wrong with being a bad painter?"

"It might be sad if you weren't any good and discovered it too late to do something else. But if you were contented being a bad artist why it makes no difference what people say. Besides, good and bad aren't always easy to judge."

"But if I worked in a bank it wouldn't be so noticeable if I was a flop. I owe something, I guess, to Mother and . . ."

"You owe her very little; you owe much more to yourself. I've no doubt you're selfish but so am I and so is your mother. The only times when we're unselfish is when we're in love and even then our unselfishness is, in a way, selfish. You should, certainly, be nice to your mother and, in the simple things, do as she wants. You may find one day that even though she's your mother you don't like her very much or that you may not like me but don't be troubled. Remember it's no fault of yours we're your parents. Don't be upset if you don't like us; for that matter, we might not like you.

"By all means be a painter, good or bad, that's your business and no one else's. Don't let your mother or anyone else talk you into being a banker or anything like that. Not many people ever know what they want to do and the few that do know should, if it's possible, do what they want. Think about that. Being a success is only important if you feel you need it to be complete. But don't try to be one for someone else."

There was nothing Bill could say. He had never known his father was like this. He was puzzled, startled. Everything his father had said was the opposite of what his mother had taught him and he didn't know which to believe. His mother loved him more; he knew that because she had told him once that never in his life would anyone love him as much as she did. He believed her but it was possible that his father knew more about the world. He could not accept his father's suggestions about gratitude. He knew he owed his mother a great deal. She had had a difficult time with him.

George went by them with a plate of sandwiches. His father took two and gave him one.

"Then you think the painting's more important than good grades in school?"

"Yes. I suppose you should pass enough subjects to graduate, to be reasonably conventional. Then if you don't go into the Army you should go on to an art school."

"And skip college?"

"If you want to. I'm really thinking aloud, thinking of what I might have done; what I should have done, I expect."

"I'd just as soon not go to college."

"Then go to an art school. After a while perhaps you'll find someone you'd like to study with or you might want to work by yourself: that might be best of all. But this is your business, not mine. You'll have plenty of time to plan your life."

"Plenty of time," Bill was hypnotized, thinking of a future where he could, amazingly, do as he pleased.

"Have you got any of your work here?"

"Not here, no. But out at the house, my mother's house, I've a few things there."

"Maybe I'll be able to come over if Roger doesn't mind."

"Oh, he won't mind." And Roger, sensing, perhaps, that his name had been spoken, came into the dining room.

"Stephen! Glad to see you. How are you?"

They acted as if they were the best of friends and, actually, there was no reason, thought Bill, why they shouldn't be. Then Roger asked Stephen how long he was going to be in the country and Stephen said he didn't know and Roger, who would quote him, asked him how long the war was going to last.

"Forever, I suppose. It seems like it already. Two or three years probably."

"Why, we'll be bankrupt!"

"It's not at all unlikely. I thought Charlotte was looking well." Stephen shifted the subject so suddenly that Roger's mouth opened and shut twice before he'd adjusted himself to the new subject. Sadly, he accepted the end of the war talk.

"Yes, she holds her age well."

Stephen laughed. "She isn't that old."

"Well, you know what I mean . . . women when they get near forty tend to lose their figures and so on."

"Fortunately Charlotte hasn't."

"No, I must say she hasn't." Roger sounded bored and Bill wondered why. Of course, the marriage wasn't going particularly well but then it never had. He had heard them fighting once:

"You make absolutely no effort with people, Roger. I can't understand it at all. You're getting terribly unpopular. I was never so embarrassed in all my life as I was when you left the Binghams' party Tuesday after dinner."

"Happened to be bored and I don't like the Binghams."

"That has nothing to do with it. *I* don't like them any more than you do . . . at least I don't like her. She was one of the Turners and they're all . . . but that's unimportant. I make an effort to be agreeable and that's why I'm popular and you're not."

"That's your business how you act; it's my business how I act."

"After all you're my husband. You have a certain responsibility."

"Perhaps you think so."

"All right, *be* unpleasant about it. Sit there like a perfect idiot . . ."

There was silence. Bill stood outside the library door listening. He had planned to go in but now he wouldn't. He didn't want to move while they were quiet because they could hear his footsteps. He stood motionless and then he heard his mother's voice.

"I don't see why you can't conform a little. After all I don't like these parties any more than you do but we have to go to them. You don't want to be unpopular . . ." Bill went away.

Roger said, "She certainly is popular."

And Stephen agreed. "She was always a great party girl."

"Yes," said Roger.

"I understand she lost a child. I was sorry to hear that."

Roger nodded solemnly. "I was quite upset when it happened. I'd been counting on a child but now the doctor tells us she'll never be able to have one."

Then Stephen excused himself. Roger and Bill poured drinks and helped arrange things in the dining room. Florence Nail came in and Bill talked with her awhile. Then she left; he'd found her unchanged.

Bill heard the sound of cars in the driveway outside. "I'll bet that's the King," he said and he left Roger and went to the window. He could hear the people in the hall and the drawing room; they were speaking louder, more excitedly. Two black cars drove up to the front door and a number of men got out of each car. Bill was too far away to tell which was the King.

He went into the hall where his grandmother stood. People were coming, casually, into the hall from the drawing room. Bill was excited. He had read so much about this King. It would be thrilling to meet him. He thought about the way he would mention the King at school. He would be casual; as casual as these people in the hall.

The door opened.

Clara Hawkins heard the cars in the driveway and she took a swallow of bourbon which George brought her. She was not excited now. She was tired. There were too many people in her house, too many noisy people. She was tired of standing up. It would be so nice to lie down on her bed upstairs and shut her eyes, shut these people out.

But she must be alert now. The King was outside. Perhaps this was a moment that would be recalled in history. How the King visited Senator Hawkins and soon afterwards the Senate approved a loan for his people. Her hands were trembling. She tried to control them. She was so tired. She had never been so tired in her life. Her heart was beating rapidly again. This was a strange day. It was so difficult to tell what was real and what was not. But at least she knew where she was. Yet she did not feel real. Perhaps she was already dead. Oh, to sleep.

The door opened.

Roger was almost as excited as Bill and, unlike the other, he showed it. He was not interested in social affairs. For that matter he was no longer much interested in banking but history fascinated him. Now for the first time he was about to come into contact with European history: not only contemporary history but centuries of historic personages would be in this one King.

And he began to think of the different things he would ask the King. He would ask about that strange shift of premiers in 1934 and was it true that the last Premier was pro-Nazi or not. "As I was saying to the King last week, he was at my mother-in-law's, Europe can never survive if capitalism in America fails. He agrees with me, a delightful fellow. And you know that peculiar coup in 1934? Well he explained it to me and . . ."

The door opened.

The King bored Stephen. He had always thought him rather dishonest: the worst sort of European politician. His royalty was unimportant. He looked at Janet; they were standing in the hall. She grinned at him. "I'll bet he pretends not to know me," she said.

"I'll bet he does recognize you. He'll tell you you look charming and he'll say something about what a pity the Germans are in Paris. He's all front, you know. Such an ass."

"Yes, but he could be rather sweet; you never saw that side of him."

"Thank the Lord." Stephen looked at Janet fondly. He wondered if he'd ever marry her or not. She'd wanted to marry him for several years and she had enough money to support both of them. She wanted him to retire. He might when the war was over. The idea of living on her money did not disturb him. But would it, in the long run, be dull? He didn't love her as much as she did him and, in time, she might dislike him because of this. He would wait a while longer. In the meantime life with her was pleasant. A few people gossiped but now, with the war, people paid a little less attention to affairs of this kind.

The King, he thought, would remember everyone's name. The door opened.

Charlotte came into the hall when she heard the cars in the driveway. She stood near her mother who nodded to tell her that this was the King at last. Her mother looked rather white, she thought. She had been drinking heavily but, even aside from that, she seemed ill. Charlotte glanced at Stephen and Janet; they were talking together but Charlotte couldn't hear what they were saying. But now something important was about to happen to all of them. The King was coming. How like a hymn that phrase was! She wanted him to be everything. He must not, he could not disappoint her. It was, somehow, so important that he be real and yet larger than reality. She must be able to imagine him enthroned. If she could imagine this then there was some hope for her; there was still a man for her, a King. He will be like Father, she thought excitedly. She was tired of ordinary men. She must know a King. She faced the door and the door opened.

Everyone was quiet as the King entered the room.

The King, alas, wore no crown.

the winter

THE FLOWERS on the lilac bushes were heavy and purple and he knew that whenever he thought of the school he would smell lilacs and remember their color.

He walked with Carter slowly down the walk to the library. This afternoon the graduation exercises would be held. After that Bill would go into the Army and Carter to the Navy. The war had not, in spite of the prophets, ended and the end seemed far away.

He was fond of Carter and he would be sorry not to see him again. At first Jimmy had been his best friend but that had changed gradually; Bill withdrew from athletics, did nothing but his painting. He and Jimmy ceased to understand one another and they moved apart. Jimmy spent his time with the athletes and Bill with the painters and writers, the odd boys. They still met from time to time in Jimmy's room but finally this almost stopped and Bill spent most of his time with Carter, his roommate, who was in love with a college girl in Boston. Bill, too, was in love this year.

They walked between the banks of lilacs, up the steps and into the library. On the first floor there was an art gallery, and an exhibition of painting. Carter wanted to see Bill's new paintings. Bill had several in the show and he'd won the first two prizes. A number of sons with parents wandered about the long, white-walled room, looking at the paintings and commenting. Like most people they didn't like Bill's work as much as the careful illustrations of the other boys. He had grown used to this.

"There it is," said Carter, pretending awe. They stood before the first prize picture.

"What's it supposed to be?" asked one gentle mother; her husband, obviously a broker (he wore horn-rimmed spectacles and a Phi Beta Kappa key) answered:

"Damned if I know. Looks like somebody sitting in an armchair."

"Queer, isn't it? They gave this the first prize, too."

"Just puzzle people and they'll think you're smart," said the broker. Bill listened; he had a great contempt for brokers but Carter was much more tolerant.

"Don't pay any attention," he said when the couple had moved down the room. "They'll be dead one day and you'll be academic."

Bill smiled. It was probably true at that; he didn't want to get any older, though. Seventeen was quite old enough. One was physically and, in *his* case, emotionally matured; one was also free of responsibilities. But one day he would be old and have responsibilities. He hated the idea. This painting would be the same and he would be changed. How terrible! how terrible life was. Death was something else: inevitable, a fact. But life changed so. Someday he would probably look back and not like this picture. He would be unfaithful to himself. The years.

"I like it the best," said Carter finally. He had watched him paint it, of course. He had often made unpleasant remarks about it at the time but now that they were leaving one another he could afford to be pleasant.

The painting was of a man in a chair but it was much more than that. Bill had noticed once that when he concentrated on a face or an object, if he looked fixedly, it changed. Certain

parts became important; others receded or vanished and wonderful things happened to light. It would congeal and become blocks upon the edges of the object. The effect was
strange, dreamlike. This was what Bill had tried to paint. It
was abstract; it was not literal: it was reality heightened.

He squinted as he looked at the painting. He was not so
enthusiastic about this particular one now but there were
some good things about it. It was a beginning. "A work of
art is never finished: merely abandoned." Valéry. The concept, of course, was all right but perhaps the man in the chair
was almost too obvious.

He asked Carter and Carter shrugged. "Haven't the faintest
notion. I think it's good enough as it is. The peasants wouldn't
like it no matter what you did. The day is coming when we
shall have to destroy the peasants, the entire proletariat. The
world must be made safe for tyrants." Carter continued for a
while on the subject of peasants. Then he said, "By the way
what time's your father supposed to get here?"

"I don't know. He said he was driving up in the morning."

"He's going to give a speech, I suppose."

"Certainly. He always gives a speech when he comes up
here." Bill's father had visited the school twice since Bill had
been enrolled. His mother had started up several times but
she'd never gotten farther than New York. She would be here
today; she was confident of that.

"What's he going to talk about?"

"The usual things, I guess. World responsibility. League of
Nations . . . all that business. I wish I could get interested in
it." Bill, who never thought about politics, always agreed with
his father. He appreciated his father's röle in world politics
but it all seemed, somehow, trivial. This new idea, this new
League, was as much his father's doing as anyone else's.

Bill had seen more of his father in the last two years than
he ever had before. His father's foreign missions were short
ones now and he was a White House advisor. Unfortunately,
unhappily, his grandmother had, before she died, politically
repudiated her ex-son-in-law, if that was possible. She mis-

trusted the Administration's plan for a world organization and she'd died trying to present her own plan.

His mother talked politics still. But even Bill, knowing nothing of politics, knew enough to tell that his mother was quoting his grandfather, usually inaccurately. She had a gift for sounding knowledgeable. In the West, that terrible summer, she'd talked knowingly of cattle and markets and rodeos (pronounced in the Nevada manner). Now her home in Washington had become a salon and she surrounded herself with government figures and she talked to them of world problems, talked brilliantly, wittily and very few people suspected that she had no idea what she was talking about. His mother was a remarkable woman and he admired her.

Carter moved down the room and Bill followed him. He glanced at the other paintings: they were so bad. Some of them, most of them, showed talent, the little talent that so many people are born with but there was no vision in their work, only illustration. His art teacher came into the room.

"Hello, Bill."

"Hi." Bill never called him "sir." He had always disliked calling people that and lately he'd stopped altogether. His mother, of course, had thought it was a good habit: it made a good impression.

The art teacher was forty and looked younger. He was a competent artist and an inspired, a zealous teacher. He wore thick glasses and he seemed, sometimes, to be trying to hypnotize his students. His temper was uncertain but he liked Bill who was his best pupil.

"Admiring yourself?"

"Sort of."

"It's fair," said Mr Forster. To the judges, to other people he'd called Bill brilliant. One of the judges had been an art critic and he'd been impressed by Bill's work. Mr Forster quoted this man often. There was some doubt in the critic's mind as to how Bill would develop. His work would not be fashionable; at least not at the moment. But perhaps in a few years, by the time he'd be ready to show, perhaps the fashion (it was so important to know the fashion) would have changed. He was fresh, almost original, everyone agreed to that. There were few very recognizable influences in his work. Everyone predicted a brilliant future and Bill agreed with them. He thought of his mother and of the pleasure she would have in being able to speak of her famous son. He would be more famous than his grandfather; that was a definite goal. He was tired of being identified as the son or the grandson. Oh, his future would be dazzling and he was almost never frightened of the years ahead. The years again.

"Yes, the light's very good. The way you visualized it in blocks." Mr Forster had said all these things before. Carter, bored, wandered around the other end of the room, mingling with the peasants, listening to them, remembering.

"Well, you'll be going tonight," said Mr Forster.

"I guess so. I'll probably drive back with my father. I don't know yet, though. My mother may come and I might take the train back with her."

"Yes, yes." Forster seemed to be thinking of something else. "You still want to go in the Army?"

Bill nodded. "I'll have to anyway."

"Yes." Forster sighed. "What a stupid thing," he exploded finally. "You should be working every day for the next twenty years. It's not simple being an artist. Talent's distributed all over the place but the vision . . . ah, that's quite a different thing." He talked angrily about vision and the lack of it. Bill had heard all of this before.

"Why don't you be a conscientious objector?" suggested Mr Forster finally, a little desperately.

"Haven't the nerve. Besides there's the family."

"To hell with them."

"Well . . . I might get something out of the war. There're so many things to see during a war."

"Granted, granted, but suppose you're killed?"

Bill had never thought of this; he looked at the top of Mr Forster's glasses and he wondered how thick they were. Would he be killed? The class of two years before had already lost a dozen boys. Would he be killed? and forgotten; remembered vaguely for a few years as that boy who was supposed to have painted well and, some people had said, would have been very good. He imagined his paintings in his mother's attic. Eventually they would be thrown away. He stopped looking at Mr Forster's glasses; he would not be hypnotized. He couldn't decide how thick they were. He looked at his painting of the man in the chair; he noticed the subtle pattern the light made. This would be thrown away and forgotten. "Oh yes young Giraud, he was killed in the war. I think he was some sort of artist, very talented they said." They would speak of him the way they now spoke of William, his dead uncle. But *did* anyone speak of William now that his grandmother was dead? No. William had not been mentioned for a long time. His picture had been put away.

"I hope not," said Bill at last; he was afraid. "I hope I won't be killed. I had an uncle who was killed in the last war, you know."

His father was in his room. He had driven up from New York alone. Just a few minutes before Bill had received a special delivery letter from his mother: "Darling, I'm so upset that I won't be able to be at your graduation but I've been having the *old trouble*." His mother's change of life was known to everyone; she discussed it freely, amusingly. "But Stephen, of course, will be there. I'm glad you finally passed everything. As I've always said you must learn to work hard because that's the only way to get ahead. I should have been *terribly* disappointed if you'd not graduated. I was upset enough at the thought that you might not pass all your courses. I'm glad you didn't let me down. Washington is hot and awful and I'm planning to spend the summer in North Hampton. I'll be there in a day or so; my address when you come is. . . ." She wrote him briefly of her activities. She had not mentioned his winning the prize. He was just as glad she'd not come; he felt guilty because he thought this but it was true. She would have made a scene about something. And she would have found

172

some excuse not to see his paintings; she would dismiss the prizes with a perfunctory "how nice." She puzzled him so.

Bill and Carter were standing among their baggage when his father walked into the room. Both were sweating; the room was hot even though it was a corner room and both windows were open. They greeted Stephen Giraud.

"Awful mess," said Bill, wearily kicking a suitcase which wouldn't shut.

"So I see." His father sat down. His hair was white at last and he looked thin and nervous in his dark blue suit. He also looked historic. Some people, Bill had noticed, looked historic and others didn't. They didn't necessarily have to be historic to look that way. His father sat in an armchair by the window and watched them pack. They talked.

"Was it a long drive?"

"No; it didn't seem long. It was such a relief to get out of the city. This is the first vacation I've had since Quebec." His father sighed.

"You were giving speeches in New York, weren't you?"

His father nodded and, mechanically, felt his coat pocket where his speech for the day was.

"I read the one about the Baltic."

"Did you like it?"

"Sure. What I understood anyway."

His father smiled, lightly accepting political responsibility for his son.

"What're we having today?" Bill finally shut his suitcase. Carter sat on it while he snapped the lock.

"Oh, world responsibility . . . all of that."

"That's what I said you'd talk about."

His father laughed. "You don't mean I'm as predictable as all that?"

"You always were," said Bill, smiling. He got up from the floor and went over to his dresser and began to comb his hair. It was just the right length now: long enough to comb back and yet not over his ears. It had turned light brown in the last few years but it was still, technically, blond. His beard (he shaved every other day now) was, fortunately, quite blond. He wondered if he should take a shower. He decided it would be too much trouble; the idea of taking clothes off and putting them on again made him feel tired. Carter and his father were talking, rather solemnly.

"Have you read any of the French writers?" asked Stephen Giraud.

"A few; not many."

"I used to read them a lot when I was your age. I think Rimbaud was my favorite."

"I like the legend," said Carter.

"Yes, the legend's attractive and perhaps, knowing it, we like the work more."

"Of course, all writers have their legends."

"Yes, but some are symbolically more important to us than others." His father looked out the window. "You know *Bateau Ivre?*"

"Yes; I like it."

"I've always liked it. The symbol of the ship . . ." Stephen Giraud stopped talking and Bill who understood his father was sorry for him; he knew how much he'd wanted to be free; he knew his father hated responsibility. His father was an artist who'd become a man of affairs. His mother had never understood this about his father. His mother had never understood.

"The one I liked best was *Le Coeur Volé*," said Carter and Bill was, as usual, surprised that Carter knew so much, had read so much.

"Yes, that's a poem for adolescence." His father managed to say this without sounding massive. "There is always a certain horror when a person sees the world for the first time. Fortunately the horror is generally cumulative for there's seldom a dramatic instant when it's fully revealed. Rimbaud, of course, had such an instant and he wrote a poem about it."

"Was Rimbaud the one who ran away?" asked Bill, remembering a little.

His father nodded. "Several times. He investigated hell, too.

Oh, he was a great traveler. I expect he was the first poet since Dante to take the full tour."

"Must've been a strange person," said Carter, sitting on the radiator. "He hated his mother."

"Yes, he hated his mother." Bill was uneasy, inexplicably so. The feeling passed.

"How come the headmaster hasn't got you yet?" he asked, breaking the tension, making a new mood, a less important one.

"He doesn't know I'm here," said his father, turning around, turning away from the window and a mood of flight.

"I guess we better go find him," said Bill. "I'll show you my pictures on the way."

"Yes, I want to see them. I had a glowing letter from your art teacher. He thinks you're quite exceptional."

"So does Bill," said Carter softly.

They went out into the sun. Bill could hardly believe that it was so recently winter: snow on the ground and the sky like iron, dark and harsh.

Several people recognized Bill's father and spoke to him. Then, free of people, they walked silently between the rows of lilacs. His father had gone to this school and he was fond of it, regarding it as more liberal than most of the others. But his father was, he knew, personally (though not publicly) opposed to education. Sometimes his father seemed to be an anarchist.

"Yes," he said when he saw the painting and that was enough praise. Bill began to like the painting again.

"And we're modern," said his father cryptically; Bill was not sure whether he was praising or criticizing or merely quoting.

"Well, it looks as if I'm going to be an artist, after all, vicariously, of course." His father chuckled.

Bill didn't know what to say. He looked about the room waiting for the proper phrase of thanks to come to him. Mr Forster came instead and that was much better.

"Mr Giraud? You remember me, don't you? I'm Bill's art teacher and we met last year."

"Yes, of course. I'm sorry I never answered your last letter. I was glad to get it."

"Well, I meant what I said." Mr Forster sounded a little truculent. He was used to middle-class parents who were not at all pleased if their sons showed signs of being unusual.

"I started out as an artist," said Stephen Giraud and Bill could tell by his voice that he'd not said this in a long time.

"Really?" Mr Forster was surprised. "Then you approve of Bill's being an artist?"

"Certainly."

"Good, good. Then you'll keep him out of the Army, won't you?"

His father laughed. "I don't know if I could. Besides, maybe Bill wants to go in the Army."

"What difference does that make? His work's much more important than anything he'd ever do as a soldier."

"That's very true but perhaps he wouldn't like to face all the discomforts of being an objector."

"An artist must show some independence."

"It's not easy at seventeen," said Stephen Giraud and he looked at the painting. Then he added, "or at any time."

"I disagree because . . ." Mr Forster was not allowed to finish. The headmaster and a number of deputies appeared in the library.

"Mr Giraud, I'm so glad to see you. We were afraid you wouldn't come at all. I had visions of you in an accident. Hello there, Forster, young man." The principal, an old pink and fat man, never recognized the boys. He had once, rather plaintively, defended himself by saying that all boys looked alike anyway. He led Stephen Giraud away and Bill walked back alone to the dormitory.

A few boys were already wearing their thin black robes although it was not even time for lunch. Across the quadrangle Bill saw Jimmy walking with a group of athletes. They were laughing and making a lot of noise. A group of younger boys stood near one of the dormitories and watched them admiringly. They admired Jimmy particularly. He was handsome, agreeable and the school's best athlete. He appealed to them. He appealed to everyone and Bill who had loved him once watched him move, gracefully, with the others.

"Wished to hell we'd never come," said Jimmy.

"It was better back home, at the other school." The leaves of the trees were already dying although it was only September. They had arrived on the train together. Jimmy was almost fifteen and Bill was fourteen. Their parents had decided, simultaneously, that they should both go to school in New England. They had left Washington together. It was different from going to camp, though. Bill was used to traveling and he'd grown tired of the high church school and the dormitory life. But it was different with Jimmy. He had never been away from home and he was unhappy though he didn't show it, except by occasional remarks about the ugliness of New England.

It was not like the South. There were hills but they weren't green and smooth, rather they were dark and hard and the trees seemed to have fewer leaves and, then, already the leaves were turning red. Bill had never seen New England in the fall and Jimmy had never been north of Washington.

"The buildings sure are big," commented Jimmy. They were standing beside the main building, a large brick colonial affair with a steeple on top and a rambling wing on either side.

Many boys walked in and out of the large central door; above the door was an inscription in Latin. They watched these boys and they envied them their ease and knowledge of this place. They shouted to one another and, in general, seemed glad to be back in school. The other new boys were easy to recognize. They looked very serious and puzzled, a little frightened, too.

Jimmy and Bill went into the building, registered and were assigned a room together in one of the dormitories.

They found the dormitory and, when the baggage was finally arranged, they were exhausted. The room was fairly large with a very large window. The building was new and

177

the walls and the linoleum floor were spotless. The dressers, the desks, the beds were not as new but they were much better than the furniture in the church school's dormitory.

They were resting on their beds when Mr Cilley, their adviser, came into the room. They had been warned that they were to have an adviser, everyone in the school had one. He was a combination (in theory) between a house master and a tutor. Actually he was more house master than anything else. Some advisers, of course, were more useful than others, or so they'd been told by a young man who, though old enough to shave, hadn't done so recently and looked quite like a defender of Bataan. Mr Cilley, they had been further instructed, was one of the most useless advisers. He was tall and thin with graying hair and glasses. He taught English and he seemed rather shy.

"Which of you is Giraud?"

"I am, sir."

"Then the other must be Wesson. I shall remember that." He looked about the room as though to find a topic of conversation hidden, perhaps, among the furniture. "You boys are from the South?"

They told him where they were from.

"Beautiful state. My wife came from Charleston but that's much farther south, of course. Either of you interested in English?"

They said they weren't and Mr Cilley sighed.

"But," said Jimmy, who hated to see anyone disappointed, "Bill here is a painter."

"Oh really?" Mr Cilley brightened. "Well, you'll get to know Mr Forster in art. A fine man and quite an unusual teacher. He used to live in France and I think he was a friend of Braque."

"I'll be glad to meet him . . . sir." Bill was impressed; a teacher who'd known Braque.

"Yes, you should get along well. Are you a modern?"

"I . . . I guess so, more than anything else. Right now I like Juan Gris about the best of the moderns."

"Good," said Mr Cilley, finding hope for himself. The rest of his advisees had been from Scarsdale. "The entire school is recruited from Scarsdale," was a lament of Mr Cilley's which Bill was to hear often the rest of the year.

"Do you do much reading?"

Bill nodded. "Quite a bit. I paint more now, though. It's hard to do both."

"All painters are illiterate," said Mr Cilley dogmatically. "And what do you do . . . Wesson?"

"I play baseball," said Jimmy modestly; he had won almost every available trophy in Washington.

"That's nice," said Mr Cilley distantly. "Well, I shall see you from time to time." He disappeared down the linoleum-floored corridor.

They decided that Cilley was agreeable, though perhaps a bit eccentric. Later Bill discovered that many of the teachers worked to develop eccentricities, to have reputations as characters; of course, some didn't need to invent a character but many found it necessary. Somehow the stranger they acted the more they endeared themselves to the boys. There was one man who had been in the school for many years and spoke with an Oxford accent acquired in Idaho. He was rude and had, therefore, developed a reputation as a wit, a schoolboy's Samuel Johnson. But Bill thought him rather a cur when he was in his class. However, most of the other boys liked him and Jimmy thought he was one of the funniest men in the world.

On this floor of the dormitory there were twenty boys and soon they knew all of them. Some they liked and some they disliked. Bill, who had been used to undisputed leadership in the other school, decided to go into school politics. He had, however, grown rather aloof since he'd taken up painting seriously; he was impatient with others and he found himself rather disliked. But, as usual, he had a group of friends and through fairly adroit politics he managed to get some of the elections he wanted. Mostly, though, he stuck to his painting and the other boys, though they didn't like him particularly, admired him; this he found surprising and very pleasing.

He was less scornful of them. As a person, however, he had changed and he was aware of the change. He had been very popular in the other school. He had acquired power and he'd exercised it. But now that he'd made up his mind to be an artist he lost interest in other things, in listening to people who bored him and, of course, the people who bored him resented this: he would contradict them or walk away; he was impatient. Sometimes, angrily, futilely, he defended modern art but most of them didn't understand, didn't care. He had been an adequate athlete at the other school but now he had nothing to do with athletics; he tried to avoid even the required exercise period.

Fortunately there were others like him in the school, other artists. Since there were over seven hundred students one could, sooner or later, find others with similar interests. He got to know these boys. He worked with them and he painted well though with little originality. He spent most of his time in the art studio under one of the school buildings. This studio had large ground-floor windows. Here the art classes were held.

"You're too romantic, Giraud; much too romantic."

Bill looked at his painting with Mr Forster and he tried to see what his teacher saw. He had done a landscape by moonlight and he thought it was good. The sky was gray and the impression of the painting was tenuous and unreal. It was literal, of course. He was not yet brave enough to do abstract work and, though he liked it, he was not sure that he wanted to be that sort of painter. Roger Gilray had dismissed the entire Franco-Spanish school of painting as decadent since Renoir. Bill had not accepted this but it had impressed him. However, he didn't have much freshness of his own. It was strange how things people said stayed in one's mind. He had read a story by Huxley which had made a great point of this: now he tried to forget what people told him. He tried to question everything, everyone. "You'll never get ahead if you're so critical," said his mother. But he tried to be critical now. There were, still, some people one had to believe and Forster was such a person.

"I can't see . . . what do you mean romantic?"

"The whole approach. It's Victorian; like one of your grandmother's speeches." Bill winced; the intellectuals of the school had very little respect for his grandmother. He had stopped defending her. His father, on the other hand, was admired.

"Why be so obvious? so familiar?"

He looked at the hills by moonlight. He had conceived the painting in an Edgar Allan Poe mood; he liked Poe and the moderns did not. The painting was not original; he realized that.

"You should give it something more," said Forster, squinting through his thick lenses.

"What?"

"Damned if I know. More of yourself is the cliché; in your own manner. See this landscape as your own not your grandmother's. Be critical." He had been right; Forster said to be critical. He had already begun to change as a person; now he began to change into an artist.

Bill thought of the school as a place of continual winter. The first winter came as the greatest shock. He hated the winter. Snow fell in November. The roads turned to ice and the sky was white and hard, like ice. Steam poured from nostrils on a winter morning and the wind which blew was wet and piercing; he had a continual earache. He hated to go outside, to move from one building to another: it was cold.

Jimmy liked it, however, and he took up skiing and, with his usual expertness, became one of the school's best skiers. He was, by midwinter, on the varsity basketball team and his athletic career was even more brilliant, on a larger scale, than it had been in Washington. He was popular. He moved without difficulty among people of all kinds; he wanted to be liked and he was liked. It was as simple as that. Jimmy was not a hypocrite. He never said anything he didn't think but when he was with another person he couldn't disagree with them or think anything unkind of them. Then, of course, he was a popular athlete and that helped. He grew handsomer as he matured. His face was serene and strong, smiling; his hair still curled slightly. Bill, who had been, in his own opinion, too soft-looking as a child, now looked more interesting. His face was thinner and his nose had finally became the Hawkins nose. He watched himself often in the mirror and he did many self-portraits; he had a reputation for being vain.

The first few months were stimulating. The athletes discovered Jimmy and Bill discovered the artists. They made separate friends and outside their room they seldom saw one another.

In the morning they went to classes. The classes were small and the boys sat at round tables while the instructors talked. The round tables were supposed to promote discussion but only a few of the instructors discussed; most of them lectured and the students recited. Bill, whose memory was not good, got bad grades. He rather liked geometry, though; aesthetically it was interesting but the measuring of lines and angles he found baffling. English was better. Latin and French bored him. The first term he managed to pass everything but mathematics. His highest mark was always in art.

"I was very sorry to see that you failed mathematics. You must learn to exert yourself. You always give in to your laziness and that's bad if you're ever to be a success. I should think that at least for *my* sake you'd try to turn over a new leaf . . ." He threw the letter in the wastebasket. He surprised himself. It was the first time he hadn't been upset by one of his mother's letters (all of her letters were reproachful or angry or threatening). He had been told to "turn over a new leaf" every month of his life. But now he would be himself. He was too busy painting to mind.

"Where're you going?" asked Jimmy; he was sitting at his desk, teetering his chair. He wore a school sweater, no tie, rumpled gray slacks and a pair of saddle-shoes, not particularly clean. He was smoking. This was not allowed in dormitory rooms and it was bad, besides, for an athlete. Bill had not yet learned to smoke. They had finished supper and, through the window, Bill could see a band of pale light in the west, under the black-blue sky. Lights were already on in the dormitories, grouped around the quadrangle.

"Going over to the studio. I've got to get my new thing finished for the exhibit."

"Jeez, you paint all the time," said Jimmy, scratching comfortably.

"Sure, and you play basketball all the time."

"Well, that's different." Bill put on his overcoat. It was cold: he had been outdoors a half-hour before and his coat was still cold. He shuddered and tried to warm the coat.

"Why don't you come out for basketball?" said Jimmy finally. Bill could see that he was coming to a point; he was maneuvering.

"You know why. I'm too busy and besides I seem to've lost interest in games anyway."

"You used to be real good," said Jimmy reproachfully. "You were on the team back at the school and you could go places here if you wanted to."

"I'm sorry," said Bill. He wanted to leave but he wanted Jimmy to finish first, come to the point if there was one.

"Well, you've sure changed a lot," said Jimmy and he brought the front legs of his chair back to the floor with a crash. He looked very serious; he frowned and Bill appreciated, as he often did, his attractiveness.

"I'm sorry," said Bill; he didn't want to hurt Jimmy's feelings.

"You won't go around . . . with the boys any more. You spend all your time with the queers, painting. You don't have to be like that. Why hell if you wanted to you could be running the school like we did the other one."

"Instead of being unpopular like I am now."

"Well . . . yes."

"We all have to do what we want, Jimmy. We have to be ourselves, no matter who doesn't like it." He realized he was quoting Mr Forster a bit too patly.

"Sure, sure, but I just didn't know you were like that, I guess."

"Neither did I till I came here."

"You sure changed," said Jimmy, shaking his head and, since there seemed no more to say, Bill left the room.

The cold air in the quadrangle hit him with a shock. He tightened the collar of his coat; his neck was always sensitive to cold. He walked quickly along the wood sidewalk which, ice-covered itself, had been put over the ice walk. He looked at the sky and almost forgot the cold. It was a beautiful, a pure sky: dark blue, almost black and the stars were large and clear, shining like illuminated ice. A crescent moon was rising in one corner of the sky. A boy greeted him in the dark. He answered him, without looking down, without seeing him. He walked on the wooden walk between the large dormitories, made flimsy, porous, by many lighted windows close together. But he noticed only the sky tonight, the clear hard winter night, stars, polished and flashing. Then he came to the building where the studio was. He looked down at the ground again, noticed the fir trees beside the door. When the snow first fell they had been dreamlike, unreal, with snow in their branches. But the snow had been blown off by the wind. He went down a few ice-covered steps, opened the door and went inside the warm building.

His ears burned. They had, as usual, been almost frozen. He would have to buy ear muffs soon. He thought they were ugly but the cold was terrible and his nose began to run as he got accustomed to the heat. He took off his coat and started down the corridor. The corridor had classrooms opening off it and he could smell the classroom smell: chalk, wood, linoleum, floor wax and young males. It was not unpleasant; at times it was soothing but when he'd not prepared his lesson it was ominous, impersonal and alien. He opened a door and stepped into the studio.

The studio was a long room with windows, large windows, down one side of it. There were paintings on the wall and, below the paintings, shelves for sculpture. At one end of the room was a magic lantern and a screen. The rest of the room was cluttered with easels and stands and basins; it was a cluttered room. Mr Forster had very little sense of order. He was not here now. The lights were on in the room and the sculptors were at work. One painter, a seventeen-year-old senior and the best painter in the school, was working at an abstraction. Another boy, tall and heavily built (he was, Bill recognized, in one of his classes), stood beside the painter, watching. Bill said hello and went to his own easel. He was doing a still life; he disliked them but Mr Forster had ordered him to do one. He was quite aware that he was imitating Cézanne and the painting disgusted him. But he worked at it. Not even artificial light could make this worse.

"How's it going?" asked the abstractionist. He was a lean dark young man with a carefully scraped blue beard. His face was ugly but interesting. His father was a Frenchman and he hoped, when he graduated, to join the Free French and eventually get back to Paris.

"Pretty awful," said Bill, beginning to put on paint. "I don't seem able to get interested in this."

"Well, it won't be any good then," said the abstractionist.

The sculptors talked back and forth and Bill envied the simplicity of their work, of sculpturing: it was just form, no color, no light to worry about. Of course, there were other problems but it looked simple to him.

"You know Carter Lane?" asked the abstractionist. Bill shook his head. He was introduced then to the large young man who, though the same age, looked much older.

Carter Lane was in the same class and he'd seen him around the campus. He was a tall heavy boy with a cherubic face, yet paradoxically, almost middle-aged in expression. He was known as a wit, and for his occasional short stories about birth control which appeared in the school's literary magazine. His manner was ceremonious, solemn and humorous.

"Superb!" said Carter Lane in his deep radio announcer's voice (he was also to have a part in the winter term play). "Such color, such tone and the line . . . the line!" His voice faded away.

Bill frowned. *"I* know it's bad," he said.

"You do?"

"Oh yes; I always do."

"What honesty! I wish I were the same," he said. "I think everything of mine is wonderful."

"Why I'll never know," said the abstractionist.

"Let's not be small or petty. We must try to be magnanimous. Seriously though I like the fruit and stuff. It reminds me of . . ."

"Cézanne; I know," said Bill.

"There *is* a certain superficial resemblance," said Carter slowly, as though he were studying each word to be sure its meaning was exact.

"Like one of your novels," said the abstractionist, still painting. "They all have a filial resemblance to the *New Yorker*."

"I have never finished a novel," said Carter Lane proudly. "I consider a completed book in the worst possible taste; it smacks of commercialism. And if my unfinished work sounds like the *New Yorker* you must remember that that magazine is the guardian of our literary morals."

Bill listened to him as he worked. Carter continued to talk in his deep radio voice and Bill found him amusing.

They decided a week before the Christmas holiday that they would be roommates after Christmas. Jimmy had already decided he would move into a smaller dormitory, one dominated by athletes. He and Bill went back to Washington together. They had decided everything in a friendly manner, and the relationship, though somewhat changed, still continued.

3

Maryland, where his mother and stepfather lived, looked bleak but, at least, not harsh. There was no snow on the ground though snow had fallen several times. The trees were brown and empty-looking. But he was glad to be home for a while, to be comfortable, to be able to sleep in the mornings. His mother was not up when he arrived but Roger was home; he was having breakfast. They greeted one another warmly. Bill was fond of his stepfather. He thought him silly at times, a bit ludicrous, but he liked him still. Roger was beginning to look old. He'd not really looked cheerful since before Charlotte's miscarriage.

"How's the school?" He put down his newspaper. He usually sat at the table alone in the morning and read the paper. Then he would go to the office. He would see his wife in the evening for the first time.

"Pretty good."

"I see where you've been getting all A's in art. That's pretty good." His stepfather, unlike his mother, only noticed the good marks. "You're not thinking about being an artist, though, are you?"

"Well . . . ," Bill was cautious. "I'd like it, I suppose."

"It's a difficult life and there's no money in it certainly. But you may not have to worry about that. I'm told it's a wonderful life, though. I was reading a book the other day about this French fellow who went to the South Seas . . . what was his name?"

"Gauguin."

"Yes, Gauguin; well, he led quite a life. You could live for nothing then, of course, and there were all those native women . . . I understand he paired off with one. So it must've been a pleasant life: no worries, no responsibilities, doing just as you please. They say his paintings sell for fabulous amounts now. It'd be nice, I suppose, to have a reputation in your lifetime. That's the trouble with being an artist. I wouldn't be one, I know. Then you have to be awfully good and, since there are so many people in the field, the odds are against your getting anywhere." After a few more remarks about artists Roger Gilray left for his office. Bill went to his room and unpacked. He was surprised to find that he was not thrilled and pleased to be back; he usually was but not this time. Perhaps if he did some painting he would feel better. Then he went out onto the landing and he saw his mother's tray in front of her door.

"Darling! How are you?" She embraced him. He sat down on the bed. There was cold cream on her face as usual, not thick and shiny, but only enough to give a curious nascent glow to her skin, colorless and strange. The gray hair about her face carried out the color scheme. She wore the triangle of adhesive between her brows to erase her frown. He noticed that the lines at the corners of her mouth were deeper and under her eyes were blue shadows, much creased. She did not look well. She had maintained she was not well ever since the miscarriage. She smoked constantly.

"How's school?" she asked. Everyone asked that.

"All right. I've been painting a lot lately."

"That's nice; did you pass mathematics?"

"No, I didn't."

She didn't frown; she couldn't because of the adhesive patch but the corners of her mouth went down. "I thought you were turning over a new leaf." How thin her mouth was, unpainted! "I thought you were going to work for a change."

"I tried."

"I don't see how you can say that. Both your father and I did well in school; you've certainly inherited brains."

"Well, I've been busy painting. I got an A in art."

"But it's the other things that count." His mother always ignored what he did well. "Well, we'll talk about this later. I'm very disappointed in you." She lit a cigarette and he noticed that her hands shook. She drew the corners of her mouth down as she inhaled.

"I've got something I want to talk to you about," she said, finally. He felt frightened. It was an unconscious reflex; it was the way he'd felt as a child when he expected a beating.

"I'm going to divorce Roger," she said. He was relieved. It was not about him. He was in no way concerned with this problem and she was not, at the moment, really interested in his shortcomings.

"When?" he asked.

She was a little irritated that he didn't show greater surprise. "After Christmas. We decided we'd spend Christmas here together; then I'll go down to Florida and get my divorce there. What do you think about it?"

"I think it's too bad . . . in a way."

"It was bound to happen. You don't know how awful things have been. We've never been able to get along. He broods all the time now. He insults my friends. I can't even go out with him any more without there being a scene. He's so unpopular. God knows *I've* tried to bring him out. He was more unpopular before I married him and, if I say so myself, I've helped him; he *did* get better about people until just recently. But I can't go on with it any more. He even acted as if the miscarriage was my fault. Imagine? I've done everything. I've given all I can. I feel I've done my part. But it was too much of a job and now I want to live *my* life for a change." She stopped and looked thoughtfully at the telephone; she seemed to be rehearsing.

It was exciting, thought Bill. He rather admired his mother for having two divorces. It made her an exceptional, a glamorous figure. She was (or she appeared to be) living on the peaks of emotion and this, he had come to believe, was the only way to live. She was an artist in the emotions. She lived importantly, angrily. Her mouth was set in an angry line, a straight line as she thought of her marriage. She looked like her mother then and Bill asked how his grandmother was.

Charlotte, irritated at being interrupted, said, "She's all right. She's had some trouble with her heart and she's claiming now that the doctor says drinking is good for her. What do you think about the divorce?" His mother had begun in recent years to discuss her problems with him as though he were a contemporary. He liked this even though he realized that she paid no attention to what he said, was barely aware that he was there; she rehearsed with him, she convinced herself of things.

"I think you ought to do what you want. It doesn't make any difference to me."

"I'll go ahead then after New Year's; when you go back to school I'll go to Florida. Now don't say anything about this to anyone." He said he wouldn't; his mother was always making him promise not to tell things which she usually told everyone herself.

"Roger knows, doesn't he?"

"Oh, yes; we've talked it over. His lawyers are making up the alimony papers. I'm having a great deal of trouble with Roger over that. He doesn't want to give me half of what I need. I've been terribly surprised by him. It takes a crisis like this really to understand another person. I'd no idea he'd be so vindictive, so mean. I hope, though, we'll be able to make some arrangement without going to court but I *will* go to court if I have to. I have a lot on that man." She nodded as though she were thinking of secrets. The phone rang.

They celebrated Christmas Eve with his grandmother in the family's house. The old house looked very gay: there were holly wreaths in the windows and a large Christmas tree in the hall. They arrived before dinner; Roger, Charlotte and Bill. It was a family evening though Clara Hawkins' secretary, Miss Whey, was also included. There were several poor cousins from Carolina, Clara's relatives, and Charlotte was charming to them, so charming that they were made acutely aware of their comparative poverty and ignorance of the great world; they hated her immediately.

Clara Hawkins was pale but otherwise seemed well. She served them eggnog from a huge elaborate silver bowl which the first Hawkins, it was said, had brought with him from England.

She asked Bill how he was and what he'd been doing and, although she knew nothing of art, she was pleased that he was doing well and liked it. They sat around the fire in the drawing room; Charlotte, gay and charming; Roger, thoughtful and tired; the relatives awkward and Miss Whey detached, thinking, no doubt, of her vanished home in Bozeman.

Bill and his grandmother sat beside each other, to the left of the fire. His mother was opposite them, surrounded by the relatives; she couldn't hear what they were saying though Bill knew she would try.

"She's told you?" Bill nodded and his grandmother looked severe. "What do you think about it?"

He shrugged; it was so difficult to think anything. It was, after all, none of his business. He was, though he would not have admitted it, indifferent to the whole business. There was a certain excitement but that was all.

"I don't know," he said; this was always the safest thing to say to a person who already had an opinion, a strong one.

"*I* told her I didn't think she should do it. Separate if she likes but not another divorce. Of course, she never listens to me. I think this whole getting divorces business, if everything isn't exactly her way, is absurd. She'll never be able to stay married to any man. Thank goodness you're almost grown and it won't affect you much one way or the other."

Bill looked across the room and he saw that his mother was watching, a dangerous expression on her face. She would call him disloyal if he appeared to be agreeing with his grandmother. Fortunately George soon announced dinner and, in this curious mood, they celebrated Christmas Eve. Charlotte, thinking of alimony; Clara Hawkins of the scandal and the effect of it, if any, on her constituents; Bill of his paintings and Roger Gilray wondering gloomily what evil he had ever done to deserve two such wives.

It was a merry Christmas Eve for the relatives, however. They finally overcame their shyness and had an excellent time. After dinner Miss Whey, with tears in her eyes, played *Noël Noël* almost accurately on the piano, the way she had in Bozeman, years before.

Slowly the first winter passed and then another winter came and went, more quickly, and finally the last winter began. The seasons in between were not real seasons: merely interludes between the long inevitable winters. He painted in these winters and, painting, almost forgot the cold. He visited his mother. She was finally divorced but she was still contesting the alimony settlement and she was, fortunately, not much interested in his failures. All of her time now was taken up with legal actions and parties. She had her own house in Washington, very small but elegant, and here she gave her amusing and often brilliant parties. Roger, it was rumored, was about to marry again, a woman Bill had never heard of. And so two winters passed and the third, the last one, was not yet ended.

He spent Christmas with his mother and grandmother. He saw his father occasionally, when he was in the country, and his father visited the school twice to make speeches. His life was more tranquil than it had been even though his mother's temper was more uncertain than ever before. She still (when she thought of it) called him lazy, a failure, critical, disloyal and she was never pleased no matter what he did. He was, finally, glad he didn't see her often. In the summers he worked in a factory which he disliked but he was, at least, financially independent. The factory was in Baltimore and he visited his mother only occasionally. Then, this last fall, he understood light and his paintings changed and he knew that he was doing the right thing at last. He worked harder than ever at his painting; this was the last winter; in June he would graduate and then the Army. He looked forward to the spring but he was a little afraid. He hated the winter but at least it was secure, in spite of the cold; he understood the winter. Then in the spring he would go in the Army, he would enlist at seventeen in one of the programs. He had decided this though his mother and Mr Forster were against it. So he painted and endured the final winter.

"I have just finished a novel," boomed Carter one evening. They were in their room. Down the hall they could hear a scuffling sound as a group of boys were trying to discover which of them was the strongest. The room they had this year was large and in a building over a century old; this dormitory was the oldest and, for some reason, most desirable senior dormitory. On the walls were reproductions of Picasso, Braque and El Greco as well as several paintings of Bill's. Carter had a reproduction of Van Gogh's "Starry Night" over his bed. "Marvelous for inspiration, like sperm in the womb: great motion."

"Yes," said Bill, he was at his desk sketching his own hand for practice; he did it literally first then abstractly. Carter was at the other desk, in front of his typewriter.

"I have written a novel twelve pages long. Jealous people will call it a short story but I regard it as my finest and certainly longest novel." Carter sat back in his chair; he looked incongruously mature for a schoolboy; his face had a certain mature heaviness about it. He was over six feet now and quite heavy. He was an important school figure. He had managed this cleverly for, though he amused people, he was not well-liked; he had a reputation for brilliance which disturbed the average boy. He had managed to be elected President of several societies as well as editor of the school's literary magazine. By what he himself described as a foul plot, an unscrupulous coup, he had not been made editor of the school newspaper, much the most desirable job since there was money to be made in it and Carter liked money. He came from a poor family and he supported himself by winning scholarships and prizes in Greek and other subjects, boring to him, but necessary for income.

"I shall read you my novel," he said, doing a favor.

"I should love to hear it," said Bill drily.

"Our scene opens in the suburban home of Mr Barnes." Carter cleared his throat and in his richest deepest voice declaimed. The story was amusing and Bill laughed in spite of himself. Mr Barnes' dilemma was whether he should enter a room where his wife was or not. He didn't want to enter because for twenty years she had asked him, "How was the office?" and he knew that if she did this again he would kill her. The story was about the difficulties of decision. It was never decided whether he entered the room or not. Bill thought it an excellent novel.

"I see it," said Carter cheerily, "bound in black cloth with silver letters. At fifty I shall write a preface, explaining, inaccurately, how I happened to write this novel and what it means. You see it is a symbol of the modern dilemma. It will be required reading in the schools. I can just see it, *Aborigine* (that's the title) by Carter Lane. I think I shall do the preface now. I may be dead by fifty and I think a long preface is necessary; it will be, of course, somewhat longer than the book."

He began to type. Bill went back to his abstractions. Then Jimmy came into the room. Bill had not spoken to him for several weeks. Bill was almost completely withdrawn from the life of the school. He had been elected President of a debating society but he had finally resigned, having lost all interest in everything not connected with his painting. He was barely aware of his increasing but rather mysterious unpopularity. His mother would have been upset to know this but he still had his circle of partisans and he was the leader of the painters; in the words of Mr Forster he was the best artist the school had ever had (which was, he knew, not much of a compliment). This pleased him, though. He knew he was the best; he accepted it naturally and others did too, even the other painters. He saw less and less of Jimmy. In the fall they had been together once but not since then. Now Jimmy stood in the doorway. Physically he had changed very little. He was slim with a deep muscular chest and a rather long waist. He moved quickly, like an animal. The texture of his face was more interesting now that he shaved and Bill had thought about painting him once or twice but he never got around to it.

"Good evening, Body," said Carter solemnly. He was the only boy in the school who was able to make fun of the athletes without offending them: peasant boys he called them and they laughed and thought he was very witty.

"Hi, Carter," said Jimmy good-naturedly. He didn't care

what people said about him as long as he was sure they liked him. "What's up, Bill?"

"Not much." Jimmy sat down on the bed nearest Bill. Carter went back to typing his preface. Bill stopped sketching and turned around in his chair. Jimmy was, he noticed, worried.

"What's the matter? Bad news?"

"Nothing much: just Alice. She wrote me saying she was in love with some soldier and that she wouldn't be able to write me any more."

"That's too bad," said Bill. He had never liked Alice himself but it surprised him that anyone could prefer someone else to Jimmy. She was a tall slim girl they had known in dancing school. She usually acted as if she were living in a novel by Fitzgerald. Jimmy had thought she was wonderful for two years now.

They talked about Alice and Carter interrupted his typing long enough to explain women to them. Carter was having a full-scale affair with a girl in a college near Boston. He planned to marry her this summer. Jimmy listened unhappily to him as he talked. Bill thought about girls vaguely. There were times when he was violently excited but most of the time he never thought of them; he worked and when he was not working he thought about his painting. He had not found time for one yet. Perhaps in the spring. Girls had been attracted to him but he usually lost interest in them once he was sure they were attracted to him. This he knew was perverse.

They were listening to Carter when the door opened and a boy handed Bill a telegram from his mother: his grandmother was dying. He must return.

He didn't know what to feel. He was surprised and not surprised. She had not been well for several years. She'd had a heart attack the day after the big reception she gave for the King. But death was not easy to understand; he had not thought nearly enough about it. He would be able to understand it once he had thought about it. He had never seen it painted. He looked at the El Greco reproductions: no, this was merely a Christian, an oriental ecstasy but not a real consciousness of death. El Greco was centuries dead. One of his friends, the abstractionist, had joined the Free French finally and was promptly killed. Now his grandmother was dying. This must be understood.

"What's the matter? What does it say?" asked Jimmy.

"My grandmother's dying," said Bill and he tried not to allow any emotion to come into his voice; he succeeded.

"Oh, gosh; I'm sorry," said Jimmy sitting up.

"That's too bad," said Carter in his lecturer's voice. "You'll be going to Washington, won't you?"

"Yes, tomorrow."

"Come on down to my room," said Jimmy.

They went down the narrow worn steps. Jimmy had a room by himself. His trophies were on the dresser, the floor, everywhere. The room was, as always, a mess. Jimmy's athletic equipment was strewn about the room. A sweat-stained basketball uniform was heaped in one corner. He cleared off a space on the bed. They said nothing for a while.

"Things get in an awful mess," said Jimmy finally.

"They do," said Bill and he tried to feel sad but he couldn't. He felt only a chill fear. Jimmy put his arm around Bill's shoulders and Bill was grateful for this.

4

She was white, almost yellow. Her face sagged and her mouth, toothless, had collapsed. The sternness was gone and there was nothing left. She had difficulty breathing. Her eyes were closed when Bill entered the room; there was a strong smell of medicines and disinfectant in the room and, or was it his imagination? the odor of decay.

Her heart was collapsing and she had, also, a serious cancer which no one had known about. She had been, according to the doctors, dying for five years. Now death was near. His mother had, very seriously, met him at the station and they drove out to the Hawkins house; she would not die in a hospital.

"It started last week. She fainted in her office. It seems she'd had cancer for years and we never knew about it." His mother sounded reproachful. She acted as if her mother had been unthoughtful, had slighted her by not telling her. Charlotte Gilray looked handsome, he thought. Her frown had, thanks to the patch of adhesive, disappeared. The lines of irritation at the corners of her mouth were not so noticeable today. The wrinkles, laugh wrinkles, under her eyes were not unattractive. She laughed a lot when she was with people. She was her happiest when she was with a group of people. She wore a black dress today, and clipped to the neckline was a large diamond brooch. Bill loved his mother's jewels. He watched the diamonds as they drove out into the country.

"How long's it going to be?" asked Bill finally.

"Today, tomorrow . . . soon. The doctors say she might go any minute." There was nothing more to say.

Now he stood in the room looking at her, looked for the first time at a person dying and he was frightened. It was too awful. One day he would be like this. One day they would all be like this. In a hundred years they would all be dead and life would continue without knowledge of them, impersonally. His stomach contracted. How could one live, realizing that this was what would, inevitably, come?

The eyes opened.

Clouded and unfocused the eyes looked about the room. The nurse came forward, "Yes, Mrs Hawkins?"

"Yes," repeated Clara Hawkins in a low voice. Then the eyes began to see again.

"How are you, William?" the voice was hoarse and strange.

"I'm just fine," he answered in a loud voice, routing the peculiar melancholy that death had cast over them all. He had to speak in a loud voice because his grandmother was rather deaf.

"Good," she said and a little color came into her face. She

lifted one thin dark-veined hand as though to touch something suspended in the air. Then the hand dropped back on the bed. "Good," she repeated. Her eyes closed and the nurse motioned for Bill to leave the room.

That night there was much activity in the house. There was a ghastly sound of choking; then, at one-thirty in the morning, the choking stopped and Clara Hawkins, a United States Senator and born a Spotsleigh, opened her eyes very wide and said in a clear voice, "No." Then she died.

"I never knew a more saintly woman, one more charitable and Christian than our friend who is no longer with us but now, mercifully, united with her beloved husband and son. For us still living on this troubled, yea, sinful earth there is nothing but a memory left of this departed woman; but from the memory of that saintliness we may draw inspiration and faith; we must emulate the example of her life. Nor should we be too sad for she is now in a state of Grace. Such is the will, the unalterable will, of God."

Bishop Southey was in excellent form, thought Bill who rather disliked him. The Bishop had visited his grandmother every day during her last illness and, according to Charlotte, the church was well provided for in the will.

There were about two hundred people at the funeral. Many less than at the Vice-President's. Close friends, relations, and a delegation from the Senate had been invited. The service was held at the Washington Cathedral in an underground, quite medieval, chapel. The coffin stood before the altar.

The odor of flowers which he now, inevitably, associated with the dead was sickening; Bill hoped the Bishop would not take long. He sat beside his mother in the front row. His mother sat erect, wearing a hat with a black veil; a dozen Spotsleighs sat with them on the front row. Behind them were the Senators and the guests. When the service was over the Spotsleighs would take the body of their most important relative back to Carolina to be buried between the impeached Governor and the captured General.

Bill squinted his eyes and concentrated on the face of the Bishop and, as it always happened when he did this, the face changed completely. Light coagulated into a separate pattern and the face became that of a beautiful woman with a head-dress like Mary Stuart. He amused himself with the Bishop's face until the funeral service was over. His mother accepted condolences gravely afterwards. Then they went back to the home in Georgetown.

It was a small but pleasant house with a narrow formal city garden in back. The maid opened the door for them and told them that the lawyers had already arrived. Charlotte took her black-veiled hat off and tossed it on the chest in the hall. She straightened herself in the hall mirror, then, like an actress leaving the wings, she entered the drawing room followed by Bill.

The room was long and narrow with a high ceiling and tall windows. There were two small marble fireplaces, one at either end. The walls were light and pale curtains of some expensive heavy cloth hung beside the french windows. A portrait of the Vice-President looked down from one fireplace; one of Charlotte from the other.

There were several men in the room. Three of them were lawyers. The fourth man was an Army officer, a Major, and, Bill knew, his mother's lover. Miss Whey sat in the corner; he had not noticed her at first; she held a damp crumpled handkerchief to her nose. Everyone stood up when Charlotte entered and she shook hands with each person. Then she offered them scotch. Everyone had a drink and, imperceptibly, the mood changed; the maid lit the fire. Bill sat in a shadowy corner of the room: he was the audience and everyone else was upon the stage and his mother, sitting by the fire in black, was the center.

They talked in low voices of the funeral. Everyone was polite and gentle with Charlotte who was, in turn, polite and gentle with them. Then Bishop Southey came into the room. No, he did not look much like Mary Stuart. Bill admired the great jeweled cross he wore about his neck, tucked partly in his sash.

"I suppose we can now read the will," announced the oldest of the lawyers and he read the will in a voice which cracked occasionally from the strain, from the importance of the occasion: the Hawkins estate. Bill paid little attention to it. He looked about the room and saw an evening paper on a table near him. Unnoticed, he picked it up and read about his grandmother. There was a picture of her on the front page, below the fold but still on the front page. It was an old picture and she looked severe and capable, not like the yellow-faced woman with the collapsed mouth. Then, while reading the paper, he heard the lawyer's voice say something surprising. The capital of the Hawkins estate was to go to Bill when he was twenty-five. The income was to go to his mother as guardian until he was twenty-five. When he was of age, by the will's conditions, a small trust fund would be created for Charlotte. All of Clara Hawkins' personal estate went to the church. Bishop Southey was to accept it and he did. Other provisions were made for Miss Whey and the servants. Bill was surprised that the money had been placed in his mother's hands. He knew of the quarrel his grandmother and mother'd had about the family estate. He'd understood that someone else would handle the income of the estate for him. How had she done it?

"We had a long talk last month when Mother was so ill." She slipped the black dress off. Bill sat at the dressing table handling the diamond clip, holding it to the light so that it would flash different colors. "I told her I thought it silly our quarreling and not getting along. *I* don't believe in holding grudges; I'm always willing to make the first gesture. She agreed that it was silly. She hadn't been well and, as a matter of fact, the doctor had told her her heart was bad. This was all just before she collapsed in her office. She must've changed the will a few days later. We decided that twenty-five would be the best age for you to get the money because, after all, you'll want to stand on your own feet and try to make something of yourself."

Bill held the diamonds close to one eye. The diamonds made another world, one of light. His mother, he discovered, was a clever woman.

He painted and nothing troubled him.

Winter became colder and the snow was thick on the hard ground. Fortunately the crust had frozen and one could walk anywhere easily. There were a few beautiful days when the sun shone bright and warm and the snow glittered. Then Bill would go and watch the skiers, many of them shirtless, practicing on the slope of a near-by mountain. Jimmy, as usual, won most of the trophies; he had recovered from desertion. His only interest now was to join the Marines, to have a uniform to wear. Jimmy did not think beyond that.

The war continued. Bill looked forward to being in it. There were times, though, late at night in a dark room, when he wished that it would end immediately. Army officers, Marine and Navy officers visited the school regularly, proselyting. It was amusing to listen to them talk; the war was like a college football game to hear them talk.

Carter had already managed to get into a Naval program which would keep him in college for a few years. "I am too young to die," he had announced when he learned he'd been accepted by the Navy. Bill was prepared to go into the Army. He accepted this interruption of his career much more calmly than did Mr Forster or his mother. Mr Forster disliked the idea of Bill's losing time, not to say, possibly, his life. His mother was opposed to the war on general principles and she didn't think he should go until he was drafted. His father wrote him to say that he should do what he thought right and he would give him his permission to enlist.

He had seen his father several times since the war started. His father had not married Janet Hamilton but he still spent much time with her. Bill rather liked her; she swore a great deal and she could be very amusing. She seemed devoted to Stephen Giraud. He liked his father now that he knew him, now that he was no longer an ironic shadow hidden by his mother. He found also that he liked his mother less. Her constant criticism was beginning to get on his nerves. He was no longer afraid of her and this made a great difference. His scenes with her always followed a certain pattern.

"Of course, I've tried to do everything for you, give you everything but you've never appreciated it. You just go on your own selfish way, not thinking about anyone else."

He would say nothing; he would sit, listening to this familiar speech. He tried to look contrite but as he got older it became more and more difficult.

"I hate to see these traits in you; they were your father's and because of them they've kept him from ever being happy. People will always dislike you if you go on the way you are."

Then sometimes she'd vary the ending a little. "The last time I saw your father he agreed with me; he thinks you're terribly spoiled." This, when he heard it the first time, had hurt him. If his father was against him, too, then he was quite alone. She saw immediately that this was an effective line. She used it again and again but he grew hard and did not believe her.

The final part, the coda, was always the same: an appeal. "After all *I* love you more than anyone else. No one else in the world will ever care for you as much as I do." And this invariably convinced him of his own selfishness and unfairness and he would resolve to "turn over a new leaf." When he was with her there were, at least, two of these scenes a week. They always started with rage and insults and ended tearfully. He was so used to them that he could tell when one was about to begin and he could almost predict how long it would take to examine some new and unpleasant facet of his attitude. But, although he recognized his mother was in the right, he grew tired of these discussions and the rages that preceded them. Each year he hoped they would cease but they never did. He preferred school to his mother's home and this made him guilty but he could do nothing about it.

In general, though he painted more, he was relaxed this

final winter in the school. He managed to pass his subjects with a minimum of work and a considerable amount of cheating during the tests. He wrote theorems and dates on his fingernails and so he passed his subjects without troubling to memorize all the things they were expected to memorize. This left more time for his painting and he worked hard at this. There were terrible days when he doubted if he would ever paint well, ever put in line what he saw. And then there were days when he felt himself completely co-ordinated, in complete control. But he was relaxed about his life in the school and he made more friends this last year. Everyone was more friendly anyway since they were all faced with the same future: the war.

Occasionally he went out with Jimmy's friends and with them he had his first woman—the girl who was known to the school as the Beaver. He was rather disillusioned by the entire business but since his illusions had never been very great about women (he knew his mother too well) he was not greatly disturbed or troubled. He remembered that first night, though.

Jimmy came up to his room. He was there alone. Carter was rehearsing for a play.

"You want to go out?" asked Jimmy.

"Well. . . ." A year ago Bill would have said no but now it was different. The winter was ending.

"Oh, come on," said Jimmy impatiently. "There're going to be about five of us. Red and Williamson, Mason . . . come on."

Bill was on amiable but not intimate terms with this group. "Whereabouts are you going?" Seniors could stay out until ten o'clock and those who wanted to stayed out longer.

"Well, Red made a date with the Beaver. He thinks we all ought to go. She doesn't mind and I'd like to play around with her; I've only been with her once before." Jimmy, now that he was free of Alice, his sacred love, had grown interested in all the available town girls. He went out several nights a week.

"All right," said Bill. This was something exciting and different. He dreamed of women often now, beautiful women; perhaps this would be something like a dream. The idea of a group was not pleasant but perhaps . . .

They joined the other boys in the smoking room. They were large well-muscled boys with fresh naive faces. They were "the boys." The school was divided between those who were the boys and those who were not. Bill stood, usually, somewhere between. They put on their coats and went outside. There was, fortunately, no wind and, unfortunately, no moon. The night was dark. The stars glittered brightly but gave no light; they walked between the dormitories, massive buildings made insubstantial by lighted windows.

They talked very little. They left the campus and walked down a steep cobbled street. At the bottom of the street was the town. The main street extended several blocks before them. The town was old and the streets were still cobbled and the sidewalks were made of brick. There was a movement in the town to pave the main street since the town was, after all, a county seat. But it would take time. Perhaps in ten years the motion would be passed and acted upon.

They walked along the sidewalks, looking in the stores and restaurants that were still open: at midnight the town would be asleep. Then they turned off the main street and walked toward the river. They stood on the bank: tall trees, a few benches and a state highway behind them; in front of them the river, smooth and dark, and, on the other side, the dark mass of a deserted factory: it had made boots for the Union Army. Sometime during the Hayes Administration the boot company had gone bankrupt; though several companies had later tried to manufacture in this factory none of them succeeded. The factory was deserted now.

"She should be along in a minute," said Red. "We always meet here." He sounded as if he saw her every night. The others said nothing. Bill found that he was trembling; the night was not that cold.

Then she came.

No one knew the Beaver's name. She was eighteen or nineteen, perhaps older and possibly younger. She was short and stocky. She wore a brown coat with rabbit fur about the neck and her hair was elaborately and untidily curled. Bill decided that it was probably light brown. The night was too dark to tell much, though.

"Anybody got a cigarette?" Her voice was high and unpleasantly New England. Red gave her one and lit a match for her. For an instant, Bill saw her face: it was plump and the front teeth protruded.

She did not seem surprised to see so many people. This was probably the usual number, thought Bill. "You bring any liquor, Red?" And to Bill's surprise Red produced a bottle. Red was an athlete who usually took his training with a boring seriousness.

"Shall we take a walk?" suggested Red. They took a walk, handing the bottle around as they did. Bill took one swallow and that was all; he disliked whiskey but he needed one swallow to keep from trembling. He and Jimmy brought up the rear. They crossed the river bridge. None of them talked very much; it was rather like going to church, thought Bill and he chuckled, thinking of this.

"What'd you say?" asked Jimmy.

"Nothing; I was just coughing." They were on the other side of the river now. They walked quickly toward the factory; Bill looked back at the lights of the town reflected in the water. It was a wonderful sight but then the factory came between them and the lights of the town.

The Beaver and Red were talking in low voices. She evidently knew what she was doing for she finally led them down into a cellar doorway of the factory. They pushed the door open and Red turned on his flashlight. They were in a cellar not much used, used, when at all, for expeditions such as this. They walked in single file toward a door at the back. The door opened after much pushing and they found themselves in a small room with a cot in it. No mattress on the cot, only sagging springs. The Beaver sat down on the cot and Red put the flashlight on the floor: the narrow ray shooting straight upward to the ceiling. Then they drank some more of the whiskey. It was cold and unpleasant in the room; there was an odor of age, of rot.

Then, after a while, it began. Bill thought it all macabre. Much against his will, he was excited. There was something strange and primitive about this group gathered around a single woman in a cellar, a cave. Bill found the act unsatisfying but the circumstances were exciting, strange.

It became a good painting. No one quite understood it except Mr Forster and himself. It was somewhat abstract, and, in symbol, phallic. Consciously he forgot the cold room and the Beaver; he remembered only the painting, his personal vision of it. He dreamed still of beautiful women.

"A peasant experience," said Carter severely when he heard what had happened. "I'd no idea you were such an amateur. I think you should now try to have a broader experience, a more, shall I say, spiritual one."

Jimmy always referred to the night in the cellar as a "hell of a good time" and Bill never knew whether he meant it or not. To Bill it had been everything but a good time: interesting, instructive, macabre, symbolic; all of these things, yes, but not a good time. But then Jimmy was essentially physical and perhaps this was what he liked. Bill realized that, actually, he did not understand Jimmy very well.

But Carter, who had now finished five prefaces to novels that he planned to write later, decided that he should take Bill to Boston to meet Roselle, the college girl who would, this summer, become his wife. It was Carter's idea that once Bill had observed the superiority of spiritual love he could then discover it for himself.

She met them at the station and they went to a steakhouse for lunch. Tonight there was to be a big dance and they were both invited. At lunch Bill examined Roselle carefully, trying to find visible traces of a spiritual love; he couldn't find this, though. She was a pretty girl, tall and fair, rather flat-chested and narrow-hipped as many tall girls are. She wore her tan-colored hair shoulder-length and her eyes were blue, a cloudy indistinct blue. She was two years older than Carter who looked ten years older than he was.

"Oh, we read all about your grandmother dying this winter; she was greatly admired here. You knew she gave a speech here last year."

Bill said he didn't know this. He couldn't imagine any very liberal person liking his grandmother's speeches and he had always heard these women's colleges were extraordinarily liberal. Perhaps Roselle was an exception or perhaps she was being polite, telling him that he was recognized and known.

"Did you get my last poems?" asked Carter and Bill looked at him to see if he could find traces of a great emotion in his eyes but they were as usual: gray and rather staring.

"Yes, and I loved them; especially the 'deciduous owl.'"

"What on earth was that?" asked Bill, struck by the image.

"One of my recent poems," said Carter distantly: a weary lecturer. "You wouldn't have understood it. He paints," he said turning to Roselle.

"'I have lost all things but a hatrack and the memory of deciduous owls beneath a slender oak,'" quoted Roselle.

"Superb!" said Carter. "I've never heard anything quite so beautiful. Say it again."

She said it again.

"What sound! . . . and the meaning. . . . An answer to all the problems of our contemporary life including the Indian," explained Carter.

"Superb," agreed Roselle, smiling.

"Yes," said Carter looking modestly at the remains of his steak.

They talked like this all that afternoon. Then Bill and Carter went back to the Inn where they would spend the night. They were to meet Roselle and another girl, Bill's date, in the lobby at seven. The Inn was full of young men like themselves though most of them were older and at least two thirds of them were in uniform. Carter and Bill were both uncomfortable about this; soon, however, they would be less noticeable.

They sat in the lobby and talked about Roselle and then they took a walk and talked about Roselle; then they came back to their room and, sitting on one of the beds, Carter talked about Roselle.

Not only was she beautiful and a perfect lover but she was also brilliant. She wrote poems and two of them had been published in *Darnoc*, the newest of the little magazines. This was somewhat disturbing since Carter had never had anything published outside the school but she believed in him and, more important, he believed in himself. He would write great novels. He had already done the prefaces to five, not counting his ten and twelve page novels which unimaginative people maintained were too short. They talked of Roselle, mostly.

She stood tall and pale in the lobby. She wore a green dress which Bill, thinking of it in terms of composition, decided was a mistake. She had a dark girl with her. The dark girl was small and she wore a dark red evening dress which made her look like a tranquil flame, if there could be such a thing. Her hair and eyes were dark and her skin was clear and light. Her mouth was wide and the color of blood.

Dinner was formal. The mood of the afternoon was gone. The formal clothes made them formal and solemn.

"Yes, I paint."

And then they spoke of painters, of the living French and the dead Italians, of the potential Americans. They talked like this all through dinner and Bill still didn't know her name; he had not heard it when they were introduced.

Then they were dancing in a large ballroom and she told him her name was Kay.

Sunday morning they looked at her paintings. Carter and Roselle disappeared for a while. They were going to have one of their interminable discussions about the future and Bill and Kay looked at her paintings in one of the University's art rooms. They were strong, intense and personal.

She was, Bill decided, unusual. She always spoke in a low voice as though she were afraid of being overheard but she said her words clearly as though she were even more afraid

208

of not being understood. But they understood one another. She was a year older than Bill but he was the better painter. He knew this and he knew, further, that she would say so when she saw his work. They talked of her work now.

She came from New York. Her father was a Belgian who owned an art gallery. Her mother was an American. Kay had spent most of her life in America but she liked Europe. She would go to Paris when the war ended.

On the train back Carter asked him how he liked Kay.

"Quite a bit. I like the way she paints. We got along pretty well."

Carter nodded. "I think she's just the girl for you and, besides, her father has a gallery." Carter, in spite of his devotion to sacred love, was also practical.

"Does Roselle's father own a publishing house?"

"Alas, no. But she has a small but secure income for life; it can support both of us in comfort. Let me tell you what we did this afternoon. . . ."

But he did not fall in love. He wondered sometimes if he ever could. He liked her, however, more than anyone else he could think of, his family, naturally, excepted. She also appealed to him physically but most important of all they understood the same things; their awareness of the world was the same. Yet he couldn't love her.

"No one else will ever love you as much as I do."

5

Winter passed slowly. Snow fell upon snow. Ice covered the streets and froze the windows. There was no sign of spring anywhere but he knew it would come and he could imagine the purple lilacs in front of the library. He bought a pair of red ear muffs and this made the cold more bearable. Sometimes he would be so cold that his hands couldn't hold a paintbrush. Then he would curse and blow on his hand until, finally, the blood moved quickly again.

The little interest he had had in his schoolwork was gone. He seldom prepared for class. When the tests came around he

studied a little and wrote the important facts on his fingernails. After three years he had developed a considerable faculty
for guessing what the important facts would be.

He went to the gymnasium class now to keep from getting
soft. He had stopped growing and he was as well-developed as
he'd ever be. Jimmy still thought he should go out for basketball; he was quick and he had endurance but he disliked
teams and games. In his first two years he had denounced them
bitterly and he'd made enemies. Now he was indifferent. He
no longer denounced anything; he painted and moved quietly
through the cold of this last winter. He was less unpopular and
he admitted, to himself, that, aesthetically at least, athletics,
games, teams were often beautiful to watch.

Kay assumed a great importance in his life. They wrote one
another regularly. They wrote mostly about their work. The
letters were impersonal and yet very personal. They could
say things to one another that they couldn't say to any one else.

Bill continued to get the same letters from his mother that
he always had. He compared his mother's letter with Kay's;
they were so different. Kay understood everything, his mother
nothing.

It was a strange, a wonderful thing to be understood (or at
least to have the illusion of being understood). The sense of
being an island was not so desperate. At least there were occasional boats from one island to another and, on clear days,
one could, looking into the sun, make out the shape of another island on the horizon. All men were separate islands:
that he knew. They were like the peaks of some great con-
tinent long since, before time, engulfed by the sea, leaving
only islands and a faint atavistic memory of the peaks connected, not separated by a sea. And Bill, like all human beings,
longed for the sea to fall back from the land.

He took an illegal weekend and went to visit Kay in New
York. He stayed in a large commercial hotel and he was
lonely when he was not with her.

Her father's gallery was large, prosperous and fashionable:
it was modern in the sense that Picasso was modern though

not, chronologically speaking, contemporary. He showed mostly European painters.

"I don't see any great sense of decay or birth in the Americans; one must be aware of one or the other or both. Since our period is one of decay the European artists paint the disintegration of Western civilization but here, where in many ways the decay is more rapid, the artists, for the most part, pretend to ignore it. In America there is such a youth and beauty fetish. It's like an old man, now impotent, who surrounds himself with beautiful young girls whose faces are only clumsy facsimiles of his desire. Your country is in love with beautiful boys who wear unstarched collars. I see so much exciting decay here, the accelerated rot of the New World and I think it a pity that so few of your painters seem aware of it. Your writer Faulkner is the only one aware of this destruction and he isn't particularly liked in this country. Your country should be producing Joyces and Picassos but it hasn't. Well, perhaps in time. You are still infatuated with youth; you still think you're young and new: as though you could escape your degenerate ancestry; you brought decay with you from Europe: you're not new at all and certainly not young. This is still the fin de siècle, the transition, and there's no sign of a new messiah yet (God help us if it's the Russians). Christianity is almost dead; it has one final fight in it and then dissolution. No, I show the pictures of the French and the Spanish because they are decaying with considerable ingenuity and faultless taste."

"Oh, I believe in the future of America. This new and vigorous nation free of the hatreds, the corruptions of Europe; we will yet save the world from itself. Our faith is ourselves and our destiny is great, must be great if we are to survive, to lead the world." His grandfather's voice had been harsh and ringing as he made his famous speech in the Senate: a platitudinous but moving reaffirmation of the American myth. Bill wondered which of them was right; the facts seemed to support the Belgian, a lean dark man, intense and superficial at the same time, a European.

Bill more than ever wanted to see Europe. Perhaps he would be sent there in the Army. He wanted to see the country he'd already seen in paintings. He wanted to see the men who were aware of the breakup, the end of Western civilization. Could a culture die, though? Could an entire generation, a century be corrupt? Or weren't all generations about the same, a few great men, a mad mystic or two, and the vast majority concerned with feeding themselves.

"But where is the faith?" the Belgian asked. That was his argument. The faith of the Middle Ages, even the 18th century, was gone; there was no longer much belief in the perfectibility of man. There was, in general, Bill knew, no faith in America and, according to the Belgian, none in Europe unless Communism was to be regarded as a faith. Bill never thought of the Christian God. He thought of death as a dark tranquil place of unawareness; the womb again.

But he could not accept all the Belgian said. The memory of his grandfather, the 19th-century idealist, was still too strong; yet he listened and he learned.

Kay's mother was a pleasant cultured woman who spoke very little. Their apartment was modern and simple. A Bernet hung in the living room and an early Chirico in the dining room. Both the Belgian and his wife were proud of Kay's painting and she showed Bill more of her work and they talked of art for hours; they seldom mentioned themselves, their emotions. Kay, he learned, was going to college because she couldn't go to Europe. When the war ended she planned to go to Paris to study. Bill decided that he would go, too.

They saw exhibits and listened to her father talk about painting. Kay decided that she would visit Bill's school in February, and she did.

"How strange," she said when she saw the man in the chair, the room in the cellar and all the others. In his letters he had showed her their construction but she was, still, seeing them for the first time. "How strange." Then she grew used to them. "How well you see things," she said at last and Bill relaxed;

this was one of the moments when he could believe: he was happy. He showed her the school and as they walked over the ice-covered snow they talked. Their relationship grew on conversation. He kissed her once but it had not seemed as intense as all the conversation. They were complete together. They didn't need other people which irritated Carter especially. Yet there was nothing obviously sexual in their relationship. Bill knew that eventually there would be a fusion and he looked forward to it but now he was in no hurry;. certain things must be done, said and experienced, first. Sex would be the final peak. They were still at the stage of recognition: the surprised awareness that another person existed in all the world.

She went back to Boston and Bill remained, living out the winter.

"An odd young woman," said Carter when she'd left.

"She is," agreed Bill. He felt complete and strong now. It made no difference if she was with him or not. He knew she existed and that was enough.

"Very pretty, too," added Carter.

"Yes, she's that."

"And, I presume, extraordinarily talented."

"Yes."

"But don't you think there's something odd about her; I mean isn't she a bit too detached from reality?"

"How do you define reality?"

"Let's not begin a discussion of things real and unreal. I only mean that it's necessary to live in the world some of the time and I don't think she does."

"She's alive."

"I never doubted it for an instant. Obviously you're in love with this odd young woman."

"Oh no."

"Oh but it's obvious: sacred, of course; not profane, or is it?"

"Neither."

"I can't believe that. You think she's so wonderful."

"No, I think she's important. That's quite a different thing from love." And it was. She was important to his life; without her he wouldn't have a single person to communicate with. But love was an ecstasy and there was, as yet, no ecstasy in this relationship. He had merely discovered that he was not the only island of awareness; that he was not completely alone.

Carter sighed and changed the subject. "I am planning a new novel about a young man who was a necrophile. It will be ghastly but amusing. I believe I shall do a preface for it now; while I'm in the mood."

6

Then it was spring. The snow melted and the gutters were full of black rushing water. The ground unfroze and became mud and the sky lost its winter clarity and became vaporous and white. There was a period of great ugliness when the trees were bare and yet not really austere, only plain. There was no color anywhere. Bill seldom went outdoors during this time but one day small fragments of green appeared on the branches, grass grew and the sun shone through the vapor. Winter ended.

Bill went back to his room. Carter was sitting there, among the baggage.

"Like Marius among the ruins of Carthage," he said.

"Is Roselle coming or not?" asked Bill, shaking out his black gown, rented for the occasion.

"No, I just had a wire from her saying she couldn't leave school. They're still having examinations down there."

"But Kay's coming."

"I know," said Carter sighing. "Young love will always find a way. Kay doesn't care if she fails or not but it's important to Roselle. Anyway I'll be with her tonight in Boston."

"When're you going home?" Carter's family lived in Michigan.

"In a week, I suppose; who knows? I'll be in college in a few weeks anyway."

"You needn't be so pleased with yourself."

"I just like to impress you with how well I've arranged my life. You don't find me rushing off to get killed. I am, as I may have remarked before, too young to die. Besides I want to live and see the publication of my great war novel. I finished it last week . . . the first chapter anyway and a rather long introduction explaining how I happened to write the book: descriptions of the village I was in overseas, my state of mind, all that sort of thing."

"But you haven't been overseas; you're not even in the Navy yet."

"I think you're being small about this; a little too carping, perhaps."

Bill smiled. "I wonder when Kay's arriving," said Bill. He had just stopped by the Inn and she hadn't arrived.

"Probably on the one o'clock train, it isn't here, is it?"

"No, I haven't heard it."

"Then she'll be here at two-fifteen; the one o'clock always arrives at two-fifteen. Just relax."

"But we start graduating at three."

"Time is relative," said Carter. "Time is only a state of mind, a habit of thought. My poem about the guppies proved it. The poet always goes beyond the mathematician."

The door opened and Jimmy came in with his mother. She was a frail little woman with fading red hair. Bill had known her all his life but he never thought of her, was never aware she existed: she was that sort of person. All he knew about her was that she adored Jimmy; he could do no wrong and Bill envied Jimmy this. He was her only child and she'd long ago divorced his father.

"How are you, Bill? Who? Oh yes, and how do you do, Carter? My but you look well, Bill. You boys grow so fast; it's hard to remember what you look like." Bill who had not grown since he was fourteen smiled tolerantly.

"All ready to graduate?" asked Jimmy, somewhat embarrassed by his mother.

"We're all packed," said Bill. Carter withdrew and sat alone in the window sill. He pretended he was polite: he always withdrew from family gatherings; he was an outsider.

"What a nice room, Bill! And much larger than Jimmy's; but, of course, there're two of you in it. Oh, I saw some of your pictures in the library and I thought they were very nice. By the way did you know that Jimmy was to get the Renkluaf award for the best all-around athlete?"

"Yes, I'd heard."

Jimmy blushed but he was pleased. His mother was proud of him. Bill envied him: this frail ridiculous little woman adored him.

"I hear that handsome father of yours is going to give a speech. I do hope you'll introduce me to him. I met him once years and years ago but he wouldn't remember me, of course."

"I will."

"Hey, Giraud, there's a girl over to the Inn looking for you." A young man, his face red from running upstairs, looked at everyone and then disappeared.

Kay wore a dark suit which made her look, somehow, cool and serene.

"I'm glad you came."

"The train was late."

"Come and see the exhibit." They walked across the green campus. The tall trees were in full leaf and the ivy on the buildings shone like metal in the sun. Boys walked slowly about the campus with their families.

"They couldn't have given it to anyone else." He hadn't told her that he'd won first prize. She had seen all his paintings before and she said nothing about them. She commented on the others. She knew what they lacked and what he had.

"You'll drive back with my father and me, won't you?"

"Will he like that?"

"Yes."

"Then I will. It was so lovely coming up on the train. What a wonderful green New England makes."

216

They talked of summer. Bill would visit his mother at North Hampton for a while. It was, fortunately, close enough to New York for him to see Kay often. She would be in the city all summer, working in a studio her family had rented for her. In July Bill planned to go into the Army. Kay said nothing about this. She accepted his decision. She knew that the Army was, in some important way, his symbol of freedom and she knew what he must prove.

They walked outside under the trees. They walked slowly. Kay told him about Roselle. She told him that Roselle was now interested in a wealthy young man at Princeton who had been recently discharged from the Army. Carter knew nothing of this and they were both sorry for him. Bill decided he wouldn't tell him, he would find out soon enough and, besides, once he was in college and the Navy he would be able to find another girl. Bill trusted Roselle to handle her desertion painlessly.

There were times when Bill knew that what his mother had said about her love was true. She would always be there; at least until she died and that was probably many years away. By that time he might have found someone else who would take her place. He looked at Kay and wondered.

"Is love like that always?"

"I don't think I know," she answered. They sat down on a bench overlooking the campus. Boys with their families passed them. Some greeted Bill, a little self-consciously.

"Have you ever thought about it?"

"Yes. Sometimes more than others."

"Is there such a thing?"

"I don't know, sometimes I think there is and sometimes I know there isn't. I think it's the best dream of all."

"Your father's very important to you, isn't he?"

"Yes, but not too important. I don't want to marry my father."

"My mother's important to me."

"I know."

"But I don't think we've ever talked about her."

217

"We never had to. It was in the paintings."

"Which?"

"The room underground, for instance. Your mother was there and you belonged to her."

He had never thought of this. He frowned. "Are you right?"

"Oh yes, I'm right." She was so calm.

"Then the painting means much more than I meant it to mean."

"That often happens. You should be glad it does mean more."

"I am; but not for the meaning. I don't think I've ever thought of my mother as more than something constant, unexciting."

"Do you like her?"

"What a question! Yes . . . yes." He stopped to think. "No one else in the world will ever love you as much as I do." Or: "Thou shalt have none other God but me." But was it true? He had questioned everything else in life but he had always accepted what she said as true. Was it true? It was almost sacrilegious to question the love of his mother. He turned to Kay. He should be angry with her but when he saw her sitting quietly beside him, watching the clouds gather, he knew he couldn't be angry but he *must* make her understand. She was probably jealous. She had said very little actually but he knew that she was questioning his mother's love and this frightened him. There had been times when he'd hated his mother and he'd made himself suffer, do penance for the moments of hatred. His mother would always be there; Kay might be another Roselle. He sighed. He didn't know what to think. He might love Kay and never know it. Would she always be there? She at least understood him, knew what he wanted to paint and, perhaps, she knew what he himself did not know: what he wanted his life to be. She was superior to his mother in this but there was no sureness about Kay: his mother had promised to be there, to be constant. He had come from her womb. He wished Kay would say something, suddenly say the words he needed to hear. What they were he didn't know.

But someday someone would have to say them. Someone would speak the incantation which would be stronger than his mother's and when this incantation had been spoken he would awake, like a Prince in a legend. Would Kay say it? Could she? Did she know enough, or more important, was she enough? Was it possible to build bridges between the islands, to dispel the vision of a vast and separating sea.

He spoke first. "There've been times when I've hated her."

"There're always such times but, most of the time?"

"What you think. Is it wrong to believe she's the only person in the world who . . . will care the most?"

"Very wrong, Bill." She looked at him, deserting the cloud-patterns. "You *must* know how wrong it is of her. She wants you to love only her."

"But she doesn't seem to be that way. She sent me away from home as soon as she could. She's always wanted me to be independent."

"In every way but emotionally. You know this."

"It's so confused. I love her and hate her and yet I'm so separate from her. I know so little about her really."

"Then perhaps it won't last much longer."

"Why do you say that? Why do you want me to lose the only thing I'm sure of?"

"Because I'll be there." She performed magic. If he didn't wake now he never would.

"You will be there?"

"Oh yes."

"Always?"

"If I can, yes. The future's not really that important. I'll be in the present with you, though. You see I understand you even better than I understand myself. Not with my mind which, I know, isn't very good, but emotionally. And I know your painting. What more do you want?"

"I don't know."

They said nothing more and Bill pondered the incantation. They walked to the dormitory and climbed the stairs.

"Hello, Kay."

"How're you, Carter?"

"Fine. Bill, you better get into your robes. The procession's forming outside."

Bill put on his black robe and cap. Carter, looking like the President of a large university, asked Kay about Roselle.

"She's well. You'd planned on seeing her tonight in Boston, hadn't you?"

"Why, yes."

"She asked me to tell you to come out to college tomorrow morning; she can't get to town tonight. She has so many tests and you know how she is: she puts everything off to the last minute." Bill admired the way Kay handled this.

Carter took it well. "I shall find amusement for myself then," he said ominously, gesturing largely.

"Kay, you'd better rush on over to the gym and get a seat; Father and I'll meet you at the side entrance when it's over." She left them and they joined the procession of over two hundred black-robed and sweating youths. There was much ceremony.

They sat in the gymnasium. The class speakers spoke and they sounded like all class speakers everywhere. Then the headmaster gave his famous speech, the one he'd given, a little tearfully, to every graduating class for thirty years.

Bill watched his father sitting on the speakers' platform. He seemed calm and at ease; he looked like Hollywood's idea of a diplomat; except he didn't have a gray mustache. Bill was nervous for his father. He was always nervous for him. His father spoke well in a low clear voice, completely emotionless. He was not a great orator the way the Vice-President had been. His grandfather had been violent, dramatic; he could make an audience weep with the most obvious platitude. He could stampede conventions into choosing Presidents; oh, he'd been a great speaker, an eminent Victorian. His father was without drama. He spoke with an impressive sincerity and an underlying desperation as though he sensed the inability of people ever to understand an idea, a figure within the machine.

"We must assume our particular responsibility to the world."

Yes, it was *that* speech. Bill relaxed a little. His father seemed so sure of himself. Bill looked down the row at Carter. Carter sat with his arms folded, his jaw on his breast; he looked like a Supreme Court Justice now. The others appeared to be listening although Bill knew they were thinking about other things. Bill squinted his eyes and concentrated on his father's face but instead of another face his father merely became a shadow. The afternoon sun shone through a window behind him; that explained it. The sunlight became red fire when he concentrated: shadow and fire, like hell. One could always see the shadows and the fire if one looked but so few people could see. Reality was indefinite, so undefined, so, in the last analysis, personal. *This* reality was but one plane of movement, one out of many. There were other planes that the human eye could not see or the mind comprehend; motion all about them, invisible; yet when one concentrated shadow and fire and another reality appeared. But not the one he wanted. He was a stranger here, isolated, and only in sudden flashes was he able to see anyone else, recognize other strangers: Kay, his father. But not his mother. She represented love on the unimportant plane and he accepted it, finding nothing better. He could not return it, of course. Something stopped him, a sense of unreality. What his mother said, what she was, to him was unreal and what she said about him was unimportant for he could not feel what she felt. He was a stranger, a traveler and only twice in his life had he met other travelers who were as real as he: Kay, his father. He was a shadow, drawn to the fire. But at least there were the beginnings of reality in his paintings. There at least he could trace the shadows, suggest the fire.

"There are no islands in the world today."

How could his father say that? All men were islands, separate from one another, and the days, the clear days, when one could see another island, were, unhappily, few. But, of course, his father was speaking politically. His father knew better.

"The senseless, seemingly inevitable, impulse that drives nations into war must stop. We cannot continue this waste if our Western civilization is to survive."

But why should it survive? Sooner or later a new period must begin, a new religion, a return to a general faith. Their civilization had obviously run its course: the golden and the dark ages had come and gone and now this was the transition, the death of the phoenix. Shadow and fire. He found he was thinking now in the words of Kay's father. He didn't really agree with him, though. He didn't really care. He was glad only that the dogma of the Christian God, the ridiculous dogma, was gone or, at least, going. He wanted only to be left alone, to find, if possible, one other stranger, to be known only to one other. And then the war . . . perhaps it was natural; perhaps it was the best thing. What difference did it make if a few million people died a few years before they might have naturally? They would die in any event. In a war they could die with some excitement about them: an adventure at least. They were, at least, free of the filing system which normally governed their physical life. He saw these things clearly. He understood.

"You have a terrible responsibility. You are growing up in a war and you must accept the chaos of your period. But when the war ends you must make an effort for peace. It is not simple to know what to do or what to try but you must do something, try something. Any agency dedicated to peace should be examined and assisted. For these insane wars must stop if any of us are to survive."

It would be unfortunate if they all were killed. Pain was horrible. Yes, pain was the worst aspect of war. Eliminate pain and war would be an acceptable pastime . . . like football games.

His father finished his speech and sat down.

There was loud applause. Bill turned around, trying to see Kay but he couldnt find her. The gymnasium, decorated with American flags, was full of middle-aged men and women. They appeared quite impressed with the proceedings. If nothing else the school was impressive. It had had almost two centuries to discover for itself the need for pageantry and ritual.

Now the headmaster was calling out the names of those to be graduated.

"William Hawkins Giraud." He rose, his heart beating rapidly as it always did when his name was said in public; he adjusted the tassel of his cap to show that he was now a graduate. Then, when they were all standing, they sang a hymn and the headmaster sent them out into the world, confident that they were men.

Kay was at the side door when he came out. Graduates and their parents wandered about the outside of the gymnasium, looking for one another.

"Did you like it?"

"Your father seems very nice." Then Stephen Giraud came out of the building, the headmaster with him.

"Ah, here's your son," said the headmaster with one of his lucky guesses.

"Yes, here he is."

"You're sure you won't stay for the faculty tea?"

"I'm awfully sorry but I have to be in Washington tomorrow afternoon and I'm driving."

"The affairs of state; I understand. Thank you, Mr Giraud, for an excellent speech, much the best we've had since Lincoln spoke here." He laughed to show he was joking. They shook hands and said good-by.

Bill introduced Kay to his father. They were polite to one another, watchful. Then they went back to the dormitory. Jimmy and his mother stopped them at the door.

"I don't suppose you remember me, Mr Giraud, but we were both at Helen Piper's wedding in 1928. Then, of course, I've known Charlotte for years, not well but . . . this is my son Jimmy (he's a great friend of Bill's) but I've felt that I've known you because I've heard so much about you."

Bill left them and went up to his room to get his baggage. Carter was there. "It's been great, old man," he said, in imitation of certain war movies. "I shall always remember these years as the best of my life and when I'm in college

223

this summer I shall put a star in my window to show that I've
a boy . . . over there." This last was whispered tearfully.
They said good-by and promised to write. Bill was surprised to
find himself feeling sentimental. He'd already said good-by
to Mr Forster who would send him his paintings in the fall.
There was nothing left for him to do.

He said good-by to Jimmy; they would see one another in
Washington, of course. Bill, his father and Kay got into the
car and they left.

He had never seen New England so green, so dramatic before. It was even better, more poignant, than the Canadian
trip. Even the stone fences which divided pasture from pasture
seemed less hard, less severe. They put the top of the car
down and drove in the open air. The afternoon sun shone
through the clouds, orange light on the green. Kay sat between
them in the front seat.

"How was the speech?" his father asked.

"Just as good as it was last year."

His father laughed. "I suppose I do give the same one all
the time. It's the only thing I think about."

"The only thing?" asked Kay suddenly. She hadn't spoken
since they left the school.

"On the top of my mind, yes."

"That's what I thought." She smiled.

His father smiled, too. Perhaps for the same reason. "Bill
tells me you paint?"

"Yes."

"I used to paint once. I wanted to be an artist. In fact I
worked a few years in New York painting but . . ." he
stopped. Then he said lightly, "I had to make a living."

"It must have been painful . . . to stop painting."

"Yes, it was."

They got to Boston at sundown and they took her to her
college. She said that she would see Bill the next week in New
York when the school was, for the summer, over. Bill and his
father went to a hotel and had dinner.

"I think she's unusual."

"Yes, she's unusual. We understand one another."

"She's probably just right for you but don't get married too young. Of course, it might be all right in your case since you'll have money someday. Still . . ."

"I don't get it until I'm twenty-five."

"That's right, the will was changed. Well, your mother has to give you some sort of an allowance."

Bill made a face.

"Yes, it'll probably be unpleasant. But you'll get it all someday. She knows that."

They talked then of the past. Usually they didn't mention the divorce but tonight they discussed it for this was an important day. Bill admitted that the divorce had never really disturbed him.

"You know," said his father finally, "that your mother wanted to get remarried."

"What? To you?"

"Oh yes. She asked me about it at that reception, the one for the King a few years ago. I was about to marry Janet Hamilton then so I was rather noncommittal. I said I'd think it over. Then she called me up a few days later and she said she didn't feel she could though she wanted to. She said she'd talked to you about it and you said you preferred living in the big house in Maryland, living that sort of life."

Bill was astonished. Then he was angry. He had never been so angry at his mother. "How could she say that? She never talked to me about it and as for liking Roger's house . . . why I was almost never there."

"I wanted to know," said his father.

"How could she have said such a thing?"

But the winter was over at last

the parallel construction

and spring began.

He joined his mother at North Hampton. She'd taken a cottage there, near a country club to which most of the summer colony belonged. They were near the northeast tip of Long Island. In the middle of the island the countryside was peaceful, English, but near the shore it was dramatic and wild, like the Scottish moors. Sand dunes, occasional cliffs, clumps of long grass and the houses on the dunes, gray, weathered shingled houses. The beach was white and the sea was generally blue but there were days when the fog, salt and damp, came from a black sea and covered the land.

He brought canvas with him and he painted the sea. At first he disliked painting it; he was bored by the vastness of the water, and what, at first, seemed to him a monotonous sameness. But then, after a few days, he became fascinated by the

227

sea's rhythm. Sometimes he painted but, generally, he sat and watched the shifting water. He was tranquil, at ease.

Too, he found it hard to paint when he was with his mother. His energy seemed to disappear when he was with her. He had been aware of this before but this summer was the first time he'd thought about it, wondered why it was. She had, of course, such energy. She managed everything so well. He felt like doing nothing when he was with her and she would grow angry and accuse him of being lazy. He spent, however, most of his time alone on the beach or at the club.

He disliked the club. The people were, for the most part, kindly and uninteresting. They belonged to that comfortable upper middle class which, in America, tries hard to be a colorful aristocracy but the puritan, the peasant ancestry is too much for them. They were neither colorful nor aristocratic. Bill had been born into this world and he had, very early, turned away from it, not bitterly, for there was nothing sufficiently affirmative or negative to dislike; he was merely bored. These people talked about their families, the children in school, which house they'd rented this year or how much they'd managed to rent their own house for. They talked, the more worldly ones, of adultery and these subjects completed their conversation.

The younger ones in their twenties, and his age, he loved aesthetically: they were beautiful animals. The girls slim and narrow-waisted with long well-formed legs and the boys like figures of Scopas, muscular, complete, always in action. He sat and watched them, infatuated with their abstract beauty; already he loved youth and himself, too, since he was young. But it couldn't last forever and that hurt him. There was no way to keep the tall godlike boys from growing fat and wrinkled, dull and bald, or the girls from becoming like their mothers, shapeless, colorless or, even worse, carefully painted and girdled. He sat in the sun of the beach and watched youth, aware, vaguely, of his own muscular body, aware that all the beauty in the world belonged together: Narcissus aware. He didn't see the fat men and the sagging women. He watched young men and women and he felt strangely warm; when he thought of them old, himself old, his sorrow was poignant and not unpleasant.

A few of the boys had been in school with him. They looked very different without their clothes and in the sun. He liked them better. He talked to them occasionally but he had no communication with them and they turned to their girls, intrigues, and drinking. Everyone was drinking a great deal this summer. Many of the boys were going overseas soon and many of them were back and everyone drank and Bill thought it a shame, aesthetically. Drinking made these boys even duller than they were when they were sober and they *were* dull. Bill talked to each of them at one time or another and he found that they had nothing to say, that they thought of nothing. The ones who were about to go overseas regarded themselves as potential martyrs to be now indulged; they would, of course, never have admitted this. They insisted on regarding the war as a football game. The ones who had been in action overseas were a little quieter than the others. They were thinking of going back to college or working. There was no interest in the non-material. Even their love affairs were physical and unimportant; they found them unsatisfying without ever knowing why. So Bill stopped talking to them. He preferred looking at them. It was enough, after all, that they were young and beautiful.

The girls were, generally, more interesting. The war had worried them; they were moved by the thought of young men dying and their emotional life *was* of importance to them. They had affairs and they tried to make something important of them but they didn't know how and the boys never suspected that love consisted of anything more than the act. Bill, an outsider, an onlooker, watched them and pitied them and himself since, in a sense, he'd not even gone as far as they had. The difference was that he knew there was something larger. He would have liked to have Kay visit him but he didn't want her to meet his mother. Every few days he went into New York to see her and, gradually, finally, it became an affair and there were signs that one day, when he was free, it would be total.

But in the days when he was not with Kay he lay on the beach in the morning. And he would watch the boys tease the girls and the girls one another or, most amusing, though saddest of all, the groups in which the young men formed, completely independent of the girls, complete without them or, rather, satisfied. This was a phenomenon which amused Bill; he was sorry for the girls who were excluded from a masculine world. The girls never formed groups of their own for very long; they needed the men.

The sun shone clearly every day for several weeks. There was no fog. The beach glittered with tiny fragments of quartz and mica or whatever it is in the sand which catches and reflects, mirrorlike, the light of the sun.

The gray club-house had colored flags on its roofs, and on the terrace there were colored awnings and umbrellas under which people had lunch and drank and discussed the difficulties one had with servants.

His mother was, as usual, very social. She was not at all snobbish or, at least, not obviously. She was better born and she'd been better married than most of these people and she felt no need to be exclusive since her position was secure; although, as Bill was aware, the older and more conservative families did not approve of her. The plain women who talked about children hated her but their husbands, *all* the men, adored her and her parties were considered the best in North Hampton. She came down to the beach at twelve. She swam for ten or fifteen minutes (she swam expertly, naturally) then she changed into slacks and had lunch. She gave lunch to a group of people or they gave lunch to her. She was never alone. Bill could hear her deep laugh no matter how loud the other voices were and they were usually extremely loud.

Bill generally had lunch alone at the end of the awninged terrace where the younger people did. He preferred to sit alone but when his mother was watching him ("you *must* learn to be a good mixer") he would have lunch with the boys from his school. He was considered rather odd by the young people. It would have been simple to exclude him if he'd been ugly but he looked just like they did. They attributed his strangeness, then, to the fact he was an artist and they thought no more about him.

At the end of the month he would go to Washington and stay a week with his father. He would go into the Army then, from Washington. Jimmy Wesson was already in the Marine Corps.

He had tried to discuss his enlistment with his mother but she'd refused to talk about it. "You're much too young. You don't know what's best for you."

Kay, on the other hand, was quite prepared for his going into the Army. She never mentioned it. She accepted this as she did everything about him. That was the best, the most unusual thing about her, he thought: she didn't want him to be different.

The first week with his mother went quickly. There hadn't yet been one of those interminable after-dinner scenes when his attitude was examined and deplored and his mother's voice grew angry, like her father's. She seemed nervous this summer, though. Her attempts to get more alimony were unsuccessful. Her affair with the Army officer had gone badly. Bill could tell this by the way she talked about him now: he had let her down. That was her favorite expression; she applied it to anyone who disobeyed her.

She was fairly polite about his paintings but he could see that she didn't understand or value them. He tried several times to explain painting to her but she always lost interest in what he was saying. She always acted as if she knew everything there was to know about art and she was very preoccupied this summer. She was also, he noticed, drinking too much. He had never known her to drink too much before. Yet there was nothing really troubling her. But at the end of the second week, the familiar scene began. Bill had returned from seeing Kay. His mother had been irritable at the table; they argued about his allowance. After dinner they went to her room.

The lines ran parallel:

the son:

The chair was not at all comfortable. It was one of those wicker chairs that all summer cottages are furnished with. A piece of the wicker was broken and it stuck in his back. He squirmed in the chair. Finally he pushed it back. She was talking and he set his face so that it would appear he was listening. But there was nothing to listen to, really. It had all been said before. He looked about the room. It didn't look much like his mother. Curious how rooms tend to look like their owners after a while. She hadn't been in this room long enough and, then, it would be very difficult to get this room to look like anyone. It was unfortunately square, practically a cube. He'd rather liked the cubist painters but they had developed so oddly later on. The original intention, of course, was exciting. All things are exciting the first time. The room under the factory; that had been exciting or had it, really? Perhaps it was more that he felt he should be excited since the others were. Jimmy really was. Jimmy liked that sort of thing. The first time they'd ever done it Jimmy shook all over. He was highly sexed. Some people are and some people aren't. Kay probably was but she was so well-controlled. He was and he wasn't. There were times yes but most of the time no. Later he would have more time; the dreams sufficed for now. He was not at all frustrated. You were only frustrated when you knew what a thing was and then couldn't have it. He'd never known what it was. The room in the cellar, the cave. . . . Was she right when she called it his mother's womb? He looked at his mother. She sat at her dressing table, her back to the mirror and the light, the white glaring electric light, shining on the left side of her face, putting the right side in shadow. He tried to imagine himself small enough to be carried inside of her. The womb was rather like a bag, a hotwater bag, most likely. And once he'd been inside of her and then, one day, he came out and the doctor cut the cord, cut the cord. She was angry now and her voice was unpleasant. He'd never liked her voice much anyway and when it was angry he hated it.

the mother:

"We've discussed this before many times. You know perfectly well that I'd do anything in the world for you that I thought was right. But I don't believe in children having too much money. Your grandfather didn't either, Lord knows. He never gave *me* a cent." (He was always selfish, William Hawkins, but he could be because he was a great man. These others . . . he sits there looking like his father. Oh, it hurts.) "I'm sure he would've wanted you to stand on your own feet. I've told you about this before but you insist on bringing it up, complaining about it. You'll never get anywhere in life with that attitude. I've told you again and again that you'll have to turn over a new leaf and stop expecting that everyone owes you a living. You know perfectly well that I haven't been able to get a decent settlement from Roger and I need all I can to live on and yet, knowing that, you have the selfishness to ask your mother for more when you've already got more than most young boys." (I'll have to see that lawyer on Monday. He's a Jew and according to Grace Willerson he's perfectly marvelous. All the Jews are clever, especially at law. I wonder if the light's too sharp on my face. God, how awful it is getting old. Well, let's hope he can get the money out of Roger. Damn these chairs they're so uncomfortable. Why they can't get a decent dressing-table chair I don't know. He sits the way his father did, ignoring me. But he doesn't look like his father. He looks like William.) "You'll find in life that the only happy people are those that give. You can't go all through your life taking. People get tired after a while and then see where you'll be. I'm getting tired, years in and year out, of doing things for you without your even saying thank you to me, to your own mother." (What a strange word "mother." I feel strange when I say it. I *am* right.) "No, go on the way you are and see where it gets you. You'll end up like your father. He may be successful finally and all that but he's quite *unpopular* and not even Janet Hamilton will marry him."

She was scowling now and undoing the work of the adhesive patches. The skin starts to sag.

She's wrong there. I shall say something and then she'll be furious but I shall say something. "I thought my father wouldn't marry Janet Hamilton. I think she's still crazy about him. They still see a lot of each other." Well, that didn't do much good, she kept right on talking the whole time I did. I wonder if she ever listened to anyone in her life. Grandfather, I guess, but no one else. She talks almost all the time. She must be getting old or else she really feels she's interesting. Men like to listen to her, though. Now she's saying that my father is a liar. Yes, sometimes he exaggerates and so do I but I've heard her lie. "Oh, yes, Senator So and So called me this afternoon," when she really called *him* on the phone. That's lying. Now she's moved and the light's behind her. That's better. I was seeing all the lines. Her face is rather hard now. She thinks only of money and she's generous and selfish at the same time. She likes to give people things so they'll thank her and think she's important. My father didn't marry Janet Hamilton but she tried to marry him. I wonder why she's telling this story. It's a reflection on her: if my father's so impossible that no women will marry him then she looks rather silly having been married to him. But she never thinks logically; in a while she'll contradict herself. How can anyone feel they're so right all the time? Her hair looks rather unattractive this way; especially with the light behind it but at least the shadows soften her face. The Browne boy; so she noticed the way he fussed over his mother's chair. Well, if she wants a charming pansy for a son she better go some place else and start over again. She doesn't know why he wasn't taken into the Army. Funny people pansies; that friend of Kay's was today at lunch. Seemed to have all the worst traits of women. Of course, technically speaking, it's not much different what they do than what Jimmy and I did; still that was a special case. I don't think I could ever go through that with another man. Women are more important, more attractive. Jimmy was important but at a different time, for a different reason.

(She looked stunning at the horse races. I wonder how she keeps the lines out of her face. She's a beautiful woman but such a bitch. At least one should keep some dignity. Now he sees the lines in my face. He sees all the defects in everyone.)

His voice isn't like anyone's in the family. "Don't contradict me!" (It's like fire, like fire.) "When I say she didn't marry him because she didn't want to I know what I'm talking about." (He's still talking while I'm talking. Now he's stopped. He'll do as I say.) "After all I know a little more about these things than you do. Of course your father may have told you something else. Your father's always been a terrible liar. Even my mother who always took his side against me admitted that. 'You can never trust anything Stephen says.' How many times I've heard her say that! I don't see how *you* can take his word over mine. But you always have. You and he criticize me all the time. You're so damned critical of everyone." (There, that's better; the light's behind my head. I wonder what's wrong with my digestion. My stomach's been gurgling for hours. I wonder if I have liver trouble. I'll get a drink in a few minutes. He sits there the way Stephen did but he looks like . . .) "Of course, your father would tell you that he'd refused to marry Janet Hamilton. That's the sort of thing *he* would say. You don't have to believe me, of course, but if you ask around you'll find that everyone knows she walked out on him. He was always so self-centered, so indifferent to other people. That's why I divorced him. No woman could live with him. And I see those same traits coming out in you. You have everything and I'd hate to see you waste everything by not being considerate; it's so easy. I suppose you noticed how polite the Browne boy was with his mother yesterday; he was quite considerate of her and I hoped you might learn a lesson from him but no you go on your way doing as you please, paying no attention to anyone. Well, you can't succeed that way." (Succeed. A good restaurant could make a fortune in Washington. If I could get enough capital and Jean that Swiss chef; of course, it'd take about a hundred thousand now with prices the way they are. Have a small very exclusive place.

Now we're deciding if I'm going to be a success or not. How important that word is to her. Yet she's the greatest failure in the world. She starts more things without ever finishing them. What an unattractive room this is. I never thought cabbage-sized roses were ever used in wallpaper any more. I wonder if she pays any attention to what she says. Anger does stimulate her, though. Her eyes shine and the blood comes to her face. That's a good way to have a stroke. Perhaps she'll have one sometime. That would certainly solve everything. But I should miss her. There were wonderful moments, but not recently, not since all the talk about money. She's talked about money for the last three years. It seems to me the only thing that can excite her any more. That's what started this whole thing. Well, I can go to the trustees of the estate and demand more. Still she has control for eight years more. That's a long time. The water-color paints: I remember. They came in a large black shiny box and she said that there was a depression and this might be the last present I'd ever get. I was so moved I could barely say anything. I don't think I ever used them. Now she's contradicted herself. Father's gotten ahead because of the wives. She's forgotten already what she said about him a few minutes ago. Why can she hurt me then when I know she's crazy? Now she's onto Kay. I shall have to defend her. Now then, as quickly as possible. "I don't see how you can say that about someone you don't even know." At least she stopped talking for a moment. Her hands shake now. She's fixing her hair and pretending not to be listening; she probably isn't. Now it starts again. She never gets tired. So now I'm supposed to be ashamed of Kay; if she only knew that I'm ashamed of my mother, that I wouldn't expose anyone to that destructiveness. But then she would be charming with Kay, the way she was with Jimmy. Only Jimmy didn't recognize that she disliked him and Kay would. No, there is no connection here between Kay and my mother. They belong in different compartments. My mother in the past and Kay in the present. The future's another thing. There may be no future at all so I had better choose Kay and have what I want while I can.

Now if Grace would put up some money; she's quite well off now that she got that settlement. I hope that Jew's good. I'll tell him what the psychiatrist said about Roger's mother complex. It would look a little silly in court but maybe we wouldn't have to take it to court. Now if Grace raised fifty thousand I could get the rest from friends and, of course, my own money. I'd run it. I've a natural talent for running things, everyone agrees. To succeed. But perhaps it's too late.)

"I've tried all my life to give you everything: I've made sacrifices. Not, of course, that I want to hold that over you. I don't demand anything of people they don't want to give of their own free will but I feel sometimes that I've wasted a lot of my life, devoting it to you, when you show so little gratitude. During the depression when we had almost no money, your father and I bought you that set of water-color paints. You barely said thank you and I had almost no money then. That was before your father got ahead in the government. Before he started going around with the right wives. That's how he's managed to get anywhere, through women. He married me only because I was the daughter of the Vice-President." (Why did it have to end? Stephen was so wonderful at first. But everything seemed to collapse. Everything ends. Some things never begin. Why must everything end in anger? Oh, it hurts. He must say something now. What is he thinking? He sits there and says nothing and he's criticizing me. Thank God, the light's behind my head.) "Now this afternoon when you could have been some help to me at my cocktail party you were off in New York with this little idiot of yours." (His voice is not at all like anyone's in the family. Well at least he's said something. I wonder what she looks like. Probably some little tart he's picked up. *He*'ll never understand women. He takes after his father.) "I can only guess about her since you haven't introduced her to me. I suggested that you have her down here; I *thought* I was being thoughtful, but you wouldn't ask her. I presume that you're ashamed of her. You'll never be able to find any girl or woman who'll put up with your selfishness.

Security without violence, without rage. Now I'm not thoughtful and considerate. I wouldn't think of doing anything for my poor old crippled mother, as if she couldn't have gotten those damned sunglasses herself. She orders one about like a servant, especially in front of people; she has to demonstrate her power. Lord what a memory she has; I'd forgotten all about that letter business with Roger.

She blames it on my father. Well she must have someone to blame things on, I guess. But that isn't true. He's been very good about not mentioning or criticizing her. Discipline. One of her favorite words. She sounds just the way she thinks a Spartan mother should sound. She still wants to command. Something in my throat; there, that's better. Now to answer: "He never did anything of the kind; he's always been very good about not talking about you. He's never said anything against you until lately and then he was only defending himself to me. He told me (should I say this? Probably not. She'll deny it but) that you wanted to remarry him and when he didn't seem enthusiastic you came around later and said that you couldn't remarry him because I'd said I liked living with Roger, with all the money." Now there would be explosions. The immediate denial. Yes, yes. So that was it. "That's quite a different thing from asking whether I preferred living with Roger or my father; you know it." I'm to be silenced I see. Now the rage begins. How wonderful she looks when she's angry. *L'orage.* The French sounds so much better. Don't interrupt me; how royal she is. Yo el Rey. Philip of Spain always signed himself that. Was Elizabeth a man? Is my mother a man? She should've been. A King or, at least, a Queen like Elizabeth. Now I'm to hear of the sacrifices. I'm to be grateful because she didn't hire a nurse for me until I was two, not three, as she says. As if I should be held responsible for my infancy. I can't remember her devotion. There's no gratitude to be got from babies but time's all jumbled in her head. Everyone's given her a dirty deal. Stephen, Roger, her parents. She's always done everything for everyone and they let her down, they disobeyed her. Oh, what a group of bastards we are.

Why if I ask you to do anything you always complain or else do it as though it was the greatest imposition in the world, doing something for your own mother." (That word. Mine is dead.) "Well, things will change one of these days. You'll find that people won't always be so considerate of you. I can go on giving and giving for just so long. I'm getting fed up now. The other day when I asked you to go over to the club and get my dark glasses from the dressing room, you acted as if I'd insulted you or something. Other people notice that about you. Even Roger did. He asked you to mail some letters for him once, several years ago, and you forgot; made no effort to mail them. Oh, everyone's noticed it about you. You'll never be liked if you're that way.

"But even now when I ask you anything you seem to resent it. I suppose you've been listening to your father. He's broken down all *my* discipline and he hasn't given you any of his own. He likes destroying me in your eyes." That was true. She knew that was true. That was the only explanation for his having turned from her, having grown cold. It had been happening for several years. I've tried. Now he defends his father. Why do my hands shake so? I need a drink. What on earth is he saying? Did Stephen tell him that? Did Stephen dare tell him that? How long has he known this? I could kill Stephen now, I could kill him. He told him that. "It isn't true! I never said any such thing. We discussed it, once, jokingly, at the reception for the King. And once I did ask you if you liked living with Roger and you said yes you did." He defends himself. He dares . . . "Don't interrupt me when I'm speaking! I know what I'm talking about. Your father's lied about this the way he lies about everything. He'd do anything to discredit me and you would, too. *You*'re disloyal to me; you always have been and now you take his side against me. After all I've done for you. When you were a baby I nursed you, I took care of you until you were three years old, without a nurse or anyone. I lost those years of my life and all for you. *My* parents didn't help me at all with money and your father couldn't.

I'm angry now. I hope I don't start shaking. Oh Lord, I hope she doesn't cry. It'll make her even more furious to cry in front of me. She understands nothing. She's a whirlwind. She's stupid, incredibly, dangerously stupid. She would destroy us all if we let her. "Obey me." She must always be right, a vessel of grace: infallible. I turned on her she says. She married Roger for my sake. She married money because she thought it was the most important thing in the world. She wanted a great house, servants and the star rubies. They're like blood. But it was my fault her marriages were a failure. My fault. Always someone else's fault. Now I'm to clear out, she's through. Fine. How easy she makes it. How can *she* say this to me? I've listened to her for years; I've never questioned her even to myself until lately. I adored her: this rage. But she'll destroy us all. The beatings and the anger. Now it will end, though. Now: "I'll go on my way if that's what you want. I've listened to you for years, to all your whinings, complaining about all of us: we let you down, we're disloyal. But no one can take it forever . . . not even a son. Roger and my father both pulled out and your mother was more loyal to you than you deserved. But nobody can take it forever. Who do you think you are that you can tell me, or anyone else, what to do? How can *you* complain about anyone when you're a failure in everything yourself; you failed as a wife; you failed on the stage, in everything you ever tried and you certainly failed as a mother: God knows, *I* know that. The fact I'm the way I am is your fault. The fact that I'm afraid of . . . of emotion, suspicious of it: that's your fault, that's the fault of your goddamned I-am-the-law attitude, your temper. You think you can say anything to anyone and their love for you will go right on but no loving can take continual anger. Never once have you said anything about my prizes, about the painting, about what I do well; you tried and you almost succeeded in destroying every bit of confidence I ever had in myself. I'm glad that I've been able to live apart from you for the last few years. I've been able to accept myself, believe in myself and see you clearly. It hasn't been easy. I loved you so or I thought I did.

Oh, I remember how he complained: you pay more attention to that baby than you do to me. But I was willing to give those years, the time when I was prettiest, to you because I thought when you're older you'd repay them, that you'd be considerate of me, that we could get along and you'd be a success and everything would be worth the sacrifice." (I mustn't cry.) "Then you turned on me. I've seen it coming. You saw more and more of your father. You listened to the things he said about me and because you owed me so much you resented me; people always resent the people who help them, who sacrifice themselves for them. Then I married Roger just for your sake. I wanted you to be able to do and be all the things I wasn't and I couldn't do it on the money I got from your father. Roger wanted to marry me and so I did but only for you. But you wouldn't take advantage of any of the things I did for you. You never appreciated them. You just sulked around with that stupid painting of yours, criticizing everybody. I went through hell being married to Roger and it was all for you and then you believe your father's lies about me. You've always been ungrateful and vicious and, as far as I'm concerned, this is the end. If you care to go on, like this, fine. Go to your father. Do as you please. I won't have you scowling around me, disobedient and ungrateful. You get out on your own, as far as I'm concerned I'm through. I'll be damned if I . . ." He interrupted me. I'll stop that. He has the nerve to . . . What is he saying? What did I say? I was never deserted. I left Roger and Stephen, they never left me. That's true. How can he say it isn't true? That's why they hate me now because *I* left them. I couldn't stand failures and they were both failures in different ways. They weren't men. My father was a better man than both of them put together. His voice is like Father's now. It's harsh and cruel; Father's voice could be cruel. He beat me once with a leather strap. But I didn't mind because he was . . . whatever he was that these others aren't. He's attacking me, my own son. How can he say these things to me? He has no right. I'll stop him . . . I'll . . . He says I've failed at everything. I *never* failed. My husbands were inadequate.

I thought you were always right. I never criticized you, even if you think I did. You've a guilty conscience; you're too sensitive to criticism. Now you think you can tell me lies and I'll believe them, that you can crack a whip and I'll obey. Well, that's over. You'd rather not have me live with you. Well, I'd just as soon never see you again. As far as I'm concerned you can go to hell and I'm leaving now since that's what you want. I sometimes think I've always hated you." Now he would leave. He was shaking. The pain, the pain; it hurt but he would leave.

And I was doing well on the stage. Yes, I've failed as a mother since I have such a vicious, ungrateful son. I'll tell him that when he stops. He looks like William. It isn't fair. He can't accept love because he's afraid. What nonsense! Love *is* violence, strong emotion. He's like his father, gutless. I'll tell him that when he stops. I *have* been nice about his prizes only I don't think he's a good painter. Those schools always give a lot of prizes. It'd be wrong to encourage him to be an artist when he isn't good, when he'll be nothing but a long-haired superior failure. It's for his own good. My son. I know what's in him, what blood, what flesh. He came out of me and it hurt; it hurts still. But now he attacks me; he turns on me. Now he says what he really thinks. Well, I'll give him a lesson he won't ever forget. I have the money for eight years more. He's leaving. . . . "I've always hated you." He's always hated me? Oh my God, what's happened? He's leaving. He has always hated me.

the beginning

IT WAS May. He reported to duty in Rastignac. Soon he would go home. His leg no longer bothered him. At first, of course, it had burned intolerably but then, slowly, the pain went away. The bone had not been damaged and he would soon be able to walk without a cane. He used it now, however. He felt strangely old and knowing, not wise, but knowing. He was the oldest man in the world and he walked with a cane. The cane had done something to him; it had assumed even greater importance than the wound itself. Now that he was going back he didn't regret (as he had many times before regretted) the influence he'd used to be sent overseas. He had been in the battle of the Bulge at seventeen, almost eighteen, of course. Everyone had been there during the winter but now he was in Rastignac and his leg was healing.

He walked down the street from the hospital. The street was cobbled and steep; it reminded him of the street from the school to the town, the school where he'd been a long time before.

The weather had been mild lately but today the sky was clouded. The sunlight was a pale yellow, diffused and gentle. From time to time a cold wind blew. He carried his overcoat with him. He would walk to the castle today.

244

He walked down the village street, an old man with a cane. Soldiers wandered about the town. They were like himself, about to be sent back to the States for recuperation. He knew they were glad but they didn't show it. No one showed much of anything. Perhaps in Paris they would become alive but now they merely wandered around Rastignac, looking half-heartedly for women and liquor. They were almost as old as he.

The town had not been damaged by the war. A medieval ugly church stood in the central square. There were cafés around the square filled with American soldiers. He passed the square and slowly he climbed a steep green rocky hill. At the top of it was the castle. He climbed carefully up the narrow worn path. Halfway up he turned to look back at the town. Yes, it was picturesque: like an illustration in a book of fairy stories. Beyond the town the fields and the orchards were beginning to turn a yellow-green. He climbed to the top.

The castle had been built by a crusader in the 12th century, the age of faith. There was not much left of it now (of faith or the castle) : a round tower made of large stones and the outlines of a building and courtyard, grown over with vines and grass. The tower was empty. Standing inside one could look up and see the sky, it was like being at the bottom of a well. He didn't go in this time. Instead he sat down on a rock beneath an arch that was still intact. He could still see where the frame of the door had been but now no one knew, or cared, where the door had led. It was an empty arch, weathered and crumbling but as yet unbroken. He looked out over the Loire valley, the fields of Touraine. He liked to look at the wide sweep of farms and towns and castles. He sat watching, not thinking. The sky was darkening in the north and there would be a storm later, perhaps at sundown. He thought of painting this scene but, at the moment, he didn't want ever to paint again. He was an old man looking at a valley, waiting for a sunset.

"Hello."

He turned around and saw a young corporal, his own age. He looked familiar. "Hi," said Bill.

"Mind if I sit down?"

"No, go ahead. We're in the same ward, aren't we?"

"Yep. It sure is pretty up here."

"Yes, it's pretty." Bill looked at the landscape and tried to see it the way the boy did. Yes, it was pretty.

"My feet hurt," said the young Corporal and he took his shoes off. Then he sat back on the stone, comfortable. "Well, what's new?"

"Nothing," said Bill. What was new?

"Did you go to the service for old Roosevelt?"

"I went to one last month, when he died. I missed the one here."

"That was some show the Chaplain put on. I guess he'll be promoted."

"It is a blow to us all and a great loss to world peace." His father had said that on the radio. It had been strange hearing his father's voice come out of a radio in France. It was probably all recorded. His father had sounded tired. He'd said all the silly things everyone else had said.

"Your old man's a big shot in the government, isn't he?"

"Yes." Bill would have denied this a year ago.

"Then how come you're only a corporal and over here?"

"I don't know," said Bill wearily. It would have taken such a long time to explain and, besides, he didn't know himself exactly why he'd gotten into this. He had wanted to prove something, of course, but he was not sure what it was he'd wanted to prove or whether it had been proven yet. Someday he would know. Soon he'd be back home, though, going, probably, to college and all of this would be forgotten. He knew already that he would forget everything except, perhaps, this view of the valley of the Loire. He held his cane in his hands; there was a crack in it near the hook and he felt this crack as he watched the valley, changing in the light.

"You going back, aren't you? You going back in the next group, aren't you?"

"Yes, I'm going back."

"Me, too. We'll probably be stuck in the same boat. I hope

they give us a little time in Paris. I've always wanted to see some of the Paris whores."

"Yes." The young corporal had very large feet he noticed, but they were in proportion. He thought of his life classes.

"What're you going to do when you get out?"

"I don't know." Bill looked at the sky.

"Well, your old man's rich; he can take care of you. But me I've got to work. I got a wife to support and a kid, too, now."

"Really?" Bill looked at the young corporal. He couldn't be over twenty.

"Yep. You want to see her picture?" Bill was used to looking at pictures by now. He nodded and the boy pulled out his wallet and showed him a picture of a young girl, slim and rather plain.

"She's pretty," said Bill.

"I think so," said the corporal. "But that doesn't seem to keep me from going with other girls over here." He said this wistfully to show that he knew it was wrong but that he was helpless.

"No?" Bill tried to sound interested. In the distance, on a hill, he could see the towers of a castle he'd never noticed before. He hadn't yet learned this landscape thoroughly; the colors were in his head, though, and the mood. Perhaps he would feel like painting when he went to Paris. Perhaps he would be able to meet Picasso. He had met several soldiers who had seen Picasso. Perhaps he felt old because he'd stopped painting.

"They got you in the leg?"

It was bad manners to mention wounds in the hospital. Mainly because the wounded liked to talk about them too much, the convalescing wounded.

"Yes, in the thigh."

"That's a real leg isn't it?"

"Oh yes." He smiled; the question was so odd.

"I got it in the stomach; went right through and came out the other side. Nothing damaged though: I was lucky. Boy, if it'd been a little lower I would've been out of commission; I wouldn't't've wanted to be alive if it'd been lower." He sighed thankfully and wiggled his toes.

"By the way," he said, finally. "You wouldn't want to help me out, would you?"

"How?"

"Well, I got this girl here in town and she and me've been seeing each other for a couple of weeks. Well, she's got this friend of hers tonight . . . a real nice girl and I wondered if maybe you'd. . . ."

"I don't think so," said Bill. "Thanks, though."

"She's a real nice girl and you can do anything to her you want."

"I don't know," said Bill, pretending to be doubtful.

"Well, think it over. Hell, but it's getting cold." Part of the sky was dark with clouds. "Let's go down now."

They walked down the hill, slowly, and Bill watched the sky turn the color of slate and the green valley looked yellow. The white bellies of the leaves turned out. Lightning flashed in the north.

There was a great deal of noise in the town.

"What're they saying?" asked the young corporal as several people passed them shouting. Bill listened.

"The war's over," he said, finally understanding.

"Which one?"

"Ours," said Bill. "This one here."

"Good deal," said the Corporal. "There'll be some celebrating tonight. Hope you can come out with me."

"Maybe I will," said Bill. Soon he would be in the States, in school. Perhaps he would come back to France and study. Perhaps Kay would come to France, too. They walked through the crowded streets to the hospital. There was less celebrating here but every one seemed more cheerful. They went to their ward and the young corporal stretched out on his bunk and listened to the radio. The ward boy gave Bill four letters; his mail had finally caught up to him. Two were from Kay, one from his father and another from Carter. He opened his father's first.

"I was glad to hear you were up and around again. I suppose you'll be back in the States in a few weeks. There's very little of interest here in Washington. The United Nations is underway and I'm quite busy. Also it takes time getting used to a new President. I may resign soon but don't say anything about that to anyone. I don't know what your plans are but it might be a good idea if you studied in Paris; that was the best place when I was young. I suppose it still is. Make up you own mind, though.

"I saw your mother at a party last week. She goes out a great deal and everyone thinks she's wonderful . . . as they always have. She's dyed her hair and, surprisingly, looks younger. She drinks too much which is a pity. There seems to be no stepfather in sight for you. She asked me about you and I think you should write her. I realize she's almost impossible to get along with but life's too short to feud with people. I'm sure she's quite sorry about all the trouble but she'd never admit it, naturally."

So his mother asked about him. There were times lately when he thought about her without bitterness; realized that she couldn't help what she was. But he would not go back.

The men in the ward turned the radio on loud and gathered around it. An announcer, an American, described the surrender.

He had tried not to think of his mother for a year now. He had managed to go long periods without once thinking of her; now his father was asking him to write her, to see her again and he knew he could not. It was the one defiant act of his life, the one gesture he'd made toward freeing himself completely from her. The gesture was much too important to be undone by even the most superficial of reconciliations. No, he would have to continue without her. He wondered sometimes if she cared at all. Her pride, her terrible angry pride, had been hurt and, for that reason, she would never forgive him. But she was probably sorry, as he was. His sorrow, however, was for the past, that vague, secure and dangerous time when he was safe and warm and she was safety and she was warmth, the center. There were times, very few, when he wanted to return to this state, to write her, to surrender but he never did write; he would never return if only for the reason that he could not. Her world would have destroyed him. He recalled how weak he'd always felt when he was with his mother.

General Keitel had signed the surrender or was he going to sign it? Bill listened carefully but nothing more was said about Keitel. Was Hitler really dead?

He remembered that his mother's affectionate moments were as intense, as consuming, as her angry ones. But generally he could only remember the times of anger and destruction. He hated her still when he remembered these times.

He would have to be a painter just to defeat her prophecy: "You'll always be a failure." He'd never forgotten the way she'd said this to him in the bedroom at North Hampton. Yellow light. Soon he would paint again and the weariness would go. He touched the crack in his cane thoughtfully.

He opened the first letter from Kay.

"I'm so happy you're getting well and relieved that you won't be in any more of the fighting. I think now that you've been there you'll be much happier, more secure. I know that you had to do it."

She was right. She understood this much more clearly than he himself did. It was something he had had to do, to be free. He had to be himself, violent. Oh, what a difficult thing it was to be a man.

"Hitler is rumored to have committed suicide in Berlin."

He read the letter. "I paint all the time. I've still got the studio downtown and now that I've quit college I work every day. You have no idea (but you do, of course) what a wonderful escape it is to work, to make something . . . it's almost as good as being alive. Perhaps someday it'll be possible to be both. When you get back. I go to exhibitions and see a few people, artists mostly. I prefer the ones like us, unknown and uncriticized: we work below the surface, invisibly. Then we rise out of the sea . . . sometimes. They say the war will be over soon and I'm glad. I want to go to Paris as soon as possible. My father's in London now waiting for France to open up. He wants to get to the Resistance painting first. I wait for you."

As much as he doubted love this must be it. Perhaps it might yet be possible to have love without violence. Now love was offered him and it appeared large and constant. And he didn't know if he could believe or answer.

"Many of the Nazi leaders are still at large but it's expected that most of them will be caught soon." He looked down the ward. Everyone in this ward could walk and they stood or sat around the radio, wearing their dark red dressing gowns. Bill was the only one not at the radio. Even the young corporal was squatting on the floor with the others, listening. This was history and Bill was indifferent, concerned only with the interior drama. He opened her other letter.

"It was good to know that you'd be back in a few weeks. Did I tell you in my last letter that I had a visit from your father? He's a charming man and understanding. I don't see how he could ever have been married to your mother. He's very gentle. He talked about you and he was worried because you'd written him that you were afraid you'd never paint again. I told him there was nothing to worry about. You're tired now; it took all your energy to create yourself but when you're rested again you'll paint."

He shuddered. This was true. The sky outside was dark now and a gray cold light came through the windows, a dingy light. The Star-Spangled Banner was played over the radio.

"My life continues about the same. I work and talk with artists. It's so gray here in New York, though. I can't wait to get back to France."

The light was gray and cold in the ward. He smiled.

"There have been some good exhibitions at the Museum but nothing really exciting. Come back soon. I wait."

He put her letters away. He opened Carter's letter.

"Dear brave soldier, your letter from the Front received and we all get goose-pimply thinking about you over there. I am, however, knitting you a red white and blue muffler with your initials carved in ivory and detachable. For those of us defending Boston from the foreign fiends and the Yellow Peril your distant battles on 'the vasty fields of France' seem inconsequential but *c'est la vie*. Roselle, that disgrace to her sex, not to mention my own, married her Princetonian. Boston is as it always was: dreary. I go to classes and parade in my uniform with the other peasants in the college. I was in New York and saw your friend Kay in the Museum of Modern Art. She was glaring at a painting, seemed quite preoccupied, so I didn't speak to her. She's pretty I admit but *so* intense. I have had time to write several novels: none of them the conventional length but they represent my best work. I have just finished a thirty-page preface to a novel about the soul. I am now trying to get Professor Babcock (a noted figure here) to do an introduction to an unwritten novel of mine but he seems to have some petty Victorian scruples about writing an introduction to an unwritten work. He shows a smallness of mind that I'd not expected in such a figure. But we are all, unhappily, but fragile vessels at best.

"By the way, according to the alumni bulletin of our beloved school I see that your friend Jimmy Wesson was killed in the Pacific. He was in the Marines, I think . . ."

"According to certain sources Hitler is supposed to be in hiding in Egypt."

Jimmy was dead. It was impossible! He put the letter down without finishing it. He would have cried but he'd forgotten how. Jimmy was gone. His mother was destroyed. He folded the letter carefully. His head ached. They were both gone: he walked slowly down the aisle, between the rows of beds; he stood with the others by the radio.

Then he turned to the young corporal. "You mind if I go with you after all; I'd like to meet your friends."

"Sure, of course. I knew you'd come around. I think we'd

better go now." They put on their coats and went outside. The sky was almost black and a cold wind blew.

"It's going to storm," said the young corporal.

Bill buttoned his field jacket tightly at the neck, shutting out the cold sharp wind; only yesterday the weather had been warm. He shivered as they walked down the street. Spring, like the other seasons, was bitter.

1947, Antigua.

PALIMPSEST

A Memoir

Gore Vidal

'I am not my own subject,' Gore Vidal used to say. But now, surprisingly, he has turned his wit and elegant storytelling gifts to a candid memoir of the first forty years of his life. Vidal's famous skills as a raconteur, his forthrightness, and his wicked wit are brilliantly at work in these recollections of a difficult family, talented friends and interesting enemies.

'A tremendous read, down and dirty from start to finish. It is also a proud and serious and truthful book'
Martin Amis, *Sunday Times*

'Wonderfully entertaining. You want high-level political gossip? You get it here. There is no-one who was anyone whom he has not met . . . [readers] will be richly rewarded, for it offers all the zing of a Dry Martini without the danger of getting drunk'
Allan Massie, *Daily Telegraph*

'Reads at times like a turbo-charged gossip column where all the anecdotes are funny or endearing . . . A storyteller of great timing and burnished phrase, Vidal achieves the wit of fine conversation . . . one of the year's best books'
Guy Reynolds, *Evening Standard*

'Quite novel and wonderfully appealing, a critical biography of himself . . . [with] an enchanting set of stories about household names – Vidal's life might even be his greatest work'
Robert Winder, *Independent*

Abacus
0 349 10800 5

THE CITY AND THE PILLAR

Gore Vidal

Revised and unexpurgated

'I knew that my description of the love affair between two normal all-American boys would challenge every superstition about sex in my native land'
Gore Vidal, Preface

Jim Willard, former high-school athlete and clean-cut boy-next-door, is haunted by the memory of a romantic adolescent encounter with his friend Bob Ford. As Jim pursues his first love, in awe of the very same masculinity he possesses himself, his progress through the secret gay world of 1940s America unveils surreptitious Hollywood affairs, the hidden life of the military in the Second World War and the underworld bar culture of New York City.

With the publication of his daring third novel *The City and the Pillar* in 1948, Gore Vidal shocked the American public, which had just begun to hail him as their newest and brightest young writer. It remains not only an authentic and profoundly important social document but also a serious exploration of the nature of idealistic love.

'The first serious American homosexual novel'
Bernard Levin, *The Times*

'Certainly one of the best novels of its kind . . . It isn't sentimental and it is frank without trying to be sensational and shocking. These are enormous virtues'
Christopher Isherwood

'A noble work'
Thomas Mann

Abacus
0 349 10657 6

Now you can order superb titles directly from Abacus

☐ Palimpsest	Gore Vidal	£9.99
☐ The City and the Pillar	Gore Vidal	£6.99

——————————— ⬭ABACUS⬭ ———————————

Please allow for postage and packing: **Free UK delivery.**
Europe: add 25% of retail price; Rest of World: 45% of retail price.

To order any of the above or any other Abacus titles, please call our credit card orderline or fill in this coupon and send/fax it to:

Abacus, 250 Western Avenue, London, W3 6XZ, UK.
Fax 0181 324 5678   Telephone 0181 324 5517

☐ I enclose a UK bank cheque made payable to Abacus for £ . . . .
☐ Please charge £ . . . . . . to my Access, Visa, Delta, Switch Card No.

☐☐☐☐☐☐☐☐☐☐☐☐☐☐☐☐☐☐☐☐☐☐☐

Expiry Date ☐☐☐☐   Switch Issue No. ☐☐

NAME (Block letters please) . . . .

ADDRESS . . . .

Postcode . . . . Telephone . . . .

Signature . . . .

Please allow 28 days for delivery within the UK. Offer subject to price and availability.

Please do not send any further mailings from companies carefully selected by Abacus ☐